The
Con Artist
of Catalina
Island

A McAfee Twins
Christmas Novel

Other books featuring the McAfee Twins
by Jennifer Colt:

The Butcher of Beverly Hills: A Novel
The Mangler of Malibu Canyon: A Novel
The Vampire of Venice Beach: A Novel

Published by Tessera Books

Copyright © 2007 by Tessera Productions, Inc.

All Rights Reserved

Published in the United States by Tessera Books, a division of Tessera Productions, Inc., Santa Monica, California.

"Winter Wonderland" © 1934 Music by Felix Bernard, lyrics by Richard B. Smith

Library of Congress-in Publication Data
Colt, Jennifer
      The Con Artist of Catalina Island: a McAfee Twins Christmas Novel / Jennifer Colt. — 1ˢᵗ ed.
          p. cm.
1. Women private investigators—California—Los Angeles—Fiction.
2. Los Angeles (Calif.)—Fiction 3. Sisters—Fiction. 4. Twins—Fiction.

1. Title

ISBN - 13: 978-1-60461-267-7

2007906636
10 9 8 7 6 5 4 3 2 1
First Edition

For the residents of Catalina —
animal, vegetable, and human. Forgive me
for taking liberties with your island paradise.

acknowledgments

Brett Ellen Block edited the manuscript for this book, but that is only the tip of the iceberg. A woman of many talents, Brett can be found falling out of a coffin dressed as Ephemera the Queen of the Undead from The Vampire of Venice Beach one minute, and writing her own award-winning fiction the next. For her friendship and support (and for being a really game girl), I thank her from the bottom of my heart.

Thanks also to Mary Whyte for doing a final copyedit. (It never ends, does it?)

Ryan Evancho designed the cover, and continues to be a webmaster extraordinaire.

Last but not least, I'd like to thank *you* for making this book possible. Thanks for reading and enjoying the McAfee Twins adventures.

The

Con Artist

of Catalina

Island

A McAfee Twins
Christmas Novel

*I*t's that time of year, a time of good cheer. Jack Frost is nipping at your toes, you're chomping chestnuts by an open fire, and Rudolph is a red-nosed celebrity, basking in the admiration of his fellow deer. You're drinking spiked nog and having so much fun, as far as you're concerned they can *let it snow, let it snow, let it snow!*

Unless you live in Los Angeles where it's sixty-five degrees and cloudless; where throwing a log on the fire makes as much sense as having a fireplace to begin with; and where Rudolph's exploits wouldn't get him a write-up in the trades, let alone a star on Hollywood Boulevard.

We imagine you on the way to Grandma's house in a one-horse open sleigh while we're snarled in traffic on the 405; sledding down the hill, laughing all the way, as we duck drive-by shooters; caroling your hearts out to the neighbors while we're here choking on smog.

Sure, we go through the motions. We hang lights and trim trees. We hum along to the carols that are piped into stores to keep people spending, the way oxygen is pumped into casinos to keep them gambling. But it seems kind of redundant to string up tinsel here in Tinsel Town, and the glitterati and the paparazzi keep the place lit up like Christmas every day of the year.

For the most part, we Angelenos grit our teeth and ride the season out, because there's no room for simple, unmerchandisable joy on the dream factory floor. If you can't package it, sell tickets to it, and promote it on *Access Hollywood*, it's not going to get much play around here—even if it is the birthday of one of the biggest stars of all times. (He's *so* two thousand years ago.)

I'm Kerry McAfee, and I hope you're having a fantastic Christmas wherever you are.

one

"*S*leigh bells ring, are you listenin'?"

Riiinnnnnggggggg.

"In the lane, snow is glistenin'."

Riiinnnnnggggggg.

"A beautiful sight, we're happy tonight…"

Riiinnnnnggggggg.

I rolled over in bed, moaning. "Okay, I get it! The sleigh bells are ringing! Whoop-de-friggin' do!"

After pounding the snooze button into submission, I yanked the covers over my head. But the jangling continued. It wasn't the Christmas song blaring from my radio, I realized. It was the phone.

Peering out from the coverlet, I squinted at the digital readout on the clock: 6:45 am.

"Who could be calling at this hour?" I grumbled. "And why isn't Terry answering. Is she in traction or something?"

I knew for a fact that my twin sister Terry was not in traction, but an able-bodied narcoleptic if ever there was one. She was probably downstairs doing her impersonation of "The Amazing Sleeping Woman" at that very moment.

Step right up, folks, and watch her snore through a nuclear attack!

I fumbled for the phone. "Hello, who is it?"

"Terry? Kerry? It's me!"

The "me" in question was Reba Price-Slatherton, my mother's aunt and one of our only two living relatives. Reba had recently moved back to Beverly Hills from Venice Beach with her son, Cousin Robert, and Terry and I were scheduled to have brunch with them that day to exchange presents. However, the crack of dawn seemed a little early to be asking us to pick up a carton of half and half or something.

"I need you girls! You've got to come right away!"

My mind was instantly filled with panic images: fire, flood, plague of frogs... When it came to Reba, the sky was the limit.

"What's the matter, Reba? What's going on?"

She drew a breath, then shrieked in my ear: "Your cousin Robert's been struck by lightning!"

She hung up. I listened to the dial tone for a few seconds, trying to decide whether it had been a bad dream. Then I reached down and pinched myself on the thigh.

It hurt.

It wasn't a bad dream. It was just my life.

Terry sleeps on a floor mattress in the front alcove of our little cabin. I walked down the stairs from my loft, made some coffee, then woke her to tell her the news.

"Give this to me again." She sat up and took the steaming mug from my hand. "Robert was *what?*"

"Struck by lightning."

She shook her head once. "In *Los Angeles*?"

"Presumably."

"You didn't *ask*?"

"She hung up before I could. And she didn't answer when I called back."

"Oh. Is he dead?"

"I think she would have said, don't you?"

"I guess so."

Terry held out the mug to me and slid off the mattress, careful not to disturb the sleeping dogs at her side. Paquito the Pomeranian was curled into a ball of fluff, and Muffy the pug was lying on her side, paws drawn into her tummy and snuffling through her mouth. Poor thing couldn't breathe through her nose. They'd bred the sinuses right out of her.

Terry stretched as she took back the coffee. She was dressed in leggings printed with pink camellias and a yellow T-shirt advertising the movie *Shaun of the Dead*. Zombie pajamas, how apropos for her.

"Sure you weren't dreaming?"

"I pinched myself to be sure."

"But how did it happen? Was he hanging Christmas lights or something?"

"You know they're Jewish now."

She gave a big yawn. "Oh yeah, I forgot."

Converting to Judaism had been a ploy on Reba's part to get her hooks into Eli Weintraub, my former boss and Terry's criminal lawyer. And ever since Terry and I had gone into the private investigation business, my lawyer too. Hanging out with Terry means you frequently need legal representation.

Reba and Eli had been romantically entangled for a time, but the affair fizzled because Reba was constantly trying to mold Eli into her idea of the perfect man. She realized her mistake and was currently trying to mold herself into the perfect woman, instead. She enrolled in Hebrew school on the theory that she'd be irresistible to Eli once they were of the same faith, but after a week she tried to buy off the rabbi so she could convert without all the tedious homework. She quit in a huff when the rabbi insisted she go through with the whole program. (Something about being "sincere in the eyes of God.")

Before Hebrew school, Reba had tried the Kabbalah Center, but she found the mysticism too weird, and once she heard how much they expected her to contribute to the temple, she bailed on that, too.

Something about being "cheap."

Ultimately she decided to slice through all the red tape, call herself Rebekkah, and proclaim herself Jewish anyway because, according to her, it was "more a state of mind than a religion, don't you agree?"

Trust me when I say there was no point in arguing the matter. Personally, I refused to call her Rebekkah until she had the papers to prove it. In the interests of humoring a senior citizen who was certifiably *meshugge*, I compromised by calling her Aunt Reb.

"What's the date?" Terry pulled back the curtain in her bedroom/alcove.

Outside was a beautifully crisp morning, a streak of sunlight shining through the blue-grey rain clouds.

"December 20th."

"It's not an April fool's joke, then." Terry let the curtain drop. "I can't believe Robert's had another disaster. You know what he is?" She gave me an impish grin. "He's a *lightning rod* for trouble."

"A little early for that, isn't it?"

She punched me in the arm. "Anytime is the right time for making you cringe."

If you're joining us on our adventures for the first time, I suppose an explanation is in order. Cousin Robert is a fifty-year-old mama's boy and artist who lives with Reba in her Tudor mansion. He had been a bit of a lush (okay, he was a lush's lush), but he slipped and fell down the marble staircase one day, and ever since that brush with death, he'd been on the road to sobriety. There had, however, been several potholes in the road.

First, he started an exercise regimen with a personal trainer and wound up collapsing in the back yard while doing jumping jacks, making everyone think he'd had a heart attack. Then, while attending a rehab program, he was allegedly kidnapped by aliens. After that he was booked, along with Reba, on a charge of decapitation murder. (They were ultimately exonerated with a little help from us.) After that, he conked himself on the head with a barbell, causing temporary amnesia. So you can probably see why I was coming to think of Robert as the unluckiest man in the world.

Now he'd been struck by lightning. I believe that's called the *coup de grâce*. At any rate, Reba could always count on Terry and me to come running when the inevitable shit hit the ever-whirring fan.

"Think we've got time to shower before we ride in to the rescue?" Terry asked.

"Sure. You first."

She blinked in surprise. "That's nice of you."

"'Tis the season."

Don't think us hard-hearted for our blasé reaction to Robert's latest crisis, but it's like the flight attendants tell you:

In case of depressurization, you should put on your own oxygen mask before trying to help the child next to you. If you're passed out in a state of anoxia, you're not going to do the little nipper any good. In our case, caffeine was second only to oxygen in terms of making us functional. We'd head east to Beverly Hills as soon as we'd polished off our morning pot of java.

two

*T*he lanes were indeed glistenin', though not with winter snow. Once outside, I found that our driveway was shining like the La Brea Tar Pits, which meant it had rained the night before and somehow I'd slept right through it. Atmospheric activity is so rare in Los Angeles, a little rainfall is as exciting as the Aurora Borealis. It's especially enjoyable as it pelts the skylight on my loft when I'm snug under Grandma's quilt, so I couldn't believe I never heard the sound.

I realized I must be depressed. Whenever I am, I sleep like the dead, though never quite as corpselike as Terry. The holiday season always brought some melancholy with it, seeing as how our parents were gone. And the ubiquitous carols with their relentless good cheer made me especially cranky, conjuring up Christmas in Burbank when Terry and I were kids.

We'd be up before dawn, sneaking into the living room to see what Santa had brought us during the night. Mom and Dad always left the tree illuminated on Christmas eve, the lights winking amid popcorn strands and gingerbread men and peppermint candy canes—a magical sight to a child's eyes. Beneath the tree we'd find piles of gifts wrapped in bright shiny foil paper, and next to the tree would be our "big presents." One particularly thrilling year we got twin starter bikes in pink with big satin bows on the handlebars.

Terry did an immediate inspection of the bikes and claimed the better one. Mom and Dad were scrupulous about treating us equally, but Terry had found a scratch on one of the fenders and she pawned the damaged goods off on me.

I didn't mind, figuring the bike was bound to get dinged coming down the chimney. What I couldn't get over was Santa's dead-on taste in gifts. How had he known it was the bike of my dreams?

I learned about Santa long before Terry did. She continued to believe in him for two years after I'd filed him away as a benevolent adult lie, but I still pretended for her sake that he'd been there and scarfed the milk and cookies in the living room before dropping off some choice consumer products. She was eight years old when she finally discovered the truth, and it hurt me to see her cover up the disappointment with the "tough bitch" act that she'd honed to perfection by the second grade. Looking back, that may have been the start of all Terry's troubles, the first of many disillusionments that would finally take her over the edge into drug addiction and prison.

However, it wouldn't account for her being an impulse control-challenged motorcycle lesbian. I'm pretty sure she was born that way.

These days our preferred mode of transport was a Harley-Davidson Softail Deuce. It was parked in the small detached garage next to the house, where it had remained nice and dry. The Harley was Terry's ride, bought with her share of Dad's insurance shortly after his death. The paint job was originally black, but she got high one day and decided it should be brain-blindingly pink.

Suddenly, as I watched her swing her leg over the Harley, I was the one zapped by lighting. I flashed on an image of the motorbike with a big satin bow on the apehanger handlebars.

Omigod, it's so obvious, I thought. *I can't believe it never occurred to me before!*

Terry had painted the Harley neon pink in an unconscious attempt to duplicate the first real bikes we had as kids, trying to recapture a time when the world was safe and predictable and filled with parental love. The realization literally made my jaw drop.

She saw the look on my face. "What?"

I thought better of sharing my epiphany with her. She didn't like me seeing through her hard shell to the soft marshmallow center. It affronted her self-image, and doing so could lead to sister-on-sister violence.

"Nothing," I said.

"What?"

"Nothing!"

She shook her head, cranking the ignition. "I hate it when you try to be mysterious."

"I don't feel obligated to share every stray thought I have with you, if that's all right."

"Moron," she said, laughing. "I *know* what you were thinking. You finally figured out I painted the Harley pink because of the starter bikes we had when we were five."

I don't know why this should have surprised me. We could often read each other's minds, but that was usually in times of duress, as when our lives were in danger or when we were extremely hungry. I suppose I'd clung to the idea that there was a corner of my mind impervious to her X-ray vision.

"Can't believe it took you so long to figure it out. You're not half as smart as you think."

Well, she had me there.

I snapped the chinstrap on my helmet, stuffed the Hanukkah presents into the saddlebags, and hopped on the bike behind Terry. She squealed off the concrete floor of the garage and roared out onto the gravel driveway, whipping into the southbound traffic on North Beverly Glen.

three

We took a left on Wilshire to cut through Beverly Hills, which was all tarted up for the season. Garlands in gold hung across the boulevard, anchored by traffic lights in the center islands. The windows of pricey boutiques were speckled with spray-on snow, offering up Christmas trinkets that cost more than we'd see in a good year. Medallions swung from street signs, encircling miniature sleighs, decorated fir trees, or little drummer boys banging their hearts out. *It was beginning to feel a lot like Christmas!*

Not.

Terry took another left onto Palm Drive and we pulled up to the gated brick fence of Reba's Tudor manse. I punched in the security code and the wrought iron gates opened with elaborate slowness, as if we were being admitted to Ft. Knox. We announced our arrival by banging on the front door with the brass lion knocker.

Griselda the housekeeper answered in a spotless white uniform. Her only concessions to the season were the red and green-striped stockings worn with her nurse's shoes and a sprig of holly stuck in her wiry gray bun.

"Merry Christmas, Grizzie!"

"For some." She ushered us inside without ceremony.

"Where do these go?" I asked, holding up the presents.

Grizzie ran the household with an iron Irish fist. You didn't dare put something where it didn't belong.

She pointed toward the living room. "In there, under the Christmas tree."

"*Hanukkah bush!*" Reba yelled from somewhere inside.

Grizzie turned to us with the expression of someone about to drag an electric toaster into her own bath.

"You can put 'em where the sun don't shine fer all I care." She trundled off to the kitchen.

"And a happy new year!" Terry called after her.

We wandered into the sunken living room and were greeted with a twinkling monstrosity—a ten-foot evergreen covered in golden tinsel, strings of lights, and enough rainbow crystals to stock a hundred chandeliers. Our gifts were going to look pretty pathetic under the fabulous tree (excuse me, *bush*), but what could you do?

Times were tough, as usual, and the presents were on a par with Bob Cratchit's. But Reba and Robert were extremely rich and could buy anything they wanted, so we had decided to focus on the things that money can't buy: health and happiness.

Cousin Robert had declared this "The Year of Fitness," so we bought him one of those pedometers that count the steps you take in the course of a day. That way he would know how many calories he burned while puttering around the house in his dressing gown, or dashing paint onto his canvasses in the upstairs studio, or being beamed up into a spaceship. The gadget had cost $1.95 with a Happy Meal, but he didn't have to know that. For Reba, we got a book by a sex therapist who resembled a hooker in her jacket photo, entitled "Get Him Back in Your Bed!"

We figured if the Jewish thing didn't work out, maybe she could lure Eli back with kinky sex.

I stuffed the packages between the overhanging evergreen branches and a tree skirt that sparkled with hand-sequined snowflakes.

"Thank you, dears. Most thoughtful. I was going to shop for you this morning, but then…" Reba paused for effect. "Tragedy struck."

"Thought it was lightning," Terry said.

I elbowed her in the back, but apparently Reba'd taken no offense.

She nodded gloomily. "So it was, so it was."

Reba sat at the glass table on the dining platform in a black silk suit and silver pumps, a long strand of pearls knotted at her collarbone. She was perfectly coiffed and sprayed, with nary a hennaed hair out of place despite the circumstances. Winking lights were wrapped around the marble columns that served as table legs, strobing festive white dots across her face.

Usually Reba would be having muffins and mangoes for breakfast, but today Grizzie had laid out a spread of lox, bagels, and cream cheese. Hey, if Reba was going to serve eats like this, maybe I'd consent to calling her Rebekkah after all.

We sat down to dig in.

"How did it happen?" Terry slathered cream cheese on an onion bagel, dotting it with capers and forking on a thin slice of lox. "Did he go out in the storm last night?"

Reba stirred her coffee. "Well, it's a *tad* embarrassing."

"We're family," I said, loading up my own bagel. "You can tell us."

"Yeah," Terry said, "we don't care if he was dancing naked in the rain wrapped in Christmas lights or something."

I kicked her in the shin under the table, but again Reba ignored her remark.

"You know how accident prone your cousin is," she began.

We nodded, chewing.

"Well, he went to the bathroom early this morning and… lightning struck at the very same instant."

Terry and I glanced at each other between bites.

"Struck what?" I said. "The roof?"

Reba made a pained face, but didn't answer.

"And this happened while Robert was in the bathroom?" Terry asked. "I'm not getting a mental picture here."

Reba let out a sigh. "It seems that the lightning hit the yard above some copper plumbing, then traveled up the pipes and into the bathroom where your cousin's *anatomy* served as a ground for the electrical charge. In short, it came through the toilet."

"*Came through the toilet?*" Terry coughed up a mouthful of lox into her napkin.

"It happens, apparently."

"No, it doesn't!" Terry turned to me. "Does it?"

I shrugged, as baffled as she was. I'd never heard of it before, but if such a freak occurrence were to befall anyone, anywhere on earth, at any time in history, it would definitely be Cousin Robert.

Still, a little clarification was needed. "Are you saying he was *sitting* on the toilet at the time?"

Reba nodded.

"Holy shit," Terry said.

"Language," Reba snapped.

Terry had finally managed to offend. I'd never doubted she would. We sat there for a moment in silent contemplation—*How weird was this?*

I finally thought to ask, "So where is Robert now?"

"In the hospital."

"And the prognosis?"

"Oh, he'll live. But they say…" Reba gave a little hiccup of grief. "They say he'll be a *vegetable*."

four

The halls of Cedars-Sinai Medical Center were decorated in multicultural splendor: blue and white for the Jewish patients, red and green for the Christians, gold and silver for the Beverly Hills residents who worshipped Mammon. The ICU nurse wore a Rudolph the Red-nosed Reindeer pin on her breast that cast a flashing red light on the underside of her jaw. Instead of being festive, though, it made her look a little spooky. A hair glowed on her chin like fiber optic cable.

"Are you family?"

"We're his cousins," Terry said, pointing to Reba. "That lady there is his mother."

The nurse looked over at Reba, whose face was obscured by enormous Valentino sunglasses. She slumped in a wheelchair, dabbing at her nose with a linen handkerchief.

"Is she all right?" the nurse asked with professional concern.

"Just overwrought," I assured her.

"Well, she can go, but you two will have to wait. We're only supposed to allow immediate family."

I gave her a baleful look. "Unfortunately, my aunt can't operate the chair."

"Oh? How long has she been wheelchair-bound?"

"Only about ten minutes. She fainted when she came through the front door of the hospital. She's had a lot of tragedy with her son. This is just the latest episode."

The nurse glanced at Reba again. "Go ahead, then. And you girls take care of your aunt. The holidays can really magnify a situation like this."

"We will," I said. "Thank you so much."

Terry grabbed the handles on Reba's wheelchair and started whizzing her down the linoleum toward Robert's private room. Reba went rigid in the seat, her hands white-knuckling the armrests.

"It's not the Indy 500!" she barked over her shoulder.

"I'm worried about Robert," Terry said, speeding along.

"He's not going anywhere, he's in a coma. Slow down!"

"Fine." Terry slammed to a stop.

Reba flew out of the chair, hitting the floor face first and sliding on her belly for ten feet, her legs in the air.

"Oops," Terry said.

I ran to help Reba to her feet, brushing off her skirt. "I'm so sorry! Are you all right?"

"Oops, indeed!" Reba glared at Terry as she wobbled back over to the wheelchair. "You might want to be a little more careful when wheeling senior citizens around. I could have broken a hip. Then you girls would be visiting me *and* your cousin in here."

"My bad," Terry said apologetically, proceeding at a snail's pace.

We entered Robert's room to find him unconscious, rigged up to so much machinery he looked like the view under the hood of a Cadillac. An oxygen tube snaked up his nose. His face was ghostly pale beneath the freckles, his rust-colored hair matted on the pillow. The EEG at his side had flat-lined, indicating Robert's cranial battery was dead.

I hadn't taken the whole thing seriously until that point, but now the awful truth was staring me in the face: My cousin was in a persistent vegetative state.

Reba leaned forward in her wheelchair and laid a trembling hand on Robert's leg. "What kind of God would take a child before his mother?" She balled up a spotted fist and shook it at the ceiling. "Is this the thanks I get for learning Hebrew? For all the money I've donated to *Thy* temple!"

"She's gonna bring down another lightning strike," I whispered to Terry.

"It might jump start the EEG."

"Don't blame God." I patted Reba's shoulder. "Sometimes things just happen."

"Don't you believe it! Everything happens for a reason."

Terry sighed. "What reason could the Almighty have for frying Robert's ass one fine December morning? You don't think He's got better things to do, like keeping the planets in motion?"

"Can't you understand?" Reba seemed desperate to convince us. "All the close scrapes he's had, all the near-death experiences... it's as if it's been *trying* to happen. It must be a punishment."

"But why see this as the wrath of God?" I said. "Robert's been doing so much better lately."

"Not Robert..." Reba removed her sunglasses, giving us soppy eyes. "I am the one who has transgressed! My whole life has been a lie!"

Terry's gaze went from Reba to the open door. I knew she was wondering how many seconds it would take her to cover the ground to the hallway, so I moved over to block her exit. With family, you can run but you cannot hide. I knew that all too well from being Terry's sister.

"What do you mean, a lie?" I asked Reba gently.

Her head drooped. "I never told him the truth. And now I'll never be able to. I was on the *verge* of it numerous times, but I couldn't bear to have my own son judge me."

I waited, not wanting to rush her into an admission of some deep dark secret. But of course Terry didn't hold back.

"What the hell are you talking about?"

"Robert's father was *not* Jeffrey Price," Reba said.

Terry and I gasped in spite of ourselves.

"He wasn't?" I ran through Reba's husbands in my mind. She'd had five of them over the years. Was Jeffrey number two? Number three?

"No, he was not Robert's father," Reba said. "Although I *was* married to Jeffrey at the time."

It took a second, but then Terry finally made the connection. "Wh-what are you saying? You had an *affair*?"

She gave us a shameful nod.

"So that would mean Robert is—?"

"The product of an illicit union," Reba confessed.

Holy cow. Was this ever a bombshell!

"It was the only time I ever strayed," Reba said, resigned to delivering the full payload now that she'd opened the bay doors. "He was a Frenchman I met on a flight to Paris. Jeffrey had been delayed by business and I went ahead alone. I was going to check into the Ritz and spend a few days shopping on the Rue de Rivoli."

"Robert's father was *French*?" Terry said, as if this were the most shocking element of the story. She couldn't have known it, but the best was yet to come.

"Oui," Reba said.

"And you got together with him in Paris?" I felt myself swaying on my feet, reeling from the idea that my great-aunt had a past straight out of a Harold Robbins novel.

"No. I never saw him again after the flight."

Another second passed while Terry and I processed this information.

"Wait a minute," Terry said slowly. "Are you telling us... you did it with this Frenchman *on the plane*?"

"Did it?" Reba shuddered. "I don't know where you get this crudeness, Terry. You certainly don't get it from me!"

"No, you're right. Apparently, what I get from *you* is congenital horniness!"

Reba spun her wheelchair to face the wall, groaning.

"Terry, please," I begged her.

"I don't believe this!" She half-laughed, half-screamed. "Robert was conceived in the Mile High Club! Why'd you name him Robert? Why not *Miles*?"

Reba pounded her fists on her thighs. "I admit it. I was weak, overcome with passion. I know you girls idolize me, but you must try to understand. I may be your great-aunt but I am also—" she threw back her head dramatically, "a *woman*."

The hospital room was spinning before me. I didn't know whether to laugh or throw up. I leaned over to steady myself on the bed, and my hand connected with Robert's shin.

"Watch it," Robert said.

"*Ahhhhhhhhhhhhhhh!*" the three of us screamed.

Amazingly, I saw that he was awake, his deep-set green eyes blinking like those of a fat, bearded newborn, affronted by the lights and commotion outside the womb. The EEG at his bedside was spiking furiously, colored lines shooting all over the place.

Robert's brain was back in business!

"Why are you screaming?" He looked around his hospital room. "What is this? A mental ward?"

Before we could answer, the reindeer nurse rushed into the room. "What's the matter? What happened?"

"Nothing's the matter!" Reba jumped out of the wheelchair and threw her arms in the air. "It's a Christmas miracle!"

The nurse frowned at me. "Thought you said she'd only been in the wheelchair a few minutes."

"That's not the miracle." I pointed to Robert.

The nurse ran to check the monitoring equipment, which was ablaze with cerebral activity. After a few moments, she turned her attention to Robert.

"Well, how about that? You're back from the dead." She shoved a bedpan in his face. "I'll let you take care of this, then."

five

$\mathcal{T}$he doctors wanted to keep Robert for observation, but he refused. He said that after his close shave with death, he had to get on with the business of living right away. He would be doing his living while seated on an inflated donut because of the second-degree burns on his backside, but other than that, he was fit as a big bass fiddle. He and Reba were now bundled in matching hospital blankets in the back of her mint green Mercedes-Benz.

"So, how do you feel, Robert?" Terry drove, inspecting him in the rearview mirror.

"Smashing, simply smashing!" Robert gave his chest a thump.

"You must have nine lives."

"Ten, but who's counting?" We all laughed, if a little uncomfortably. "You know, I've had so many close calls, I'm beginning to think I've been spared for a reason."

"What reason would that be, dear?" Reba asked.

"It must be so that I can get to know my real father."

Reba's mouth fell open. "You heard that?"

"Every word, Mumsy!"

Reba began scrabbling at the door handle. "Let me out! Let me out right here!"

She got a grip on it and sent the door flying, throwing herself outside. Only the shoulder harness prevented her from being dashed to the asphalt. She hung suspended from the belt like an elderly rag doll, arms waving in the wind.

Robert's reaction time was excellent for a recent coma patient. He grabbed Reba and jerked her back inside the car. Terry spun around to see what was happening and, as she did, accidentally wrenched the steering wheel, causing the Mercedes to veer into oncoming traffic in the opposite lane. I tried to warn her, but my scream strangled in my throat. I yanked the wheel back to avoid a head-on collision with a Hummer—but not before the Hummer's front bumper snapped off the Mercedes' open door like a pop-tab pulled from a soda can. The door bounced along the street as brakes squealed and cars swerved and my sanity flew my being.

No one in the Mercedes spoke for several seconds. The only sounds were a high keening noise coming from Reba and the shallow breathing of people who had barely cheated death seconds before.

"I'm so humiliated." Reba covered her face with her hands. "I want to die!"

"Yeah," Terry said. "But *we don't.*"

Robert sat there, smiling and placid as the Buddha. "There, there, Mumsy. Let's not exaggerate."

Terry pulled across three lanes of traffic to the side of the road. We turned to see if the Hummer had stopped for an accident report, but it was long gone. The driver had probably never even felt the impact, ensconced in his urban assault vehicle. Cars moved deftly around the severed door, the same way they did for crates of grapefruit or used mattresses or gas-powered lawnmowers that regularly fell off of the backs of trucks.

"No harm done," Terry said. "No cops in sight. I say we make a run for it."

"Go!" Reba kicked the back of Terry's seat. "Take me home!"

Terry pulled out into traffic again.

"You know, Mums, you did the right thing telling me," Robert said. "Even if you did think I was comatose at the time."

Reba peeked out from behind her hands. "I did?"

"To be perfectly honest, I always felt like a foundling. I mean, I felt close to *you*, of course. But I never felt that same affinity for my father."

"He did pass away when you were five," Reba pointed out.

"I always nurtured a fantasy that my real father was the Green Hornet, working to bring arch criminals to justice. Later, when I got into my teens, I imagined he was Elvis. I'd practice my hip gyrations in front of the mirror for hours in preparation for the day when he'd come to take me home to Graceland. When I grew up and discovered my passion for art, I pretended Pablo Picasso was my *papasita*."

"You *do* have me consorting with a number of strange men," Reba sniffed.

"I never really believed it, Mumsy. I was only compensating for being fatherless. And in a sense I was right, wasn't I? My real father was unknown to me."

"Your real sperm donor, you mean," Terry said.

I smacked her on the back of the head.

"Ow!" She smacked me back.

"But he's more than that," Robert insisted. "He's a flesh and blood man, with a history, a life. Dreams fulfilled and ambitions thwarted. When you think about it, I owe him my very existence. Without him, there'd have been no *me*."

"True enough," Reba agreed.

Robert studied her face. "But... does this mean you never loved Jeffrey?"

"Nonsense. I loved him dearly. He was my sweetest husband, and he lived the longest. I have to give him that."

Five years constituted a marriage marathon for Reba. Her husbands seemed to have been chosen for their wealth and infirmity, in reverse order. When they died, she attended their lavish memorials in chic black suits, mourned for a week, and was back on the dating circuit before you could say "merry widow." To her credit, these men never showed outward signs of terminal illness. But I couldn't help thinking she had some sort of sixth sense that they were about to cross that line into the great beyond. And as we all know, *you can't take it with you.*

"But if you loved him so much, why did you...?" Robert let the question hang in the air.

"I wish I knew," Reba said. "It was as if I were under some sort of spell. I was drawn to the man, and he to me. It was almost mystical."

"What was his name?"

Reba gazed out the window. "I don't remember."

"Come on, Reba," Terry said. "You do, too."

"It's the truth! Although I may have repressed it out of guilt."

"What did he look like?" Robert wanted to know.

Reba adjusted her sunglasses, thinking back. "Oh, he was handsome... in that rumpled, French-intellectual way. He had long black hair that—if we're to be completely honest—could have used a shampoo. He claimed to be a film director."

"A film director?"

"Yes. He'd been doing a publicity tour here in the States, he said. That's all he managed to tell me before..." Reba blushed, quickly changing the subject. "That must account for your artistic temperament, darling."

"But *which* French film director? Who was directing films in the Fifties? François Truffaut?"

Reba shook her head. "No, I'm sure it wasn't."

"Jean-Luc Godard?"

"Hmm. I don't recall a double name."

Robert twisted a bit of copper beard between his fingers. "Shouldn't be too hard to track down a French director on a press junket in 1954."

I expected Reba to react badly to this, but she merely shrugged. "It was so long ago. What are the chances that someone *I* was involved with has survived half a century?"

"Not very good," Robert admitted. "Still, I'd like to know something about him. Perhaps he was an unsung genius of the

French cinema, like Alain Robbe-Grillet, making obscure but highly symbolic films about the futility of existence."

"A regular Spielberg," Terry quipped.

"I might even have some half-siblings. An interesting cousin or two."

"Well, if *we're* not good enough for you," I said, feigning indignation.

"Don't be a dunderhead, Kerry, they don't come any better than you two. But if you had a biological counterpart somewhere out there in the world, wouldn't you want to meet him or her?"

I suppose the correct answer would have been *yes.* But the biological counterparts riding in the car with me seemed like more than enough to deal with in this lifetime. Terry cracked a smile, obviously thinking the same thing.

"Enough of this dwelling on the past," Reba said. "We've been given a new start! Let's take a trip, the four of us, as a family. I don't feel right about spending the holidays here, what with everything that's happened. What do you say?"

Something told me this was a ruse to keep Robert from exploring his roots, but I went along with it.

"A trip? You mean right now?"

"Yes. I know, how about Catalina?"

"But I was going to try to find my French family," Robert protested. "You can't drop something like that on me and expect me not to check into it."

"*This* is your family, dear. No matter who may have contributed some genetic material in the beginning. Let's forget about it, at least until the new year. If you insist on pursuing it, you can do it then."

"Catalina might be fun," I said, warming to the idea. "It's just a couple of hours away, isn't it?"

"It's only twenty minutes by helicopter," Reba said.

"Helicopter?" Terry jerked a thumb toward Robert. "You think I'm getting on a helicopter with Mr. Death here?"

Reba ignored this. "It's the quaintest little place. Have you been there before?"

"No," I said. "But I always meant to."

"What about it, then? Do you have any work?"

"Not at present."

We'd been sporadically employed since the previous summer, when we uncovered a blood-drinking cult in Venice Beach. (Long story.) A couple of months after that, we were hired to baby-sit a megastar pop tart in the Hollywood Hills. (Long, disastrous story.) There'd been a smattering of day jobs in the intervening months, but nothing that demanded our immediate attention.

"Then it's settled. I haven't bought you girls a gift. It'll be my treat. Why don't we go, say, day after tomorrow? I'll get us a reservation."

"I could stand a change of scenery. What do you think, Ter?"

"Beats sitting around here getting struck by lightning and sideswiped by Hummers."

"Wait. What'll we do with the dogs? I don't feel right calling Lance at the last minute to baby-sit during the holidays."

"How about a kennel?" Robert suggested.

"For their first Christmas?" I recoiled at the idea of the pups locked away in cages while we enjoyed an island vacation.

"Can we take them with us?" Terry asked.

"I don't know about that," Reba said. "We usually stay at the Hotel St. Lauren, a darling Victorian inn facing the bay. I doubt they allow dogs."

"I'm sure we can think of something," I said.

I knew that a "Plan B" usually presented itself when you needed it, from long experience with a series of botched "Plan A's."

"All right, then." Reba bounced in her seat. "We're headed to Avalon as a family!"

six

Our friend Lance Manley was a newly minted deputy in the Malibu sheriff's department, who was convinced (with some reason) that he owed me his life. He was always anxious to "work off his karma," but it turned out that he was headed home to Redwood City for the holidays. He offered to take the dogs along with him to his parents' house, but Terry and I declined. We didn't think a five-hour car trip would be their idea of fun.

We inquired into kennels, but we couldn't bear to leave our babies with complete strangers for a whole week. We'd never been separated from them for as many as twenty-four hours since they'd come to live with us.

Reba called with the solution just as we were about to cancel. Grizzie had declared that going to Catalina with her employers would be a mockery of a vacation, so she offered to sit the dogs at Reba's house.

"Think they'll be alive when we get back?" Terry asked. "Or will she pull a Cruella de Vil? Turn them into tea cozies or something?"

"Nah. After a few days with these little guys, even her hard old heart will melt. We'll have to pry them away from her with a crowbar."

Terry went shopping at PETCO, and on the morning we were scheduled to leave, we gave Muffy and Paquito their Christmas presents. They ripped into the packages, shredding the paper, almost fainting from excitement as each new treasure was revealed. Chew toys, bouncy balls, plastic squeakers, even a stuffed kitty-cat that was immediately beheaded. I lifted up one particularly strange object that resembled the wing of a vampire bat, turning it around in the light, fascinated and repelled at the same time.

"What is this?"

"Pig ear," Terry said.

I shrieked and tossed it across the room. Paquito and Muffy took off after it like twin shots. They snapped the ear up in their tiny maws and played a game of tug-o-war with it.

"Hey kids, don't play with that icky one!" I waved around a stick chewy. "Here's a nice piece of rawhide!"

Terry snickered.

"What?" I turned it over in my hand. "It *is* rawhide, isn't it?"

"It's called a bully stick."

"And?"

"According to the clerk at PETCO, it's a desiccated bull's penis."

I flung the bully stick away, gagging. The dogs dropped the pig's ear and darted after it.

"No, don't touch that!" I started to get up from the floor, but Terry grabbed the hem of my pants, holding me back.

"Get over it! They're carnivores!"

"So am I, but you don't see me snacking on scrotums!"

"Yeah, I noticed that." She gave me a sly wink. "Where is Mr. Boatwright these days, anyway?"

I kicked myself for handing her that set-up. John Boatwright was a homicide detective in Beverly Hills and my on-again, off-again love interest. I had started to pull back from him because he was making noises about commitment. I liked the guy a lot; I maybe even loved him. But when I thought about being Mrs.

Boatwright—Mrs. *Anybody*—for the rest of my life, I got a severe case of the heebies, complete with physical symptoms like upset stomach, chills, and tremors. I figured as long as my system couldn't distinguish between a husband and an intestinal parasite, I was better off postponing matrimony.

Complicating the situation was a sort of *thing*, for lack of a better word, I had with an FBI counterterrorist agent named Dwight Franzen. He worked undercover, which made it hard to explore any sort of relationship. But I was definitely hung up on him. Or at least on his memory.

"Boatwright's dad died last month," I said. "He had to go back to Arizona to be with his mom. I thought you knew that."

"He didn't invite you to go with him?"

I shook my head, but I wasn't fooling her.

"Yes, he did. But you told him you couldn't leave me on my own at Christmas."

I shrugged. "Something like that."

"Well, I wouldn't pass up great sex for you any time of the year. I just want to be upfront about it in case I'm ever given the choice. Hanging out with you or getting some, I'll take getting some. We clear?"

"As a bell."

That was a bald-faced lie. No matter how exasperating it could sometimes be, Terry and I were bonded for life. When she was in prison, it felt like I was living on borrowed air. I wasn't complete until she was back on the outside driving me insane.

Go ahead. Call me codependent. You wouldn't be the first.

Terry rolled back on the floor and whistled for the dogs. They romped over to her, biting her hair and licking her face, scampering around to the sound of crinkling wrapping paper.

"I'm gonna go wash my hands." I headed for the bathroom. "And I'm telling you now, you guys are never licking *my* face again."

"Don't listen to her," Terry whispered to the dogs. "She's got issues."

Grizzie drove up in the repaired Mercedes and waited for us to load the dogs into the car. They whimpered inside their traveling cages, breaking our hearts. They knew they were being dumped.

"Bye bye, honeys," Terry cooed, as she placed them in the backseat.

"Sure you don't mind watching them?" I asked Grizzie.

"Better'n celebrating Hanukkah with yer bloody aunt. Scraping menorah wax off the table. Settin' food out for some prophet's ghost. Gives me the shivers."

"Uh, thanks a lot. Here's everything you need to do." I handed her a page of instructions. "And here are their beds and bowls." She watched impassively as I stuffed the paraphernalia next to the kennels. Then she folded the instructions, stuffed them into her bra, and took off without another word.

Terry and I stood in the driveway, waving goodbye, swallowing our guilt as the threesome disappeared around the corner.

Was it cruel and unusual punishment sending the dogs home with her? Would this be the year the Griz stole Christmas?

seven

*W*e arrived at the helipad in Long Beach, with only a duffel between us. The friendly Japanese pilot loaded it on the chopper.

"How long will the trip take?" I asked him.

"Fifteen minutes. Twenty-two miles."

I looked inside the helicopter. Robert and Reba were already strapped in their seats.

"You think Robert's luck will hold on the trip over?" I whispered to Terry.

She wrung her hands, doing a dead-on impersonation of Reba. "What kind of God would take a son before he's met his biological father?"

"From your lips," I said, climbing aboard.

Inside, Robert raised his pant leg to show off the pedometer on his chunky ankle. "Love the counter, girls. It's perfect. I'll be much more conscious now of doing things for the aerobic benefit. Burned off fifteen calories just toting the luggage down from the taxi to the helipad. Five hundred, thirty thousand, eight hundred and twenty-one calories from now, I'll be a reed blowing in the wind."

"How on earth did you work that out?" Terry asked.

He patted the laptop computer at his side.

"You brought a computer just to count your calories?"

"No, I brought it because I've placed a personal ad in Paris looking for Dad. I asked for an email response."

Reba lowered her sunglasses, rolling her eyes. "That's like trying to find a needle in a haystack. Paris is a city of millions."

"It's a very targeted ad," he told her.

She reacted in alarm. "You didn't mention me by name?"

"Certainly not!"

"Thank goodness."

I was dying to know how the sex book had gone over. "Did you open your present from us, Aunt Reb?"

"Yes, but I didn't bring it with me," she said snippily. "I was fresh out of brown paper to wrap it in. Honestly, where did you girls ever get the idea that I was so interested in sex?"

The three of us just stared at her.

"Never mind." She turned to look out the window.

The pilot hopped into his seat and started the engine, rotors whirring noisily overhead. He welcomed us aboard, making sure we were buckled in with our headphones on. We began our journey by lifting straight up in the air.

Next thing I knew we were soaring out over Santa Monica bay.

Down below, sailboats with billowing sails cut through the water, churning up slender white wakes. The sky stretched before us, shimmering a pure, unpolluted blue. Terry tugged on my sleeve and pointed toward the horizon, where a breaching whale was displaying its enormous barnacled back. Then a fountain of water shot up from its blowhole, the droplets raining back down like sunlit diamonds.

Santa Catalina Island loomed just ahead of us, a craggy, verdant lump in the middle of the turquoise sea. The coast was lined with white buildings beneath a sheer, rocky cliff. Thousands of boats bobbed at anchor in the crescent-shaped bay. The top of the island was a wide expanse of valleys, peaks, and untrammeled grassland.

At least I thought it was untrammeled, until—

"Buffalo!" the pilot said.

He pointed to a large herd on a hilltop, wall-to-wall black bison, grazing peacefully like something out of the old west.

"Paramount Pictures made a cowboy movie here in the Twenties and left the herd behind!" the pilot explained.

Suddenly, the buffalo set themselves in motion across the hills, their humped backs moving in perfect concert. The dust rising from their hooves gave the impression they were being conveyed on a cloud. It was an even more breath-taking sight than the breaching whale.

A few moments later, the skids touched down in Avalon. After waiting for the pilot to give us the signal, we unbuckled our seatbelts and disembarked.

Terry high-fived the pilot on the way out. "Great flying!"

When I stepped onto the tarmac, I looked back at the mainland and saw smog hanging over the city like iodine-soaked cotton. But here was freshness, here was untouched wilderness, here was a herd of buffalo, which I had thought were pretty much extinct courtesy of the white man.

A van pulled up with the legend *Hotel St. Lauren* on the side. A tall brunette bounded out from the driver's seat. Her long, tan legs were clad in shorts despite the chilly temperature; her straight, sable hair was blowing in the wind. She gave us a broad smile, and thrust out her hand. "Hi, I'm Nikki, your driver. Welcome to Santa Catalina Island."

Terry darted in front of me to grab the girl's hand. "Hi, I'm Terry. This is Kerry."

Robert climbed out of the helicopter, his red hair wind-whipped into a peak like a Dairy Queen cone. He was dressed in his artist's togs—a paint-splattered yellow guayabera shirt, baggy khakis, and ratty old penny loafers worn like scuffs due to the mashed-down heels, and he had one arm through the inflated donut, wearing it like a big rubber bracelet.

"I hope he doesn't think that thing will float him," Nikki said out of the corner of her mouth.

Terry chuckled. "It's not an inner tube, it's a butt donut. He was hit by lightning and suffered second-degree burns."

"For real?"

"Yep, that's our boy. Cousin Robert."

Nikki gave Reba a hand down from the chopper. The pilot rolled up a luggage cart and tipped his cap to us. He wished us a nice stay and then proceeded to the terminal.

Nikki picked up our duffel and threw it into the luggage compartment at the back of the van. "By the way, we just had a cancellation, a newlywed couple that got into a fight. The bride ran out on the groom, so he left. The manager put you two in the honeymoon suite for the price of a regular double. It's got the best view in the whole hotel."

"Honeymoon suite?" Terry said. "Cool."

"The only thing is, it has a king-sized bed. If you don't want to share, they can bring up a cot."

Terry pointed to me. "She'll take the cot."

I found my investigator's instincts aroused by what Nikki had just said. Kerry McAfee, girl sleuth. Couldn't leave it alone, even on vacation.

"Where did the bride go?" I asked. "Back home?"

"Don't know. She just took off. The guy was devastated. Said he didn't want to stay in the suite by himself. You can't blame him."

"And where is he now?"

"I don't know exactly, but he hasn't left the island. I've seen him around."

"I wonder what the fight was about."

"Hey, if my husband was playing golf on our honeymoon, I'd be ticked off, too." Nikki slammed the hatch. "He says he only played nine holes, but when he got back, her bags were gone and so was she."

"Did he tell the police?" I said, trying to sound nonchalant.

Nikki shook her head as she helped Reba into the backseat. Robert followed, teetering on the running board as if he were about to tumble off. Terry threw her shoulder into his butt, vaulting him inside the van.

"Ouch!"

"Sorry. Forgot about your little problem, there."

Robert tossed his donut on the seat and positioned his posterior in the hole. "My fault. I've *got* to do something about these extra pounds. The good news is that I've burnt off five calories walking from the helicopter to here!"

I climbed into the van behind Terry. "So the groom hasn't reported her missing?"

"Nope. I'm pretty sure he didn't." Nikki hopped behind the wheel. "She's probably off sulking somewhere. When she's made him suffer enough, she'll turn up."

Maybe. But I had a sense of foreboding all the same.

eight

$\mathcal{T}$he van traveled west on the main drag, Casino Avenue, skimming the coastline past waterfront hotels and outdoor cafés. In the harbor, sailboats masts were wrapped in colorful Christmas lights. Wreaths of holly hung on the cabin doors of pleasure cruisers. One yacht featured a life-size mechanical Santa in red suit and sailor cap waving from the railing. Another boasted a group of reindeer hauling a sled full of toys.

"Isn't it charming?" Reba said. "What an excellent idea this was, if I do say so myself."

Cobblestone streets led uphill from sea level, lined with curio shops and T-shirt vendors. They appeared too narrow to allow for regular traffic.

"How do you get cars up and down these streets?" I asked Nikki.

"Very few of them are allowed here. This is a conservancy, so cars would be disruptive to the environment. But the inhabited part of the island is only a mile long. It's easy to get around on foot or on one of those." She motioned to a golf cart coming in the opposite direction.

"What about motorcycles?" Terry asked.

"A few. I have a Yamaha myself back on the mainland, but I left it at home when I moved here. Do you ride?"

"We have a custom Harley Softail," Terry said. "The bane of bikers the world over for its shocking pink paint job."

Nikki laughed, as she weaved around a group of tourists that had spilled out onto the street. "Where's home?"

"Los Angeles. My aunt and cousin are from Beverly Hills."

"Me, I'm from Tarzana," Nikki said. "I've been here about a year."

"Why'd you move?"

She waved an arm at the gorgeous surroundings. "This or the Valley? It's a no-brainer."

We passed a peninsula jutting out into the harbor, on which sat a cream-colored stucco rotunda with a red tile roof. Beneath the building's eaves were Moorish arched windows opening onto a circular balcony. A cupola was perched on the top of the structure.

"What's that building over there?" I asked.

"That's the Casino," Nikki said. "It houses a dance hall that was built in the late Twenties. They used to do live radio concert broadcasts from there with big bands like Jimmy Dorsey, Woody Herman, and Duke Ellington. Then it was used for Hollywood parties in the Fifties and Sixties. The Rat Pack—Frank Sinatra, Dean Martin, Jerry Lewis—they all came over here to play. Some of the greatest acts of all time have performed there."

Who knew this little island was so interesting? I'd expected a few hotels and beaches, not all of this living history, lovingly maintained. Maybe Christmas wouldn't be so depressing this year after all.

"They're having a holiday party there tomorrow night sponsored by the tourist bureau. You should check it out."

We passed a fountain in the main square that was covered in hand-painted tile with images of mermaids frolicking amid strands of kelp.

"That's the famous Catalina tile," Nikki told us. "They're currently refurbishing a lot of the old Art Deco murals around town. You'll see more arts-and-crafts era tile work here than anywhere else on earth."

I spotted a couple of men in wet suits walking along the narrow beach. "Is there a lot of scuba diving?"

"I'm actually a scuba instructor, myself. I do the shuttle thing to supplement my income. The diving's good, but not like the Caribbean or anything."

"Any night life?" Terry wanted to know.

"The *Chi Chi* dance club and a few bars, but I'm mostly into water sports, so I don't do much partying."

"I'd like to get some diving instruction," Terry said. "Is it too cold for it now?"

I knew immediately that diving wasn't all she had in mind. Nikki was definitely Terry's type.

"Not for us diehards," Nikki said.

Terry elbowed me excitedly. "Let's do it!"

"*You* die hard. I'm here to relax."

Nikki pulled a business card out of the pocket of her shorts and handed it back over her shoulder. It read:

"Catalina Dives — Nikki Edwards, Licensed Instructor."

"Call the number and set up an appointment," Nikki said. "Ask for me."

"Sure will."

Love—or at least a crush—was blossoming in Terry's dilated pupils. I was just wondering if she was going to get lucky during this trip, when Nikki suddenly slammed on the brakes, jerking us against our seat belts.

"Ho, there," Robert said. "Did we hit a tourist?"

"Sorry about that, everyone. We have a little situation here." Nikki leaned on the wheel, talking to someone through the windshield. "It's called driving on the right side of the road, lady."

A golf cart blocked our progress, angled toward an outdoor café. The woman driving the cart was a pudgy, middle-aged blonde with pale legs in white shorts, a pink golf shirt and matching anklets, her spotless white trainers betraying a complete lack of athleticism. She was probably a suburban housewife who'd thrown back too many umbrella drinks.

"Do you need a driver's license to use one of those carts?" I asked.

"Sure, but sometimes people think the usual road rules don't apply."

The woman peered up at us from under the roof of the cart. She had a bobbed hairdo, framing a face like an aging cheerleader's—bright blue eyes, chubby cheeks, upturned nose—but her cherubic face was contorted in fury.

"She looks like Doris Day," Robert said. "Only much, much angrier."

"More *psychotic*," Terry muttered.

The woman jerked up her right hand, middle finger extended. Her lips were pulled back in a hateful snarl. It was such an incongruous mix of perkiness and malevolence that it caused us all to gasp.

Nikki leaned back. "Hey, you're in paradise, remember? Collision averted. Let's get on with our lives now, okay?"

The woman fumed another few seconds, lips trembling with the effort of sneering. Finally, she withdrew her hand. The golf cart backed up and swung around the van to continue down the main drag.

"You had the right of way," Terry protested. "She came straight into your lane."

"Maybe she just got here and hasn't had time to unwind," Reba said. "Perhaps we should send her a complimentary massage."

"Or complimentary anger management classes," Robert suggested.

Nikki shook it off, pointing to a sprawling Victorian house on the edge of a cliff. "That's the Inn on Mt. Ada, originally William Wrigley's home. He bought ninety-nine percent of the island in 1919—"

"Wrigley?" Terry interrupted. "Like the gum?"

"The very same," Nikki replied.

"We have him to thank for our least favorite pickup line."

Nikki glanced at her in the rearview mirror. "What's that?"

"Can I double my pleasure, double my fun tonight?"

Nikki laughed. "Well, I don't think you can hold a grudge against him, especially not after you've seen the Inn. He chose that setting for his home because it received first sunlight in the morning and the last rays at sunset, and named it Mt. Ada after his wife. The Inn sits three hundred-and-fifty feet above the town, so the views aren't too shabby. Construction was completed in 1921. While the Wrigleys lived there, they entertained Calvin Coolidge and the Prince of Wales, among other bigwigs."

"How did they get all the building materials up there?" I asked.

"They brought horses to the top of the cliff, then harnessed them to lifts for hauling the lumber and other stuff. Everything was dragged up, piece by piece."

Nikki took a right onto Metropole Avenue. "Wrigley owned the Chicago Cubs at the time. They used to have spring training right up there." She indicated the bluffs high above us.

"Great spot for it," Robert said. "Why did they stop coming? Didn't like running the bases with buffalo?"

"Actually, World War II broke out and the island was used for training and quartering troops, instead." Nikki took another right onto Beacon Street and pulled up in front of a hotel on the corner. A gingerbread Victorian with white cornices and window frames on a background of pink, it looked good enough to eat. "Okay folks, here we are!"

Reba and Robert thanked her and walked ahead into the lobby. A uniformed doorman came out and proceeded to unload their matching Louis Vuitton luggage.

"It's so great to be here," Terry said, reaching in to grab our duffel. "Nice to get away from work."

"What do you guys do for a living?" Nikki asked.

"Private investigation." Terry hoisted the duffel on her shoulder like a sailor on leave, cocking her hip rakishly.

"You mean, like detectives?"

"Yeah." Terry shrugged modestly. "We've received medals from the mayor for valor."

Nikki seemed genuinely impressed. "Really?"

"It was nothing. Just brought down a few terrorists on a plane is all."

"That's off the hook." Nikki paused for thought. "You know, I might actually be in need of your services."

"Why? What's up?"

"It might be nothing, but—"

"If you've got a problem, we'd be happy to help."

"It's probably my imagination. But I've had the feeling lately that I'm being followed."

"When?" I asked. "While you're driving the van?"

"No, more in my off hours. I've thought I heard someone outside my window at night. When I go to check, there's no one there."

"How long has this been going on?"

"A week or so."

"Have you told the police about it?"

"Nah, I don't want to go to the sheriff until I'm sure. I'd feel dumb, you know?"

"Don't worry about that. You can never be too careful, an attractive woman living alone." Terry emphasized the word *attractive*. "Have you been bothered any other time?"

"It's… I don't know, a vague feeling. When I'm going home in the evenings or when I'm out food shopping. A sense I'm being shadowed."

"It doesn't sound like you *may* need our services," I said. "It seems you definitely do."

"Are you expensive?"

"I can be had for the price of a diving lesson," Terry said.

I knew for a fact she'd been had for less.

"Better not take chances," I told Nikki. "Don't worry about the cost."

"But are you sure you want to do this on your vacation? It's Christmas, and you just said how happy you were not to be working."

"No problem. It would spoil our trip if anything happened to our favorite tour guide."

Nikki let out a breath. "Thanks, I appreciate it. But like I said, it's probably nothing."

"Sure, probably nothing," I echoed, in an attempt to allay her fears. But I knew that "probably nothing" usually meant *something*.

Something none too good.

nine

$\mathcal{T}$he honeymoon suite, like the entire Hotel St. Lauren, was furnished in classic good taste. The floral curtains and matching bedspread complemented the persimmon walls, cherry wood chairs, and silk striped cushions. Two overstuffed armchairs were arranged in front of a gas fireplace with a hand-carved mantelpiece. It was warm and inviting, but the room's real charm lay in the view. Terry threw open the balcony doors, sighing appreciatively at the sight of Avalon Bay.

"This puts the su-weet in suite!" she exclaimed. "New plan, Ker. We're gonna give up our lives on the mainland and move here."

"Oh really?" I fell back on the bed, hands behind my head. "And what'll we do for spending money?"

"Bison rustlers?"

"Think again."

"Gotta be sunken treasure out there in that harbor. We could be treasure hunters."

"You haven't even had your first diving lesson."

"Let me dream, okay?"

As the sun began to set, the islanders fired up their Christmas decorations, green, red, and white lights against an indigo sky.

"Stars!" Terry exclaimed. "They have stars here!"

I joined her at the window and saw a spray of white pinpricks in the darkening mantle above us. "I'm pretty sure they have them everywhere."

"Yeah, but you can't see them in LA... *Look!* A falling star." It streaked down in an arc of sizzling white. "What does that mean?"

"It means a star burned out. It's probably a black hole of anti-matter now, sucking all the neighboring stars into its void."

She gave me a frown. "Buzz kill, man."

"Sorry."

"You depressed?"

"I guess so. Christmas, you know."

"I don't see how you could be depressed with that view. I could really get used to this."

"We'll see how you feel after being marooned here with Reba and Robert for a few days." Reba had made dinner reservations at a restaurant down the street from our hotel, named Le Metropole. I dressed in stiletto heels and a flirty skirt, a concession to the restaurant's five stars in the AAA guide. Terry wore tight black pants stuffed into knee-high platform boots, topped off with a white lace camisole and a woolen shrug. Glam outfit or no, she still walked like a stevedore.

Le Metropole had certainly earned those stars. The tables were draped with crisp white linen. Long green tapers flickered in centerpieces of pink poinsettia leaves. Place settings were white china rimmed in gold, paired with antique silverware and sparkling cut-glass stemware. A tuxedoed maitre d' led us to a harbor view table where Reba and Robert sat waiting for us.

"Listen, girls. I have our itinerary for tomorrow." Reba excitedly retrieved a handful of brochures from her purse. "How about this? We'll do breakfast at the hotel, then meet at the Pleasure Pier for a ride on the glass-bottom boat. Afterward, we'll take a trip up to the top of the island to see the buffalo, then we'll have lunch—"

"Sounds good," Terry said. "Except…"

Reba looked up from her brochures. "Except what?"

"We just took a job. We may need to do some investigating tomorrow."

"You took a case on our family vacation?" Reba sounded hurt.

"It's not really a case, more like a consultation," I said. "Our van driver has a little… situation."

"What sort of situation?" Robert seemed as keen on this new mystery as he was on the breadbasket that had just been delivered.

"A stalker, possibly."

"Oh dear. Well, I'm not surprised." He fished a warm roll out of the basket. "She's a pulchritudinous young thing."

Terry gave me a quizzical look.

"Hot," I translated. "It may be nothing, but we said we'd check it out for her."

"And how do you propose to do that?" Reba asked.

"We're going to her place after dinner to see if there's any evidence of a peeper. And we'll make sure her apartment's secure. If we don't get a good feeling, we'll encourage her to stay somewhere else and contact the police."

"You mean to say she hasn't *been* to the police?" Robert was aghast at the notion.

"She's afraid of being an hysterical female," Terry said.

"I'm going to get hysterical if I have to listen this dreary shop talk at dinner." Reba gestured for service.

An elderly waiter appeared at the table, wearing a black dinner jacket and maroon cummerbund. He looked like he'd been waiting tables since Benny Goodman was tooting his horn.

"Good evening. Any questions on the menu?"

"None, thank you," Reba answered. "We'll have the buffalo steaks, medium rare."

My gag reflex kicked in. "The *what?*"

"It's our specialty," the waiter informed me. "Served with a red wine mushroom sauce, accompanied by lyonnaise potatoes and steamed asparagus."

I was trying to express my revulsion at the idea of consuming mammoth meat when Reba gave my hand a pat.

"When in Catalina, do as the Catalinians do."

"May I recommend a nice cabernet?" the waiter inquired, taking the menus from us.

"Lovely," Reba replied.

The waiter was gone before I could voice an objection. Seems I was about to sample filet right off the hoof.

"They *eat* the buffalo?"

Reba smoothed her napkin over her knees. "Of course. What else would they do with them? Throw a rodeo?"

"This is a preserve, isn't it? It's a strange way to preserve something, turning it into steaks."

"I'm sure they'd become too numerous if left to their own devices," Robert said, copiously buttering a roll. "They'd overrun the place."

"I can't eat a buffalo!"

"Why not?" Terry said. "It's just like a cow, only bigger."

"But they're so ugly! They have those huge necks and big heads and those little tufts of hair on their foreheads that remind me of some old lady in curlers."

"You'd rather devour a cute little Beatrix Potter character like a bunny or a duck?" Robert asked.

I frowned, caught in my own contradictions.

"You won't see chickens winning any beauty contests," Terry put in. "And you eat plenty of *them.*"

"What would you have done if you'd come west in a wagon train?" Reba said. "You'd eat buffalo or starve."

"Oh, and I suppose *you'd* be out there like Annie Oakley, shooting your dinner between the eyes."

"Pretend it's sirloin." That was Reba's final word on the matter.

When the steaks arrived, I had to admit they looked delicious—thick and juicy. I watched everyone else dig in, and when I could no longer ignore the watering of my mouth, I took a bite, savoring the rich meat.

"Hey, this is pretty good. Tastes like beef. Only bigger."

Robert agreed. "What say we come back in the morning? I'd love a little *oeuf* and turf for breakfast."

After a dessert of sorbet and coffee, Terry and I said our goodnights, and then headed back to the hotel to meet Nikki. She pulled up in a golf cart, still attired in white T-shirt and blue shorts, a dark blue sweater tied around her shoulders. Her hair was pulled back in a long ponytail, aquamarine drop earrings dangling from her ears.

"I appreciate this," she said, as she took off with us down the hill. "I'll bring you back up to the hotel as soon as we're done."

Nikki lived in a modest apartment building on a side street, two blocks up from Crescent Avenue. It was a one-story structure with a private fenced-in area in front of each unit. We followed her through the fence door, crossing a miniature courtyard planted with banana trees and succulents. She unlocked the sliding glass door with an apologetic smile.

"It's kind of small."

It was, in fact, a claustrophobic shoebox of an apartment with a pint-sized bathroom and a kitchenette. Diving gear was piled in one corner. The table next to the door was covered with maps and books on sea life.

"So where did you see this intruder?" My eyes settled on the louvered window above the day bed.

Nikki knelt on the bed and pulled up the bamboo shades. "There, in the backyard. I installed an outdoor light, but it's burned out again."

By "backyard" she meant a five-foot strip of grass fronting a small alley. Across the way stood the back wall to another apartment building, glowing pastel green in the roof lights.

I peered out into the yard. "Let's take a look. Got a flashlight?"

Nikki found one and we exited through the kitchen door. I shone the torch below the window and saw that the ferns had been trampled and an aloe plant was crushed. Scattered around were the shards of a broken light bulb. I swung the flashlight up and illuminated the jagged glass remains in the overhang socket.

"You definitely have a peeper, a determined one. He broke your light so he could spy on you without being seen."

"Oh, terrific." Nikki appeared to be doing a quick mental review of her activities the past few days, trying to remember whether she'd performed them naked.

I shone the light around the ground again and found several deep footprints. "He's a big guy, heavy."

Suddenly there was the slap of shoe rubber on asphalt, the sound of pebbles being flung underfoot. The three of us spun around to see someone running down the dark alley. Before I could stop her, Terry gave chase in her high heels.

"Terry, wait!" I ran after her, yanking off my stilettos as I went, cursing at the rocks cutting into my feet.

"Oof! Ouch! Shit!"

Then there was the sound of crashing, and I came upon Terry rolling next to a garbage bin in the center of the alley, cradling her knee.

"Goddamn girly boots!" she yelled. "He knocked over the trash can as he went!"

I jumped over her and sprinted to the end of the alley, the flashlight beam crisscrossing the darkness. I saw nothing but small houses obscured by bushes and banana trees. Then I caught sight of a figure turning the corner down the block. The man was medium height with curly, dark hair. One of those people who looked like there'd been a mistake matching up the torso and limbs—the top half of his body was big and broad, the legs short and spindly. He had overlong arms, like an ape's. I realized there'd be no catching up to him, and I wouldn't know what to do with him even if I did. I hobbled back up the alley to find Nikki helping Terry to her feet.

"I'm so sorry about that," Nikki said. "Are you okay?"

Terry bent over to check out her torn pants and scraped knee. "Nothing a little Bactine won't cure. Where are your shoes, Ker?"

"Kicked 'em off." I tiptoed to the side of the alley to retrieve my pumps. "Why did you chase him?"

"Because he was there. Why did *you* chase him?"

"Got caught up in the moment, I guess." I slipped on my shoes and the three of us started back toward the apartment. I looked at Nikki. "Any idea who that was?"

"No," Nikki said, her voice shaking.

"Well, he's seen us now. And he knows you're aware of him, too."

"Is that a good thing or a bad thing?"

"Hate to say it," Terry told her. "But it's probably not good."

Back in the small bed-sitting room, Terry doctored her knee with ointment. The two of us tried to persuade Nikki to call the sheriff, but she declined on the grounds that the guy was long gone, and we'd probably scared him enough to keep him away for the night. She promised to file a report the next day.

"We'll go with you," Terry said. "I can give a good description of him. When I crashed into the bin, he turned around to make sure I was down. I got a decent look at his face."

"I only saw him from behind," I said. "But he's built like an ape."

Nikki handed Terry a Band-Aid. "Thanks, but I can file the report by myself. 'Ape-man' probably covers it. There can't be too many of them roaming the island." She headed for the kitchen. "I could use a beer. How about you guys?"

"Sure," I said.

Terry stretched the Band-Aid across her knee, while Nikki retrieved three longneck Bohemias from the small fridge along with a saucer of limes.

"Do you have any idea what he's after?" Somehow I didn't think we were getting the whole story from her. "Or is he a random pervert?"

"I don't know."

Nikki gazed out the kitchen window, then came back and set the beers on the table for us. Crossing one foot behind the other, she lowered herself to the floor, sitting with her back against the bed.

"The population of the island is only three thousand in

the winter." She squeezed a wedge of lime into the bottle. "Everybody knows everyone else. I suppose he could be a passenger on one of the boats."

"But why victimize you?" Terry asked.

"There is one possibility."

We waited, and at length she continued. "Um, my boyfriend... former boyfriend. I just found out he's married."

Terry's face fell on hearing the word 'boyfriend.' Still, you never knew when someone was a lesbian-in-training.

"Married," Terry repeated. "Not happily I take it."

"Guess not. Anyway, he never told me."

"And you think your stalker could in some way be related to him?"

Nikki stared at the floor. "I didn't handle it all that well when I found out he was lying to me. I yelled at him."

"He didn't appreciate that, huh?"

"Nope." She gave an embarrassed smile. "And then I did something pretty stupid. I threatened to tell his wife."

"How did he react to that?" I asked.

"He got eerily calm. Stopped yelling and said very quietly, 'I wouldn't do that if I were you.' Something about the way he said it—real low and slow—it gave me the willies."

"Was that the last you heard from him?"

"Yeah."

"And how long after this conversation did your stalker show up?" Terry asked.

Nikki corkscrewed her way back up to her feet, and crossed the room to the kitchen again. "No, I'm sure there's no connection. I don't even know why I brought it up."

"But you must have suspected there was a connection if it came to mind at all," I said.

She stood with her back to us. "It's just, your description of the guy..."

"Yes?"

"Well, it sounds a bit like someone I knew, but it couldn't be."

"Why not?"

She turned around to face us again. "Because he's in prison for assault."

I tried to hide my shock that a girl like Nikki would be acquainted with a convicted felon. "How did you know this person?"

"I worked with him. Long time ago."

A momentary silence followed.

"I tell you what," Terry said. "Why don't we stay with you tonight?"

"No, that's silly. You're paying for a room. I can't let you stay here."

"Then why don't you come back with us to the hotel?" I suggested. "We won't sleep if we think you're not safe."

"Seriously, I've imposed on you enough for one day. If anything happens, I'll call the sheriff."

"What about your neighbors?" Terry asked her. "Are you friendly with them?"

"Yeah, Max, he lives next door, used to be a tour guide. I'll tell him to watch out. You know how it is with old people, they never sleep."

There was no point in pursuing it. Her mind was made up.

"Well, okay. If you're certain, then we'll call it a night," I said.

"I'll phone the dive shop tomorrow and see about those lessons," Terry said. "I mean, if you're still up to it."

Nikki smiled. "Absolutely. Being in the water always makes me forget my troubles."

ten

$\mathcal{N}$ikki waved goodbye after dropping Terry and me in front of the St. Lauren, and we entered the lobby to find Robert seated on the couch watching a flat-screen TV.

"Girls! Come here, quickly! You have to see something on CNN!"

"What's going on?" Terry rushed to his side. "Not a terrorist strike, I hope."

He chuckled. "Depends on your definition of terrorist."

There was an early-morning shot of the Eiffel Tower on the screen.

"A new billboard has created quite a stir here in the city of lights," the bemused anchorman said. *"An unnamed American is apparently convinced that his natural father, a man he never knew, is a resident of Paris. However, his methods of genealogical research are a little unorthodox…"*

The live feed cut to a lighted billboard on the *Périphérique*, the highway encircling Paris. Terry and I gasped simultaneously, covering our mouths.

There was Reba, decades younger and bigger than life, posed like a screen siren next to a pool. She reclined on her elbow in a polka dot bathing costume with bra cups like nose cones, the skirted bottom hiked up over one hip. Her head was thrown back, a red ponytail dangling between her shoulder blades, crimson lips parted in a *Hello, Big Boy* smile. One thin but shapely leg was crooked over the other, which was stretched out alongside the water, and a long fingernail was caught between her teeth, hinting at sexual delights to be had.

My great-aunt the pin-up.

The best part had to be her shoes. Reba wore chunk-heeled, red patent leather sandals with miniature bunches of fruit attached to the insteps—papayas, bananas, apples, and grapes. It looked like she'd mugged a tiny produce vendor.

The female announcer took up the story from there.

"Êtes-vous mon père? Which translates to 'are you my father?' If you met this woman on a Delta Airlines flight from Los Angeles to Paris in 1954, you may be the one. Please respond to the email address below."

The male announcer sniggered. *"That ought to wake them up in Paris."*

"Any idea who she is, Jim?"

"So far, her identity is a mystery. But you can bet someone's going to find out who she is before this is over."

"I'd hate to be in her shoes," the female announcer said. *"Even if they weren't decorated with papayas."*

The story then changed to a police chase on the L.A. freeways.

"Omigod!" I screeched. "Where did you get that photo?"

"Found it years ago," Robert said." Stashed it away for a rainy day. Didn't know when I might need to blackmail the old girl. It was ideal for my purposes. No man who had carnal relations with that woman would be likely to forget it."

Terry slapped her forehead. "I wonder if Reba gave your father the finger-sucking treatment when she passed him on the way to the airplane bathroom."

"It's getting more attention than I ever dreamed, on satellite hookups from Hong Kong to Paraguay," Robert said, beaming.

"Even if the man isn't in France, he's sure to see it wherever he is."

"Provided he's not dead," I said. "How long has the billboard been up?"

"They just mounted it—*pardon*—last night. I was afraid there'd be pile-ups of Citroens and Renaults on the morning commute, bloody berets strewn across the expressway, but fortunately none has been reported."

"Have you considered how Reba's going to react to this?"

Robert smiled wickedly, enjoying this just a little too much, in my opinion. "She'll have a *cow*, naturally. Or perhaps a bison, given our current locale."

"But you believe she deserves this because she kept you in the dark about your true father, don't you?"

"Absolutely."

"And here I was thinking this was going to be a dull vacation," Terry said.

Just then a flash of a movement caught my eye. I saw a diminutive woman in large Valentino sunglasses and a headscarf, tiptoeing toward the hotel entrance, a Vuitton overnight bag in her hand.

"Reba, *stop*!"

Robert and Terry turned at the same instant. The would-be fugitive froze like a doe in the headlights, then made a mad dash past the startled doorman.

"Reba, come back!" Terry raced after her with me on her heels.

I plunged through the front door and found Reba hopping into a golf cart with the keys still in the ignition. "Where do you think you're going!"

"South America!" She brandished a teasing comb like a switchblade. "Don't try to stop me!"

The doorman ran outside. "Ma'am, there's no way off the island this time of night."

"Watch me!" Reba cranked the motor and sped off. Terry chased after her, jumping on the back of the cart.

"Reba, it's just a stupid billboard!" she yelled, clambering into the front seat.

After a few seconds, the cart ground to a halt. I caught up with them just as Reba slumped forward on the steering wheel.

"I'm ruined!" she wailed.

"It's not the end of the world," Terry said.

"I should never have told him the truth," Reba sobbed, her shoulders heaving. "I should have taken the secret to my grave. At least I could have lived out my later years with some dignity. Why did he do this to me? My own son?"

I gently nudged her across the front seat and took the wheel, turning the cart around. "It'll be okay."

"*Okay*? Being an international laughingstock is okay? Having your dirty laundry strung up across all known continents is okay? Oh, kill me now!"

"Not now," I said. "Maybe later. For the moment, you're going to have a nice nightcap and go to bed."

"I'll have facial surgery, that's what I'll do! I'll make sure nobody can recognize me, then I'll check into a nunnery."

"You can't 'check in' to a nunnery," Terry said. "It's not a day spa. Besides, they don't have Jewish nunneries."

"To hell with that!" Reba blurted out. "What's the use of converting now? Once Eli sees that picture, he'll want nothing to do with me!"

"I'm sure that's not true." Eli hadn't wanted anything to do with her for months, but this was not a good time to point that out.

"You think he wants a relationship with a whore?" she said. "A whore with *fruit shoes?*"

"I loved those shoes," I lied.

She sniffed up some tears. "They *were* all the rage at the time."

"You know what? I'll bet that's exactly what Eli wants."

"What?" Reba said hopefully. "A whore?"

"Of course not. But maybe somebody who's a little more accessible, a little less perfect. He's had you on a pedestal, you know."

"Perhaps you're right. Perhaps I should tone down the perfection, just a tad."

"We don't even know that Eli will see the story," Terry pointed out. "They don't watch CNN at the sports bar."

"They don't?"

"Only ESPN. Anybody who tried to change the channel would get the shit beat out of him."

"That's heartening, I suppose," Reba said.

I parked the cart in front of the hotel, and then took Reba's hand to help her down from the front seat. "You're going to get a good night's sleep. And you'll see, the whole thing will blow over by tomorrow."

"Let us hope." Reba raised a hand to her brow. "Meanwhile, be a dear and get Auntie some aspirin, will you? I feel a mega-migraine coming on."

Terry and I tucked Reba into bed with a hot water bottle, a pint of vodka, and the last four aspirin tablets from the vial in her vanity case. We made sure there were no other pills in her luggage, in case she was tempted to take the easy way out of her problems during the night.

Robert didn't seem to feel the least bit guilty about what he'd done. He was in fine spirits as he bid us goodnight at the door to our room.

"She'll get over it. She's nothing if not resilient. How many women bounce back from a husband's death quicker than the common cold?"

"That's true," I admitted. "But she's cancelled on the sightseeing tomorrow. I think she's gonna hole up in her room for the rest of the trip."

"I'd better cancel, too. Wouldn't want to miss it if I got a response to my ad."

He'll get responses all right, I thought. *From every old Parisian pervert on the planet."*

"So much for family togetherness," Terry sighed.

Robert bussed her on the cheek. "Want me to wake you if I hear something from Dad in the next few hours?"

"No, thanks. We need to sleep."

"Very well," he said, waddling down the hallway. *"Hasta mañana!"*

Finally, it was lights out in our suite. I snuggled down under the covers of my cot, trying to get comfortable. It wasn't bad for a rollaway, but it certainly wasn't the honeymoon king.

"I get the big bed tomorrow," I said.

"Fight me." Terry rolled around in ecstasy. "I'm the one who usually gets the floor, remember?"

As I lay there, my thoughts went to Muffy and Paquito. "You think the pups are having a good Christmas?"

"I think every day is Christmas for a dog. They're always having fun, just like little kids."

"Yeah. No memories of what used to be. No regrets."

She waited a second, and then said, "Sis?"

"Huh?"

"I miss Mom and Dad, too. I'm sorry we couldn't have them around in their golden years. But we do have each other."

"Right."

"And our memories."

"Yeah."

"And Reba and Robert."

"Don't push it."

"At least we got to know our dad, not like poor Robert."

"That's true."

Suddenly, Terry burst out laughing. "You remember the Christmas when Reba almost choked to death on a cheese log?"

"Omigod, I'd forgotten that!"

"Dad gave her the Heimlich maneuver and they crashed into the tree, knocking it over and smashing all the ornaments."

"I couldn't laugh at the time, I was too worried about our presents. But in retrospect, how hilarious was that?"

"She went to the emergency room. I think to get treated for humiliation."

"And Robert went with her in the ambulance, so it was just the four of us that year."

"We played football with Dad on the lawn. He let us tackle him, pretending to be hurt."

"Mom baked us chocolate chip cookies."

"And read us *The Night Before Christmas*."

"We sang those dopey carols at the piano."

"You sang carols. I played with my new Thundercats toys."

"*Thundercats, ho!*" we said together, and then laughed.

"Dad barbecued a turkey that year," Terry said. "Remember?"

"Butterball, baby."

"The best."

We both yawned.

"You know, Ker," she said. "One day we'll have our own kids and we can make all new memories. Until then—" She stopped mid-sentence and let out a snore.

"Night, Ter," I said.

Terry's right, I thought. We should cherish the past, but we needed to look forward to the future, too. Tomorrow was another day.

But as it turned out, today was far from over.

eleven

At first I thought I was dreaming. I was dragged out of a dead sleep by the sound of scraping at the door. A large figure slipped into the room, backlit from the hallway. I saw his shadow crossing the room to Terry's bed.

What's he doing? I thought in annoyance. *We told him to wait until tomorrow.*

"Robert. What are you—?"

He jerked around, surprised at the sound of my voice. I had barely formed the thought—*That isn't Robert!*—when he covered the room in one leap and pounced on top of me. Two hundred pounds minimum, smelling of sweat and wet wool.

A rough hand went over my mouth, stifling my scream. His knees pinned me to the mattress. I twisted my body, struggling to get free, kicking my feet under the covers. He dropped down on my shins, causing me to cry out in pain. But his thick hand muted my cry.

What was he going to do? I felt his other hand clamp down on my throat, choking me. My mouth and nostrils were blocked. I couldn't breathe.

Terry, wake up! I beamed to her.

It was like sending radio signals to a brick wall. She continued to snore contentedly, oblivious to my desperate straits.

My larynx was on the verge of collapsing. I was blacking out, lights flashing as my brain began the process of shutting itself down.

This is the end. I'll never see my family or the puppies again.

That's when the cot collapsed under our combined weight, crashing to the floor. I prayed the noise would finally penetrate Terry's stupor. My attacker let out an involuntary yelp of surprise, his hand coming off my mouth.

"Terry!" I screamed.

"Huh?" she said. "What?"

The attacker hesitated, unsure which one of us to go after. Terry had no such dilemma once she realized what was happening.

"Son of a bitch!" She flew off the bed.

The man jumped up to fend off her attack. Terry hit him on the head with a bedside lamp, seized in mid-flight. He grunted in pain, scuttling toward the door. Terry leapt through the air again and landed on his back, screeching and clawing like a rabid badger.

He cried out as she ripped at his face, his eyes, his curly hair. The door flew open, admitting enough hallway light for me to see him.

It was the Ape-man from the alley.

Terry clung to his broad back, her arm around his neck. Then he used brute strength to wrench himself out of her grip, tossing her away like a bag of garbage. She hit the floor hard.

He fled the room, slamming the door behind him.

Terry scrambled to her feet and lunged for the doorknob. I shoved her back into the room.

"No!" I threw the lock. "Terry, get a hold of yourself!"

She rushed me, full of unreasoning fury. "Out of my way!"

"Let him go, for Christ's sake! We're alive! Leave it alone!"

She kept up a pattern of footwork on the floor like a boxer spoiling for another round. Finally, she slowed down and her senses seemed to return.

"You're right," she said, huffing. "You're right."

We remained there for a moment, gathering our wits. Then she flipped on the light and I saw her clearly for the first time. Her hair was sticking out in all directions, her face stark white.

"Do I look as bad as you?" I rasped. It felt like someone had taken a razor blade to my vocal chords.

"Worse. You all right?"

"Yeah, I'm okay."

"I'll call the police," she said.

twelve

The responding officers arrived in fifteen minutes. Deputy Rain Whitehorse had black hair in a long braid. She was mid-thirties, with high cheekbones and steely black eyes. Her partner was the aptly named Deputy Billy Young. Ten years her junior, he was blond and baby-faced, the tan Stetson adding another six inches to his considerable height. He seemed completely flabbergasted that this sort of attack had happened here on Catalina. Maybe he thought he'd spend his twenty giving directions to tourists and citing tipsy golf cart drivers, not actually doing police work.

But Whitehorse was all over the situation, hungry for action. I thought she was probably in the wrong place for that, our little episode aside. Catalina is not known for its assault rate.

"You're sure he was the same man you saw at Ms. Edwards' apartment?" Whitehorse asked, taking notes.

Terry nodded impatiently. "Have you sent someone over to check on her?"

"How do you know it was the same man?" The deputy was too focused on her own line of questioning to be diverted.

"He has a distinctive kind of build."

"Describe it, please."

"He's a big ape." Terry's irritation was evident. "Have you sent someone over or not?"

Whitehorse glanced up at her. "Yes. Didn't I say that?"

"No you didn't!"

Whitehorse nodded to Young, who clicked on his shoulder radio. "Hurley, come in, over."

A man's voice crackled over the speaker. "Hurley, here."

"Have you located Ms. Edwards, over?"

"She hasn't answered the door. Want me to call, over?"

Whitehorse shook her head. "Probably out for the evening."

Terry glared at her. "She doesn't *go* out."

Whitehorse returned her gaze calmly. "I thought you just met her today."

"Yes, but she did happen to mention that she doesn't go out in the evenings. And tonight she was going to lock herself in."

"She's a grown woman, isn't she? She could have gone to stay with a friend."

"Oh, forget it!" Terry stomped toward the door, intent on taking matters into her own hands. "I'll go check on her myself."

Young blocked her exit. "Ma'am, we're not done here."

"*I'm* done." She tried to shove past him.

"Hold on, Ms. McAfee." Whitehorse clicked on her own radio. "Can you see in the window, Hurley, over?"

"Ten-four. The blinds are open."

"Shine your flashlight through the apartment. Use the bullhorn. Wake her up if she's there."

We waited a few moments, and then the radio squawked again. "No sign of a break-in. No one's there. Unless she's in the bathroom or on the kitchen floor."

"Ten-four. Whitehorse out."

Terry's hands went to her hips. "It's okay with you if she's lying on the bathroom floor, bleeding to death?"

Whitehorse didn't react to Terry's anger, which only inflamed it.

"Tell me something. Why would she leave the blinds open if she had a stalker? Even if she went to a friend's house, why would she give him a full-on view of the interior of her place?"

"Maybe she figured if the peeper saw no one home, he'd get discouraged."

"That doesn't make sense!"

"You let us worry about that. Now, you said the man looked like an ape. Can you be more specific?"

"Was he covered with fur? Did he beat his chest and go *hoooohoooohooo*?" Young pounded his pecs à la King Kong.

We all stared at him, open-mouthed. It was an unfunny joke at best, totally inappropriate at worst.

Young's cheeks went pink. "Just trying to lighten things up in here."

Whitehorse let out a breath and turned her attention back to us, waiting for an answer.

"He has bowed legs," Terry said. "His torso's too big for his lower body, and his knuckles look like they would drag on the floor."

"His hands were rough, like a laborer's," I added. "No fur on him, but his hair is curly and dark. He has very broad, sloping shoulders."

Whitehorse wrote it all down. "Anything else?"

I rubbed my sore neck and shrugged. "Like what?"

"Did you hear his voice?"

Terry and I shook our heads simultaneously.

"Only some grunting when Terry hit him in the head."

Terry pointed at the lamp on the floor. "There may be blood on that. Give it to your lab people."

"Don't have any of those," Young said wistfully. "Wish we did. We'll have to send it to L.A." He started to bag it up.

"Great," Terry said. "What about fingerprints?"

"There'll be somebody along later for that. It's tricky, though, in a public place like this. We'll do our best."

"There is something else," I said. "Nikki thought his description matched someone she'd worked with."

"Did she give you a name?"

"No. She seemed to change her mind about that when she remembered the guy was in prison."

"Right, well if he's in prison, he can't be her peeper," Whitehorse said. "We'd appreciate it if you'd come to the station tomorrow and work with our sketch artist."

I said we'd be there first thing in the morning.

"Not first thing. He's a volunteer. Works on one of the tile projects over at the Casino. He can usually spare an hour around lunch, okay?"

"What if the big ape hops the next ferry out of here?" Terry said.

"No chance of that." Whitehorse shut her notebook. "We'll have deputies on the dock in the morning searching for him. Later, we'll post the artist's rendering on a wanted poster all over town."

"Sure hate to upset the tourists," Young said. "This being Christmas and all."

"I think they'd be more upset if they got assaulted," Whitehorse said pointedly.

Young's shoulders sagged. "I just meant—"

"Anyway," she said in a low voice. "We've got that other thing."

"Other thing?"

"You know." She stole a glance at Terry and me. "Those *other* people coming over tomorrow. They'll want to see his picture."

"You think he's their guy?"

She gave her head a little shake as if to say: *Not in front of them.*

Terry crossed her arms. "Want to tell us what you're talking about?"

"Can't." Whitehorse angled for the door, looking back at me. "You sure you don't want to see a doctor?"

"There's nothing to be done for it."

"All right. Take care of yourselves, ladies. We'll be downstairs talking to the manager if you think of anything else." She motioned for Young to follow her.

"Thanks," I said, my voice still husky.

"It's our pleasure *and* our duty." Young gave a little bow, doffing his cowboy hat.

Whitehorse rolled her eyes and walked out the door. Young scooted out after her, practically treading on her heels.

Terry watched them leave as she sat down on the bed. "Should we wake Reba and Robert and tell them what happened?"

"Why get them all keyed up in the middle of the night?"

Somehow the two of them had missed the flurry of excitement. Most of the other guests on our floor had come running, but not our nearest and dearest. Robert was likely conked out on butt pain medication, and Reba had probably swilled the whole bottle of vodka to blot out her newfound infamy.

I coughed, wincing in pain.

"Hurts?" Terry asked.

"A little."

"Take the big bed."

She got up shoved me down on it, then moved toward the door. "I'm gonna check on Nikki. You stay here."

I came off the bed again, yelling, "No!"

Damn, that hurt.

"She's a client and she needs protection."

"She's not *there*."

"And that doesn't bother you?"

I'd been too concerned for myself to worry about Nikki—a realization that made me feel ashamed.

Terry pulled on her pink leather jacket with the fringe. "If I need you, I'll call the room phone."

"Forget it." I got up and retrieved my black motorcycle jacket from the armoire. "I'm coming with you."

thirteen

$\mathcal{T}$he lobby was quiet. The deputies were probably inside the office, interviewing the manager. We snuck out of the hotel and hiked down the hill, then took Crescent Avenue in the direction of Nikki's street. I doubt I could have found the place again on my own, but Terry's in-born GPS led us straight to it.

She had a great sense of direction, but I had a finely honed sense of survival. It's what made us a good team.

I saw no cop cars in the vicinity. "They're gone."

After slipping inside the fence, we peeked through the plate glass door. The apartment appeared empty.

"Maybe she went somewhere else to spend the night after all."

"We're gonna make sure." Terry fished a small leather case out of her pocket. "Brought my trusty lock pick with me."

"On Christmas vacation?"

"I like to be prepared." She took out two small levers, inserting one into the slot above the door handle to secure the tumblers, using the one below to release the locking mechanism.

I didn't object to the illegal entry. Now that I was more fully recovered from my own trauma, I agreed that the deputies had been too casual about Nikki's safety. They didn't seem all that concerned that there was an attacker at large, one who'd brought me very close to death.

The door was open in seconds. We entered the dark room, our senses alert.

"Nikki?" Terry whispered. "You here, girl?"

There was no answer. No one was visible in the studio apartment.

I headed for the kitchen while Terry went to the bathroom. We flipped on the lights. When neither of us saw a dead body, we quickly turned them off again in case the cops were stationed nearby.

"Not here," I said.

Terry reached for the flashlight, shining it on the table next to the door. "She left a note."

I picked up a folded square of paper with our names on it, and read the handwritten note inside:

Dear girls,

I've decided to leave for my parents' house early. I'm spending Christmas with them. Hopefully all the other stuff will be sorted out by the time I get back. Thanks a lot and happy holidays,

Nikki ☺

"Good," I said. "She's gone home."

Terry read the note herself, then stuffed it in her jeans pocket. She shone the flashlight around the apartment, stopping at the flippers, tank, and diving mask piled in the corner.

"Her equipment's here."

"It's not as if she can go deep-sea diving in Tarzana."

"I don't like this."

She began opening the drawers of the pasteboard dresser one by one. They were full of clothes. So was the closet. A black suitcase sat on the top shelf. "None of her clothes are gone, and her suitcase is still here."

"Maybe she travels light. Took a duffel, same as us. Obviously she didn't want us to worry. That's why she left the note."

Terry gave me a patronizing look. "If the note was to keep

us from worrying, how were we supposed to get it? She left it inside her locked apartment."

"Oh."

"And how's she getting off the island in the middle of the night?"

"You know, the oxygen was cut off to my brain for several minutes when I was being strangled."

"Good excuse, but don't think about using it again after tonight." Terry let her gaze move around the apartment, as if she were afraid of missing something. "I guess there's nothing more we can—"

Suddenly, the phone rang, causing us both to jump. Terry made a dive for it.

I grabbed her arm. "What if it's the sheriffs? We broke in!"

She brushed my hand away and snatched up the phone, then held out the receiver so we could both hear the open line.

A man's voice, "Are you there?"

We held our breath.

"Nikki, is that you?" There was a lengthy pause. "You're gonna pay for this, bitch," he said, then the line went dead.

Terry stared at the phone in her hand. "She doesn't have Caller ID."

"Hit star sixty-nine."

She punched it in, but Nikki apparently didn't have the automatic callback service either.

"She's *going* to pay?" Terry said softly, setting the phone back in its cradle. "Or she already has?"

"But if he wants *her* to pay for something, why did he come after *us*?"

"Maybe that was the boyfriend. He sent the Ape-man to intimidate Nikki. After he saw us here, he followed us to the hotel."

"But that doesn't make sense. He tried to kill me. What purpose would that serve?"

"If her private investigator was attacked, Nikki might think twice about telling the wife about their relationship."

It was my turn to be patronizing. "He didn't know I was in

the room. I surprised him. If he had followed us, he would have known there were two of us. Besides, who would ever suspect us of being investigators?"

"Okay, then. So he's not connected to the boyfriend. He's just some mad rapist on the loose."

"That's reassuring."

"Hold on. What about the old guy who lives next door? What did Nikki say his name was?"

"Max, I think."

"She said he never sleeps. If he's an insomniac, he probably wouldn't mind answering some questions."

"Two complete strangers knocking on your door late at night?"

"Come on, let's try it."

We went back outside and passed through the neighbor's fence, then drew back at the sight of an old man pressed up against the plate glass door. He was dressed in pajamas and a threadbare housecoat, the sparse white hair spiking on top of his head. His mouth was wide open, his fingers splayed on the glass. He looked as if he'd seen a ghost, or maybe had become one.

"Max?" I called from the fence.

He nodded.

"May we talk to you?"

I read his lips through the glass: "Who are you?"

Terry pointed to the next-door apartment. "Friends of Nikki's."

He fumbled with the lock, tugging the door partway open. "I heard noise over there. Thought it was that big fella again. I was gonna call the sheriffs back out here."

"Big fella?" Terry said. "Do you mean the one who's built like an ape?"

"That's the one. I've seen him outside in the bushes. I wanted to call the law, but the little tramp said not to."

The little tramp? Nikki had said she and Max were friends. That was a strange way to talk about your pals.

"Why didn't she want you to call them?"

"Have'ta ask *her* that," the old man sneered. "Who the hell knows what she gets up to over there. You're probably just like her. Men coming and going at all hours." He started to close the door.

"Excuse me." I pushed back on the handle. "Nikki was afraid of that man, the one you saw. She hired us to find out why he was stalking her. We're private investigators."

"Well, she's off with another one now. I wouldn't worry about her."

"Another man?" Terry frowned at him. "Who?"

He shrugged his bony shoulders. "Some beach bum."

"But what did he look like?"

"Like a bum!"

"Dark-haired. Blond?"

"Dark hair. Light-skinned, though."

"When was this?" I asked.

"Couple hours ago," the old man said, reaching for the door handle. "I got better things to do than keep track'a you little tramps and your boyfriends."

"You're sure she went willingly?"

"Ain't one *yet* she didn't go with willingly."

Terry glanced over her shoulder at the fence. "But how could you see them? Were you standing at the fence?"

"A man has a right to know what's going on next door to him," he grumbled.

I took that as a *yes*. He'd been spying through the fence and had seen her leave. But how good could his eyesight be?

"Did you tell the officers about this? The ones who were here earlier?"

"I told ya, I got better things to do."

Before we could ask another question, he slammed the door closed with more strength than I would have expected. He locked it and waved us away from the glass, as if we were a couple of neighborhood brats trampling his prize geraniums.

fourteen

$\mathcal{J}$erry and I were too wound up to do much sleeping that night. I heard her thrashing around on the cot as I struggled to let my guard down and get some z's.

It was useless; I couldn't stop worrying about Nikki—wondering if the Ape-man had somehow gotten to her. Max had seen her leaving the apartment with someone. *Who was it, and where was she now?*

I finally gave up on sleep at seven o'clock, just four hours after we'd gone to bed. When I got up to go to the bathroom I saw that Terry was wide awake, hands behind her head, staring at the ceiling.

"Couldn't sleep?"

"Nope."

"That's a first."

"Hurry up with the bathroom, okay?"

Once we were showered and dressed, we started down the hallway to catch the elevator. We passed Reba's room just as her breakfast was being delivered, along with the morning newspaper.

"Uh-oh," Terry said. "Here comes trouble."

We'd already seen the front page of our own complimentary L.A. Times. It featured the story of a randy Beverly Hills matron doing her Rita Hayworth impersonation in a full-color photograph above the fold. On top of that, some ace reporter had ascertained Reba's identity.

We covered our ears as we bolted into the elevator, but we still heard her blood-curdling screams all the way down to the lobby.

Robert was sipping coffee in an overstuffed chair next to the window. A shaft of sunlight struck the front page of the paper next to his saucer. "Good morning, lovelies!"

"Not so good." I said. "Didn't you hear that screaming?"

"Yes, indeed. What was it? Sounded like a seal being attacked by a shark."

We glared at him until he flipped over the newspaper to hide Reba's photograph. "Mumsy?"

We nodded.

"I'm sorry she's taking it so hard, but I have the right to know my natural father. It's anyone's right."

I crossed my arms over my chest. "I wish you had found a less public method of locating him."

"Like what?"

"Ever think of hiring a private detective?" Terry said sarcastically. "I wouldn't have minded flying to Paris on your dime."

Robert actually blushed. "Egads! Here I was in the presence of two highly accomplished snoops, and the thought never occurred to me. I suppose it's hard for me to think of you girls as anything other than those knobby-kneed, freckle-faced little things in pigtails."

"Well, the damage is done," I said. "And I don't think there's any chance she'll join us sight-seeing."

"Probably not," Robert agreed glumly.

"How about you?" Terry asked. "Want to try the glass-bottom boat?"

He shook his head. "Got to man the phones. You never know when someone's going to respond to my ad."

"Any takers so far?"

"No, but I remain hopeful."

That's when I noticed a Santa suit draped over the chair next to Robert—a peaked cap with a white pompom, red pants the size of a circus tent, and a thick black belt.

"Hey, check it. Santa got naked and forgot his suit."

"Oh, that's mine," Robert said.

"What do you mean, *yours*?"

"I've been scouted by the hotel for the Christmas party over at the Casino. Apparently, their Santa got drunk and drove his golf cart into a canyon last night. He's laid up with a broken leg. Can't very well have the little children climbing onto a plaster cast, asking for their hearts' desires, can we? I'm the only one around with the right girth to play the old boy." Robert expanded his stomach proudly.

"But... do you think you're the right one for it? You're not such a big fan of kids."

"I was practically made for the part! All the great thespians had roles they were born to play. Barrymore had his Hamlet. Olivier his Othello—"

"And you've got your Kringle," Terry said.

He pulled the cap down over his kinky hair. "I'm told it's only for an hour or so. It's the least I can do for the children of this fair island. By the way, I told them you would help out, too."

Terry narrowed her eyes at him. "Help out how?"

"You know—Santa's helpers. Bringing the children up to my throne." He trilled the "r" in throne.

"All right, but no little elf outfits. I draw the line at little elf outfits."

"I'm sure you can wear whatever you please."

Terry looked at me. "Okay with you?"

"Okay, I'm in." It sounded like we were already committed, and anyway, it might be fun. Just the thing to take our minds off the more nefarious goings-on here on the island.

Terry reached for the coffee carafe and poured a Styrofoam cupful for me. "Let's fuel up, then go to the dive shop and see if we talk to some of Nikki's co-workers. Maybe they have her phone number in Tarzana."

"Your stalker victim?" Robert asked. "What's going on?"

"Should we tell him?" Terry asked me.

"Tell me what?"

"What you slept through last night."

She gave him a quick rundown of the attack, as well as the trip to Nikki's afterward. His little green eyes got rounder and rounder as she recounted the story.

He yanked the cap from his head, starting up from the chair. "We should leave here at once! I had no idea Catalina was so dangerous!"

Terry pushed him back down on the donut, which gave a squeak of protest.

"What kind of detectives would we be if we wimped out anytime things got dicey?"

"Do you mean to say you're going to stay and follow through on this case? Even after being attacked in your own hotel suite?"

"Please don't tell Reba about it," I begged him. "She's got enough to cope with."

"Very well," Robert said, pouring himself some more coffee. "But I have to say, you girls are something else. Where you go, trouble follows."

You are so not one to talk, I thought.

The dive shop's window was decorated with tempera paintings of tropical fish, flowing kelp, and scuba divers blowing bubbles. A cardboard clock hanging on the door indicated that the store would open at ten a.m. It was just past eight.

"Hmm," Terry said, tapping on the clock. "Can't talk to them, can't go to the sheriff's office yet."

"Shall we take the glass-bottom tour?"

"Gotta do something. All this *hurry up and wait* stuff is making me nuts."

"Easy. You're in paradise, remember?"

We ambled along the main street, watching the morning's activity out in the harbor. People were drinking coffee on deck,

enjoying the morning sun, or pulling up anchor to do their pleasure cruising and deep-sea fishing. We took our place in line at
the ticket booth near the Pleasure Pier.

The glass-bottom boat was weathered wood, with a small
house-like structure sitting on the flat bottom. It reminded me
of *Tommy the Tugboat,* minus the expressive eye windows and big
smile on his smokestack.

Inside, wooden benches were arranged around a pane of
glass that took up most of the floor's surface area. Passengers
leaned on a blue plastic barrier surrounding the glass to watch
the underwater show. Our guide was a short woman in her fifties with a dark, silver-streaked pageboy and a holly-jolly attitude.

"Welcome one, welcome all, aboard the famous glass-bottom
boat!"

The captain tooted 'Tommy's' horn and we started out into
the choppy water. A cool breeze blew inland, as the boat rocked
over the swells. Seagulls cawed hungrily when a teenage boy
began to toss chum off the side of the boat.

Almost immediately, orange fish with electric blue stripes
materialized beneath the glass. The passengers leaned forward,
oohing and *ahhing* at the sight of scales flashing golden in the
sun-dappled water.

"You're looking at the Blue-banded Goby fish," the guide began.
"And those pure gold fish are the famous Catalina Garibaldi."

Greenish-yellow leafy stalks brushed at the base of the boat,
swaying in a slow, undulating waltz. "...This is the kelp forest.
It's cultivated by the Catalina Conservancy and is harvested for
food and clothing products."

I was captivated by the watery habitat, strange and forbid-
ding in the murky light. I could see why mermaids figured so
prominently in the mythology of this island—you could almost
picture them playing hide-and-seek among the stands of kelp,
weaving it into garlands for their shiny green hair.

"...And those are the Blackeye Goby. They travel in very large
schools, as you can see, feeding on the smaller fishes inside the
kelp forest."

We passed over a school of pinky-silver fish with bulging raccoon eyes. They moved as one organism, darting this way and that, angling towards a source of food, or perhaps fleeing some perceived danger.

I spied something large and white below the school. The Goby had discovered a bonanza, a large dead fish to feed on.

Yet on second glance, the object didn't resemble a fish at all. It was large and white, with a hint of blue showing through the swarm.

"What's that big white thing they're hovering over?" I asked the guide.

She leaned in toward the glass. "Where?"

"Right there."

Several others also tried to see, but it was too late. We'd passed over the spot.

"It may have been a dead stingray," the guide said, returning to her spiel for the other tourists.

"Didn't look like a stingray to me," I whispered to Terry. "It was more elongated."

"Dolphin?"

I got up from my seat, grabbing her by the sleeve. "Let's go outside for a minute."

Terry and I hustled out to the aft deck. Beyond the wake, I spied something floating in the water. A woman's blue tennis shoe.

"See that?"

"It's a shoe."

"You know that 'stingray' we just saw?"

"Yeah?"

"Something tells me it wasn't a ray."

She squinted into the distance. "You're imagining things."

"Maybe, maybe not. I'm going to talk to the captain."

I noted a landmark so we could find our way back to this spot, a snazzy yacht at anchor, semaphore flags flying from the crow's nest. Her name was *All That*.

I knocked on the open frame of the captain's door. He popped his head outside, a welcoming smile in his wind-burnished cheeks. "Want to take over the helm?"

"No thanks. I was wondering, did you see that shoe back there in the water?"

"You lost a shoe?"

"No, but I saw one bobbing on the waves, right back there."

"I wouldn't worry about it. Things fall overboard. I'm sure its owner can live without it."

"The reason I ask is, um, we passed over a large white object at about the same time. The fish were eating it."

He frowned curiously. "White object?"

"The guide thought it might have been a ray. But don't you think it's a little funny that a shoe is floating there in the same spot? I mean, I'm not saying it was necessarily a human body, but—"

"Whoa, Nelly. You have some imagination. Are you a movie writer or something?"

"No, my sister and I are private investigators. We're here on vacation."

"Well, Ms. Investigator, keep your eyes peeled on the way back. We'll get a look at your white object."

"Hope you don't think I'm paranoid, but we're from Los Angeles. Being paranoid is a way of life."

"Sure. A person's gotta be crazy not to be paranoid these days." He ducked back inside, and I overheard him telling a crewmember about our conversation, followed by muffled laughter.

Terry leaned on the railing, enjoying the wind blowing across her face. "You tell the captain what you saw?"

"Yep."

"Did he treat you like an hysterical female?"

"Yep."

"Good. 'Cause you are."

"Terry, Nikki was wearing blue tennis shoes last night."

"And so were a thousand other people."

We waited out the next hour on deck, at one point coming across a family of seals. They cavorted in the waves, rolling and barking and splashing, having as much fun as a pool full of five-year-olds. I was unable to appreciate their carefree attitude, too caught up in my morbid imaginings. I prayed that I'd been hallucinating, but the lead weight in my stomach told me otherwise.

Eventually, we were headed back toward the *All That*, and Terry and I moved to the prow of the boat.

"Ahoy!" I yelled, pointing out in front of us. "There's the shoe!"

Terry squinted. "I see it."

I knocked on the door. The captain poked his head outside again. "Did you enjoy the tour?"

"There's the shoe I told you about."

He brought a pair of binoculars up to his face.

"I see it." He sounded less amused with the situation now. "I'm pretty sure it's nothing, but we'll check it out."

While the captain turned the boat around, I dragged Terry back into the main cabin where the guide was wrapping up her presentation. We squeezed onto the bench between a kid with a white buzz cut who was punching his little brother in the arm, and an older woman with half-glasses who watched, enthralled, as the kelp forest passed underfoot.

"Keep your eye on the glass," I said to Terry.

"Fish and leaves. How scintillating." She hunched back against the hull.

My gaze was glued on the bottom of the boat. Soon a school of silver fish appeared below. They rode along with us, merging with another identical school, a massive conglomeration of twitching tails and glittering scales. They swirled and pitched around a large white object.

"There it is!"

It had been snagged in the kelp, but the motion of the glass-bottom boat caused the object to be released. Slowly, it floated up toward the window.

It was a woman.

Her dark hair trailed behind her, her arms floating weightlessly at her side. Her large blue eyes had turned milky in the water. There was a bloody mass where her facial skin used to be, the white teeth forming a lipless grimace. Bits of tissue floated towards the water's surface, where hundreds of silver fish nibbled on them with tiny, relentless bites.

Her forehead bumped the glass, the eyes staring up at us sightlessly.

Women and children screamed.

fifteen

They anchored the boat at the spot. The first mate and chum boy attempted to snag the body with a net and grappling hooks, while the tour guide hustled the passengers to the opposite side. They crossed a gangplank to another boat that had arrived to return them to shore, sneaking peeks over their shoulders as if they expected a homicidal maniac to come rising out of the waves.

People on nearby yachts and sailboats craned their necks to see what was going on. Drinks in hand, they talked excitedly, like spectators at a sporting match. It was bloodthirsty American voyeurism at its best.

After we told the captain that we thought we knew the dead woman, he asked us to remain onboard to make an identification.

"How did you know her?"

"She was our van driver to the hotel," Terry told him. "She was having problems with a stalker and hired us to look into it."

"And how did you know she was in the water?"

I flinched at his suspicious tone, though I understood the

reason for it. What were the odds that we had both worked for the woman *and* sighted her body in the water?

"We didn't know she was there." I removed my sunglasses so I could meet his eyes. "It was pure coincidence that I saw her shoe out there."

When the last of the passengers was on the way back to Avalon, the crew hoisted Nikki's body up on the port deck. A rush of water came with her, pooling under her bloated body.

Terry and I bent over her. An aquamarine earring still clung to her right ear; the left one was lost. It was the same outfit she had worn the night before, along with the remaining blue shoe.

Terry shook her head sadly. "What a waste."

"Here come the sheriffs," the captain said. "You can tell them all about it."

A speedboat with an L.A. Country Sheriff's insignia was buzzing up to the starboard side of the boat carrying Whitehorse and Young, along with a man in a medic's uniform. A red flasher announced their urgent mission in the otherwise peaceful harbor.

"She wouldn't be dead if they'd done their job," Terry said angrily, watching them approach.

"Don't take that attitude," I warned her.

"You know it's true!"

"No, I don't. She could have been dead long before they got to her apartment. Anyway, don't be hostile with them."

"If they're hostile to me, I'm hostile back."

Terry was taking this personally. I knew she'd had a crush on Nikki from the first moment she saw her. It couldn't be fun to witness the untimely death of someone you'd spun romantic fantasies about. It wasn't much fun for me, either.

"Whatever you do," I said, "don't mention the note."

"What note?"

"The one we found as a result of breaking and entering? The taking of which could be construed as tampering with a crime scene?"

"But what if it's material? What if she was in the middle of writing that note when she was abducted or something?"

"Max said she left willingly with the guy."

"You believe him? He's just an old man who hates anyone with a life. He's got a bug up his butt about her male visitors."

I thought about Max's cranky reaction to the mention of Nikki. "What's weird is, she said he was a friend."

"Maybe *she* considers them friends, but he seems like dementia has set in. One minute you're probably his best buddy, the next minute you've stolen money out of his wallet. I think we can discount anything he says."

The deputies glanced over at us as they boarded, and I was once again struck by the contrast between them. Whitehorse was stern-featured and straight-backed, her hair as tightly knotted as her personality. Young was soft and almost comical in his cowboy hat, like a chubby kid poised on top of a birthday pony. While Whitehorse spoke to the captain and inspected the body, Young remained a few feet away with a nauseous cast to his face. It was probably his first homicide.

That is, if it *was* a wrongful death. Somehow against all reason, I was hoping there had been a boating accident or something more benign to account for it. Though I don't know why it mattered. Either way, Nikki was just as dead.

The medic opened up his box and began to process the body. Whitehorse spoke to him in low tones, and then walked over in our direction.

"Look innocent," I whispered to Terry.

"I *am* innocent."

"Sorry. Habit."

"We meet again." Whitehorse skipped the niceties as she pulled out a notebook and ballpoint pen. "I'm told you recognized the body."

"It's Nikki Edwards," Terry said. "You remember, the one we told you was in extreme personal danger? Which you chose to ignore?"

Whitehorse took Terry's tone in stride. "How were you able to make the identification? Her face is gone."

"I noticed her legs," Terry said. "They were, well, memorable."

"Is that all?"

"We also recognized her clothes, her hair, and an earring," I added.

"Are both of you gay?" Whitehorse turned to Terry. "Or just you?"

Terry's jaw dropped, but nothing came out of her mouth. I can honestly say I'd never seen her at such a loss for words.

I stepped in front of her protectively. "I hardly see the relevance of that question."

"You don't? Well, let's try this. You were with the girl last night. You had a story about how she 'hired' you to investigate a stalker. You claim to have been assaulted by this stalker, but nobody saw him except you—"

"Nobody?"

She shook her head. "Not the manager, not the night doorman, not any of the staff or the guests. And now the girl is dead. Want to change your story?"

"No!" Terry shouted. "We didn't kill her!"

Whitehorse's black eyes lingered on hers. "Never said you did."

"You implied it," Terry shot back. "You were thinking it."

Deputy Young walked up wearing a genial grin. "Now Ms. McAfee, we know you're upset, but—"

Terry jerked away, in no mood for his gosh-golly charms. "You yokels better get a clue. That girl was the victim of a stalker. We *told* you she was in danger and you did nothing about it."

"I've got this covered, Billy," Whitehorse said. "You stay with the victim."

Young gave a nod and made his way back to the body.

"Mind if I ask you a few more questions?"

Terry crossed her arms. "Do we need our lawyer?"

"Entirely up to you. Just trying to get a little information, here."

"Ask," I said.

"You say this woman hired you. Do you have a contract?"

"It wasn't a formal arrangement," Terry said. "It was more of a… casual thing."

"How casual?"

"What do you mean?"

"Did you have sex with her?"

That did it. Terry blew out a disgusted sigh and stormed away, leaving me there to fend for both of us.

"In point of fact, Nikki thought the stalker might be connected to an ex-boyfriend. The girl was straight. Ergo, no lesbian sex. Sorry to disappoint you."

"Did you get a name of this alleged boyfriend?"

"No."

She made a note. "Boyfriend, no name." The irony was in the words, not in her delivery.

"I'm sure you could get the information from her friends or family."

"Mmm-hmm." She looked up from her pad. "How'd you know where the body was?"

"I knew because I saw it under the boat."

"According to the captain, no one else did. He said you insisted on going back to the area and that's when it was seen by everyone else."

"By the time I alerted the guide we'd already passed it. She thought it might have been a stingray. After that, I saw a shoe floating on the waves. I put two and two together and asked the captain to go back to see if they were related. And here we are."

"Yep. Here we are." Whitehorse glanced over at the corpse. "Looks like they're related, all right. Excuse me." She started to walk back to the rest of her team.

"Would you do me a favor, Deputy Whitehorse?" I called to her.

She turned.

"Would you ask around about us? We're known in the Sheriff's Department in Malibu and the Beverly Hills PD, also the FBI. It'll save a lot of time if you stop treating us like your prime suspects."

She flashed me a quick smile. "I have checked on you. From what I hear, you and your sister are a couple of showboats, always putting yourselves at the center of things. Now, it will save a lot of time if you let me do my job, Ms. McAfee."

I gave her my back and walked over to Terry, who was slumped on the railing, staring down at the water.

"Does this suck or what?" She kicked the base of the rail. "She was such a nice girl."

I didn't know what to say. I put my arm around her shoulder.

She blinked tears from her eyes. "They can't really think we had anything to do with it, can they?"

"Last people to see her alive, first people to spot the body. A story about a stalker no one's seen but us." I paused. "And Whitehorse obviously has a thing against lesbians."

"No, she doesn't. She was just trying to provoke me. Can't believe I fell for it."

The voices of the law enforcement types floated over to us on the breeze.

"How long has she been in the water?" Whitehorse asked the medic.

"A few hours."

"I've seen bodies come out of the water before," Young said. "Drowning victims, mostly. But I never seen anyone had their whole face eaten off."

The medic snapped a photo of Nikki's head. "It wasn't eaten off. The tissue was already exposed and bleeding. Big attraction for the fish."

"You mean her face was gone before she went in the water?" Whitehorse said.

"See that?" The medic pointed to the area beneath Nikki's jaw. "Looks like it's been cut with a knife edge. Her face was excised."

"What do you mean excised?"

"Surgically removed. By a pro."

"A pro?" Whitehorse echoed. "You mean a surgeon?"

"Or a fisherman. Someone skilled with a knife."

We heard the roar of an engine. A water taxi was headed straight for our boat. A lean, wiry man was clinging to the windbreak. He had thick, salt and pepper hair and a deeply tanned face, with a strip of white skin showing just below the hairline. There was another conspicuous tan line on his biceps. He was either a golfer or a pig farmer. My money was on the sport of kings.

The taxi pulled up next to the glass-bottom boat. Before it came to a complete stop, the man catapulted himself on board, slamming onto the deck with a thud.

"Where is she?" he shouted.

Whitehorse and Young hurried down the deck to head him off. Whitehorse's hand twitched toward her holster.

"Can we help you, sir?" Young said.

"Let me see her!"

Young tried to restrain the man, but he knocked the deputy's hand away.

"I need to see her!"

Whitehorse raised her gun. "Sir, we're going to cuff you if you don't calm down. Now, tell us why you're here."

"I want to see my wife!" He strained to look past them. "It's her, isn't it?"

"We don't have a positive ID on the victim yet," Whitehorse said.

"Then get out of my way and let me identify her, you idiots!"

The deputies stepped back and he ran past them to the body, stopping five feet away.

"Don't touch anything," Whitehorse cautioned him.

Needlessly, as it turned out.

The man stared down at the faceless young woman, his own expression a mask of revulsion. He was immobilized by the vision of gruesome death. The deputies walked up beside him.

"Is that your wife, sir?" Whitehorse asked, holstering her weapon again.

The man brought his eyes up to meet hers. "It's not Anna," he said, his lips trembling.

Then he stumbled over to the railing and retched his guts out into the water.

$\mathcal{W}$hen he'd recovered sufficiently to speak, the man gave his name as Steven Petty. He told the deputies he was "in real estate" in Newport Beach.

Terry and I suspected he was the former occupant of our suite, the one whose bride had dumped him. Our suspicion was confirmed when they took him into the passenger section for further questioning. Terry and I hung around within eavesdropping distance, peering into the window from time to time for a glimpse of the proceedings.

"When did your wife go missing?" Whitehorse asked Steven Petty.

"She left the day before yesterday," he answered petulantly. "Do you think she could be dead?"

The deputies looked at one another. Then Whitehorse said, "Why do you ask that, sir?"

"Why?" Petty shrieked, his blood pressure rising along with his voice. "You're asking me *why?*"

"It's sort of a strange question."

"It's sort of strange coming across a woman's body with her face eaten off, don't you think?"

Whitehorse waited a moment for Petty to calm himself down. "Sir, we want to help you, all right? Did you report your wife missing?"

"No, because she wasn't missing. We had a fight and she left."

"Tell us about it."

He let out a long sigh. "I guess it was selfish of me, but I played nine holes on the first day of our honeymoon. You probably know how it is with golfers..."

"I sure do," Young said.

He shut his mouth when Whitehorse threw him a silencing glare.

"I thought she'd get over it," Petty went on. "We had a whole week here. Surely I could get in one round."

"What time did you return to your hotel?" Whitehorse asked.

"About six. Plenty of time for dinner."

"And when did you realize she was gone?"

"When I went into the room and saw that all her suitcases were gone!"

"What did you do then, sir?" Young asked.

"I got drunk."

"Didn't call anyone?"

"No."

"Why not?"

"Who would I call? Her mother?" He gave a sour laugh. "That'd be beautiful. My nightmare of a mother-in-law flying in to grill me on what I did to her baby."

"And what *had* you done to her?"

"I told you. All I did was hit the links. Jeez, you'd think I'd beaten her up or something."

Whitehorse made a note. "How long have you been beating your wife?"

"I can't believe you're making a joke about this!"

"I'm not joking, sir."

"*How long have you been beating your wife?* is a joke," he insisted, though some of the bravado had gone out of his voice.

"According to who?"

"Where are you from? Mars?"

"I'm a member of the Shawnee nation."

Terry looked over at me, shaking her head. She mouthed the words: "Petty is such a dick." I tried not to laugh.

"Okay, maybe it's not a joke there," he said after an awkward pause. "Anyway, I never laid a hand on her. I did everything she wanted. The big rock, this honeymoon trip—"

"The location was her idea?" Young asked.

"Yes."

"The big rock. You mean a wedding ring?"

"A green diamond, ten carats. Nothing else would do. Cost me a hundred grand."

Young whistled. "That's an expensive ring. You make a lot of money?"

"I do all right." His tone said, *Better than a pissant sheriff's deputy.*

Whitehorse took over again. "Let's get back to the hotel. Your wife's luggage was gone. Had she checked out? Did she say anything to the hotel staff about where she was going?"

"I didn't ask."

"You didn't think there was cause for concern?"

"I was pissed. If your new wife ran out on you on your honeymoon, you'd be pissed, too."

"I think I'd be worried," Young said.

"I was. Later."

"Yes, you seemed very concerned when the body was found in the bay," Whitehorse recalled. "You were convinced it was her. Why was that?"

"I don't know. I just panicked."

"Did you have any particular reason to suspect it was your wife?"

"I was... I guess I was *afraid* it was her."

"And now you're relieved it isn't?"

"How can I be? You have some sort of murderer running around here! How do I know he didn't get to Anna too?"

"I guess we don't know that," Whitehorse said matter-of-factly. "Do you have a picture of your wife?"

Petty pulled out an expensive leather wallet and passed it to Young, who lingered over the photo. "She's a pretty girl, sir."

Petty didn't respond to the compliment.

Whitehorse took the wallet. "She's a good deal younger than you, Mr. Petty."

"So?" He ripped the wallet out of her hand and stuffed it back in his pants pocket. "Can I go now?"

"You got something pressing, sir?" Whitehorse asked. "A tee time?"

"No, I want to pack and get off this godforsaken tourist trap."

She feigned surprise. "One minute you're afraid your wife has been killed, and the next minute you're out of here?"

"I realize now I was wrong. Anna's probably back home meeting with a divorce attorney as we speak. I'll go try to make it up to her."

"I have to ask you not to leave the island just yet."

Petty's body went rigid. "Am I under arrest or something?"

"No, sir. Nothing like that. I'm asking as a personal favor. Just until we can locate your wife, here or on the mainland. We'll be in touch with NBPD to make sure she hasn't come to any harm. You'd want to know that, wouldn't you? That she hasn't come to any harm?"

He glowered at her. "Of course."

"Where are you staying, in case we need to reach you?"

"The Motel Six."

Young couldn't suppress a laugh. "On your honeymoon?"

"We were at Hotel St. Lauren. I checked out after Anna flaked on me."

"Why did you do that?"

"I should pay top dollar to sit in that hotel alone? If she came back, I wanted her to wonder where I had gone. I thought she should have a taste of her own medicine."

"Very good, sir," Whitehorse said, closing her notebook. "We'll get back to you after we talk to the hotels and house rentals."

"What if she's gone home?"

"We'll check with the ferry service and airlines, too. Thank you for your cooperation."

Petty stood awkwardly, fists jammed into his front pockets.

"Thank you," he said.

"It's our pleasure to serve you," Young replied. "And please enjoy your stay on Catalina."

Petty lurched out on deck to hail the water taxi.

"Yeah, right," he muttered under his breath.

seventeen

*A*fter Nikki's body was removed to the local mortuary, Whitehorse took us to the station on Sumner Street to meet with the sketch artist. I knew she'd be watching to see whether we waffled on the details or contradicted each other, since she seemed to think the Ape-man was a figment of our imaginations.

We waited in a small break room that was bare except for a gray Army surplus table, molded plastic chairs, and a coffee carafe containing a thin layer of black sludge. Finally, the artist entered the room. I got a glimpse of long muscled legs between khaki shorts and distressed work boots, olive green socks bunched over the tops.

Then my eyes traveled up the length of his slender body.

He was nothing short of gorgeous. His dark hair was parted in the middle and hung down to his shoulders. He had soulful, deep brown eyes with lashes so long they could be used for feather dusters, strong eyebrows and a nose that belonged on the Mediterranean, and possibly the most beautiful mouth

I'd ever seen on a man. His intelligent face had *artist* written all over it.

I cringed when I realized that I was having palpitations over someone who looked like the man of the hour. The guy was a dead ringer for Jesus.

"This is David Solomon," Whitehorse said. "Our police artist."

Terry offered a hand. "Nice to meet you."

He shook with her and then held out a hand to me. I immediately turned into a babbling idiot as I gazed into those bottomless brown eyes.

"We're twins," I blurted out.

"No kidding?"

In my peripheral vision, I could see Terry gawking at me in disbelief. She made it a point to savage anyone stupid enough to ask if we were twins, and here I was, volunteering that painfully obvious information.

I held David's hand just a hair longer than necessary but released it before he could notice.

"I'm Kerry," I said. "She's Terry."

He smiled and pulled up a chair between us. "Okay, let's give this a shot." He placed a large sketchpad on the table, holding a soft-lead pencil between his fingers, a gum eraser clutched in his palm.

"I got the best look at him," Terry said.

David nodded, waiting for her to continue.

"He's close to six feet tall. Big through the shoulders and chest, if that makes any difference. Long arms like an orangutan. Kind of bandy-legged."

"Bandy-legged?"

"You know, his legs were bowed."

David's hand started moving across the paper without touching the lead to the paper. He was loosening up, like a runner stretching before a sprint.

"Tell me what you remember about his head."

"Big head."

He started sketching. Random marks coalesced into a skull. "Round?"

"No, more of a blockhead."

He squared off the top of the skull, then used the gum eraser to obliterate the rounder outline he had begun with.

"He had curly dark hair, longer than his ears."

Wisps of curly hair emerged in a flurry of strokes, which he shaded with his finger pads. He switched from eraser to lead to fingers with the dexterity of a sleight-of-hand magician, teasing the intruder to life.

"Right!" Terry said. "It was just like that!"

Young and Whitehorse stood nearby watching the image unfold.

"What about his features?" David asked.

"Um… little eyes, far apart. And sort of a broken nose."

He sketched in small eyes over a broad nose with a flattened bridge. "Like that?"

"Uh-huh. And I don't think he had any eyebrows."

"None at all?"

"Maybe just a hint."

He sketched in the faintest brows over the beady eyes. "What about his mouth?"

"Don't remember it."

"Wide? Small? Full lips? Thin lips?"

Terry screwed up her face, trying to call up an image.

"Did he have a beard?" David asked.

Terry's eyes popped open. "Yes, a dark goatee."

He drew a Van Dyke beard, and added an off-kilter set of thick lips.

"That's it!" Terry was astonished. "How did you do that? It's a perfect likeness!"

"Because I know him." David made a few final smudges with his thumb. "He's one of my laborers. His name is Beaver."

"Beaver?" Whitehorse leaned over David's shoulder to see the drawing. "Beaver what?"

"It's a nickname. He's from Beaverton, Oregon. He's on my crew over at the Casino. I thought it might be him when she described his body, but I wanted to hear about the facial details before I jumped to any conclusions." He ripped the page from the sketchpad and handed it to Whitehorse. "I can take you to his motel, if you want. He didn't show up to work today."

"Didn't he?" Terry shot Whitehorse a victorious grin.

Whitehorse stood for a moment with her lips pressed together, staring at the sketch. Was she disappointed that our Ape-man had not been a fabrication? "Never seen him before," she said.

"He's only been here a couple of weeks."

"Does Beaver have a real name?"

"Ben Kirch."

"Okay," she said to David, inclining her head toward the door. "Let's go."

Terry started to follow. "We'll go with you and make an ID."

Whitehorse held up a hand. "Oh, no."

"Why not?"

"Because it's not standard procedure. We don't like to parade complainants in front of the suspects. It puts them in potential danger."

"You want to bring him in for questioning?" I asked. "Put him behind a two-way mirror?"

"That's the general idea."

"And what if he won't go along?" Terry said. "We're willing to take the risk. It's on us."

"That would be highly irreg—" Young started to say, but Whitehorse cut him off.

"Might be interesting to see how he reacts, coming face-to-face with two of his alleged victims."

She was getting on my nerves with all her "allegeds."

Truth to tell, I wasn't anxious for a confrontation with the man who had attacked me in my bed, but Terry left me no choice, short of sissying out in front of the hot sketch artist.

"I'm game!" I said, a little too gamely.

Terry gave me her patented *Oh, brother* look.

"I need you to stay here and make copies of the drawing," Whitehorse told Young. "Work up a wanted poster in case we don't find him."

Young's face went pitiful, like that of a dog commanded to wait outside for his master.

"We need a copy for those other parties," Whitehorse said in a near whisper. "They should be here today."

"Oh, yeah." Young eagerly took the drawing from her. "I keep forgetting about them."

"Try to remember," she said wearily.

Whitehorse drove her cruiser to the Sunspot Motel, a one-story structure of turquoise cinderblock with orange doors, and a yellow plywood sun propped on the roof. Whitehorse went inside to talk to the manager, then returned with a key on a green plastic tab. The three of us piled out of the car and trailed her to room number three.

"Sheriff's department," Whitehorse called out, pounding on the cheap wooden door.

There was no response.

Whitehorse knocked again before putting the key in the lock. I went tense when she turned the knob, having been through enough of these "no answer" scenarios lately to make me jumpy. It almost always meant someone was dead inside.

Except on this occasion.

The door was filled by a hulking individual with a chestful of matted hair, dressed only in dirty grey workout pants. Extremely muscular on top, his short legs were bowed in the cotton sweats. His eyes were little, mean, and red. Seeing him made me shiver, as I remembered his rough hand over my mouth, his misshapen bulk pinning me to the cot. But the goatee Terry had described was now history.

Whitehorse glanced over at Terry, who gave her a nod—*This is the one.*

"What the f—?" Beaver roared, before registering Whitehorse's uniform. "Uh, sorry. What can I do for you, officer?" He glanced over at Terry and me. "Ladies?"

"Mr. Kirch?" Whitehorse said. "Did we wake you?"

"Yeah." He rubbed his eyes sullenly. "Most people call me Beaver."

"We'd like to talk to you if we may." She held out her hand to shake—a strange gesture, under the circumstances. In my experience, investigating officers usually kept a professional distance from whoever they were questioning.

Beaver wiped his hand on the side of his sweatpants and enfolded hers. She smiled amiably, giving him a hearty shake.

"What do you want to talk to me about?" He searched our faces, curious but not apprehensive. There was no sign of recognition when it came to Terry and me. Nor was there a greeting for his crew boss, David, who was standing just behind us.

"It's about a murder," Whitehorse said.

"A murder?" Beaver frowned, gripping the doorframe.

"A young woman named Nikki Edwards. May we come in?" He stepped back. "Uh, sure."

Whitehorse walked in first and the rest of us followed her. The dark room was small with a double bed and connecting bathroom. A razor was visible through the open bathroom door, sitting on one edge of the sink. Used towels were wadded up on the counter.

Beaver sat down on the bed, which looked like it had been the scene of a wrestling match. He rubbed his bare chin, unconsciously feeling the smooth new skin. Whitehorse took a chair from the small table next to the window and sat across from him. She brought out her notebook and ballpoint pen.

"That's a nasty gash," she remarked. "You might want to see a doctor."

Beaver's hand shot up to the right side of his head, just above the ear. He realized his mistake and yanked his hand down. "I don't have no gash. What are you trying to pull?"

She sandbagged him. "You've been identified as the person trespassing on the murder victim's property last night."

"Identified?" He drew himself up. "By who?"

"By me." Terry stepped forward.

The big head rolled in her direction. "Who are you?"

"An acquaintance of the victim's. I was there."

His blank demeanor—the frank lack of recognition—would have convinced me if I hadn't known without a doubt he was the one in our room. I recognized his smell.

"Good for you," Beaver said, then he looked back at Whitehorse. "I don't know nobody named Nikki. Don't know where she lives. And since I don't know her and I don't know where she lives, I can't be the person *she* thought she saw." He smiled, proud of his unassailable logic.

"You were also identified as a suspect in an assault at the Hotel St. Lauren last night."

His eyes got even smaller, and his voice became threatening. "Somebody's got it wrong, babe. I mean, Deputy."

"I see you've shaved off your beard," Whitehorse said. "When did you do that?"

"Last night."

"May I ask why?"

He broke into an ugly grin. "Why would I want to hide this face?"

"Mr. Solomon, here, tells us you didn't show at work today."

Beaver jerked as if he'd been spritzed with cold water. "David?"

David spoke from his station by the door. "Hi, Beaver."

"I didn't even see you there, man! Sorry, I decided to quit. I was gonna let you know later."

Whitehorse eyed Beaver curiously. "Do you wear glasses, Mr. Kirch?"

"I probably should. I'm kinda near-sighted."

"Can you tell me how many fingers I'm holding up?" She held two fingers out to her side. Six feet separated her outstretched hand from Beaver.

"What is this?" he grumbled. "A friggin' vision test?"

She didn't move.

"Two fingers, okay?"

Whitehorse pulled back her hand. "Want to tell us where you were last night?"

"Right here." He slapped the mattress.

"All night?"

He nodded. "After ten o'clock."

"Where were you before ten o'clock?"

"At the bar. Lining up my evening's entertainment."

"Which bar is that?"

"Don't remember the name."

"Do you have any receipts?"

"No. I paid cash."

"Did you hook up with someone?"

Beaver winked. "A sweet one."

"What's her name?" Whitehorse readied her pen.

"Who knows? Amber? She said the goatee was bothering her, so I shaved it off. We went at it all night."

Whitehorse wrote on her pad. "Where would we find Amber?"

"Probably at the clinic, getting treated for beard rash."

No one laughed at his revolting joke.

"You don't know where she lives?"

"No."

"Did you get a phone number?"

"I wasn't gonna marry her. I was just in it for one night."

"I suggest you find her," Whitehorse said. "You're going to need an alibi."

"Alibi, shit! Here's your alibi!" Beaver stood and ripped the covers off the bed. "Oh, I forgot—she swallows." He threw me a sickening leer. "How about you, honey? Do you?"

"That's enough trash talk," Whitehorse said in a warning tone.

I desperately wanted to get out of there. "Deputy Whitehorse, do you need us anymore?"

She shook her head, dismissing me.

Terry indicated she'd stay, but David opened the door and I practically flew past him into the parking lot.

"What an animal!" I said, as he slammed the door behind us. "You hired that guy?"

"Can't be too picky. Labor's not easy to come by here."

Nevertheless.

"What job are you working on?"

"Restoring a tile mural at the Casino."

"The guy can't see and he's doing intricate tile work?"

"No, he hauls materials, mixes concrete, builds scaffolding. Stuff like that."

"Still, he must be blind as a bat if he didn't recognize you standing five feet away."

David glanced back at the motel room door. "Yeah, but what's strange is, I never had the impression he had bad eyesight."

"Never saw him wear glasses?"

"Nope."

"Or saw him squinting?"

"Not even."

"Hmmm." The two of us stood there for a second. "Did he strike you as a violent person?"

"No. Just sort of brutish."

"Well, I think you called that one."

The conversation stalled. I noticed David staring at my face intently. His eyes seemed to turn a deeper shade of brown as he took me in. I began to sweat under his lingering gaze. If he didn't say something soon, I was going to start bleating or something weird.

"Your thoughts?" I asked casually.

"I like your face."

"Then I guess you like my sister's face, too."

He gave my glib remark serious consideration. "Yeah, it's funny. I know you're identical, but you seem completely different to me."

"I do?"

"Yeah, I... I can't explain. It's as if when I look at you, I'm seeing more than your features." He gave me a half-smile and took a step closer. "Maybe I'm reading your soul."

"Maybe you are."

And then, just as things were getting interesting, Terry and Whitehorse came back out of the room together.

"What happened?" I asked, seeing that Beaver was not under arrest.

Whitehorse walked to the cruiser. "In the car, please."

Once inside with the doors closed, she turned to look at us through the open backseat barrier. "This guy stinks."

"In more ways than one," I said.

"The shaved beard, the flimsy alibi. You're absolutely sure he's the man you saw at Ms. Edwards'?"

"Yes." Terry said. "And he was definitely the guy in our room."

"His hands *were* rough, like you said."

So that's why she'd shaken hands with him. The cunning little minx.

"Why didn't you make an arrest?" I asked her.

"Not enough evidence."

We'd identified the creep who assaulted us, terrorized Nikki and most likely killed her in cold blood. And there he sat in his rented room, free as the proverbial bird, bragging about his prowess with a chick who had never existed. This "Amber" was probably the December foldout in *Juggs Magazine*.

I glanced over to see Beaver peering out the window at us. He immediately dropped the curtain and slunk back into the darkness.

"I asked him to submit to a DNA swab and he started talking lawyers." Whitehorse said. "I need to get a case together. I'll go for a warrant, see if the judge will allow it based on your eyewitness testimony. There may be something we can extract from your lamp for a comparison."

David was quiet throughout all of this, seemingly lost in his own thoughts. Were those thoughts about me? I wondered.

Color me self-absorbed.

"There's someone else who can place him at Nikki's," Terry said. "Although he may not be the most reliable witness in the world. Max, the old man who lives next door. He said he saw a 'big fella' hanging out around the apartment."

"Very good."

"What else can we do to help?" I asked.

"You can swear out a statement. Meanwhile, if you'd stick around in case we need you…"

"Stick around? How long?"

Whitehorse made a *who knows* gesture.

"Doesn't matter," Terry said, puffing out her chest. "However long it takes for justice to be done. Right, sis?"

"Absolutely," I said.

David smiled, but I don't think it was on account of our thirst for justice. Unless I missed my bet, he was happy I would be sticking around.

Minutes later, Whitehorse dropped David off at the Casino. As he let himself out of the cruiser, he gave me one last glance. "Want to see my work?"

"Sure!" I'd vaulted myself halfway out of the car when Terry yanked me back in.

"Sorry, we have stuff to do," she told him.

"Later?" I said hopefully.

"Anytime." He held my eyes for another second, then closed the door.

I turned in my seat for the posterior view as he walked down the street. He had straight carriage and a fluid stride. Tall and thin, yet broad-shouldered—a very fine specimen of manhood.

I whipped back around in my seat, mentally swatting myself on the hand. *You've got two back on the mainland,* said a prim voice in my head. *Don't be a man hog. Leave some for the other girls.*

Back at the station, we met with the stenographer for an hour, swearing out a statement that Ben "The Beaver" Kirch had been our attacker.

Afterward, as were taking our leave from Whitehorse, I asked her about the runaway bride. "Do you think she's another murder victim?"

She shook her head. "More likely she wised up. Didn't run away so much as stage a prison break. You saw the husband, you know what I'm talking about."

Terry handed her one of our business cards. "If you need us, call our cell phone. We're at your disposal."

"Double Indemnity," she read, then stuffed the card in her shirt pocket. "Cute."

Whitehorse reached out to shake our hands. I was so surprised I almost forgot to squeeze back. She gave us a sincere smile with teeth and everything. Then she dropped my hand and the smile at the same instant, and strode across the hall into her office, slamming the door behind her.

"She's coming around," I whispered to Terry, as we headed for the front door. "She doesn't seem to hate us so much anymore."

"No one can resist our charm forever," Terry replied.

eighteen

$\mathcal{T}$he walk back to the hotel took us past an outdoor café on Crescent Avenue, its patio packed with wooden tables, umbrellas glowing golden in the low afternoon sun. Surrounding the eating area was a waist-high fence covered in magenta bougainvillea vines.

"Don't look now." Terry poked me in the ribs. "But our pal Steven Petty just stopped in there to wet his whistle."

"You sure?"

She nodded. "You know, there's something not right with him. All that panic over the body, when he supposedly believed his wife had gone home."

"I had the same thought."

"Let's go have a chat with him."

"Why?"

"There may be more than one mystery on this little island."

I sighed. "And I guess we have to have our fingers in all of them."

We had just seated ourselves, when Petty came back out of the restaurant, carrying a club sandwich and a glass of beer from the self-service counter.

"Here he comes," Terry said. "The jilted groom."

His eyes widened when he saw us, then he hurried to the far side of the patio, sitting at a table with his back to the street.

We ambled over to his table. He sensed our presence, lowering his head.

"Hi, Mr. Petty. Mind if we sit down?" Terry asked, not waiting for an answer. We snagged the two chairs across from him.

"I'm just grabbing a quick bite," he said defensively, as if we'd implied some guilty behavior on his part.

"Nothing wrong with that," I assured him. "Nothing wrong with playing golf on your honeymoon, either."

"I don't expect you to understand." He ripped into the sandwich with his teeth. "You're women."

"I have a ten handicap myself," Terry said, buffing her fingernails on her shirt. "But I don't get to play as much as I'd like. Maybe you and I could get in a round in the next day or two? I mean, if you're not too busy looking for your wife."

"You probably think I should be looking for her."

I made a neutral gesture. "We don't have an opinion one way or the other. But you seemed pretty concerned a couple of hours ago that she'd been the victim of foul play."

He shrugged and took another bite. "I overreacted. Must have been the shock of seeing that dead girl. She looked a bit like Anna."

"Could we see that picture of your wife?" Terry asked.

Too surprised by her request to refuse, he took out his wallet and opened it to a photo of a lovely brunette against a cheesy studio backdrop. Her hands were folded atop a pedestal to showcase her engagement ring, a large green stone that was surrounded by smaller, gem-cut diamonds. She was easily fifteen years younger than Petty—the perfect type to have on your arm if you're an Orange County mover and shaker.

Terry and I took our time looking at the photograph.

"Nice," Terry remarked, finally handing it back to him.

He slapped the wallet closed, replacing it in his pocket. "I hear you're private detectives. Is that right?"

"Yes, it is," Terry said. "Why?"

He was about to answer, when we were interrupted by the sound of a woman's voice calling from the street.

"Yoo hoo! *Yoo-hoooo!*"

We looked over Petty's shoulder to see the strange woman who'd flipped us off in traffic, the "psychotic Doris Day." She sat at the wheel of a golf cart, waving in our direction, thrashing her underarm flab.

"There she is again!" Terry said.

Petty whipped around in his chair to get a look.

"Happy honeymoon, asshole!" She cackled and then took off, weaving along the street like some kind of crazy inebriate.

"What the hell?" Terry looked back at Petty. "Was she talking to you?"

Petty shot up from his chair, banging his head on the underside of the umbrella. "Gotta go." He pushed the chair back, sending it crashing to the ground. He righted it hurriedly, and hustled out of the restaurant without a backward glance.

"Wait!" Terry yelled after him. "Do you know that woman?"

But Petty was long gone, hot-footing it up the sidewalk in the opposite direction.

Terry stared at the remains of Petty's sandwich, the half-drunk beer. "What the heck was that about? Does he know Psycho-Doris?"

"Something tells me she's a ghost of Christmas past," I said.

"Let's go online and see what we can dig up on Steven Petty. It would be interesting to see if he has some connection to that nutcase."

A light bulb went off over my head. "Hey, I just had a thought!"

"I'll alert the media!"

"Shut up and listen. Petty and his new bride were the occupants of our room, right? If we scoured the place, we might find a clue as to her disappearance."

"Or the housekeeping staff might have wiped out all trace of her."

"We could check the drawers and whatnot. You never know."

"Thought you had enough mysteries on your plate?"

"Changed my mind. Woman's prerogative."

We left the restaurant and hiked up the hill to our pink hotel. Upon entering the lobby, we heard a deep voice booming from inside the bar. Terry and I both recognized it at once.

"Barrrrtennner, another Armagnac if you please! Chop chop, old man! I'm dry as a bone!"

We hurried into the lounge, and what to our wondering eyes should appear? Cousin Robert in a red velvet suit with an ermine collar, slouched over an empty snifter. One of his elbows was resting in a nut dish, and his shiny red nose would have put Rudolph to shame.

Santa was shit-faced.

"Robert!" Terry ran to his table. "What are you doing?"

The mustachioed bartender poured another snifter. "Hey girls, are you Santa's helpers? I'm not so sure he should be driving the sleigh tonight, if you catch my drift."

"Keep that drink," Terry said. "Or better yet, I'll take it. And get some coffee brewing, stat."

"You got it." He handed her the glass, then started loading the copper-faced coffee machine with grounds.

Robert frowned up at Terry, bleary-eyed. He came out of his chair, snatching at the glass in her hand. "S'my drink!"

She yanked it out of his reach, giving him a hard shove with her other hand. He landed on the chair with a burst of donut flatulence. "Robert, what's gotten into you?"

"You deflated my donut!"

"Never mind that. You're obviously feeling no pain." She set the drink down and shook him by the fake ermine collar. "Why did you get toasted, Robert? Was it the pressure of playing Santa Claus?"

"Don't be a dumb bunny." He jerked the collar out of her hands, leaving them covered with white fur. "I not afraid of a few excited tots. Jus' don't feel like inflicting myself on a celebration."

Terry slapped tufts of fur from her palms. "That's the booze talking."

Robert laughed, a sharp bark of despair. "Ha! The world would be better off without me. I killed a geniush of the French cinema!"

"*What?*" Terry and I said in unison.

He thrust a piece of paper at me. It was an email from a law office in Paris written on behalf of one Madame de Pontbriand. Terry read it over my shoulder.

Cher Monsieur,

I regret to inform you of the sudden death of M. François Gautier, your late father. According to his landlady, Mme. de Pontbriand, M. Gautier died from an infarction of the heart. Mme. de Pontbriand heard M. Gautier cry out in horreur and entered his room to help. She found him pointing to the television, which contained your advertisement with the very attractive lady.

He screamed, "C'est moi!"

Then he very sadly expired.

Mme. de Pontbriand asked me to convey this tragic news, and to inform you that she will be forwarding the ashes of M. Gautier and some of his personal belongings, along with a bill for six months' rent, which was in arrears.

She begs me to tell you that M. Gautier was a very nice man and she is sorry to cremate him so quickly, but there was another tenant eager to move in.

Sincerely,

Pierre Latour, Avocat

"Sorry, Robert." Terry handed him back the letter. On second thought, she handed him back the drink, as well. "That's a real blow, huh?"

"He lived in squalor! I could have helped 'im! I could have financed a retr'spective of his films so he could go out in a burs' of glory, instead of...a burs' of artery." Robert's head drooped, the chin bouncing on his heaving chest.

"It's not your fault, Robert," I said, although I realized a decent case could be made for Robert's having killed the old guy. But would that bring him back?

"She's right," Terry said. "You can't blame yourself."

"Oh, can't I?" Robert drained the snifter, slamming the glass on the table. "Barkeep, ano'er!"

"How's that coffee coming?" Terry called to him.

"Right up!"

"Ho ho ho... *horreur*!" Robert blubbered. "He screamed in *horreur*!"

"Robert, listen to me." I sat down at the table. "People only go when it's their time. You must know that from your own experience. You've been through so many life-threatening situations, you should be dead now. But it wasn't your time, so you survived. Right?"

"I s'pose there's truth to that." He picked up a cocktail napkin and honked into it.

"Sure there is."

"Figure it this way," Terry said. "At least he died knowing his seed didn't go to waste."

I gave her a horrified look.

"Just trying to be supportive," she said.

I picked up the red hat, holding it out to Robert. "Come on, Santa. Put on your cap and a smile. It'll make you feel better to see a bunch of happy, hopeful kids."

"I'll pass. I'm not–*hick*–in the holiday spirit, having just committed *patricide*."

"I think it would be the perfect tribute, bringing Christmas joy to the children. Your father would have appreciated that."

"You really sink so?"

"I'm absolutely positive."

"Oh, a'right." He pulled the red velvet cap onto his head and cinched the thick black belt around his waist.

"Good!" I said. "Now let's have some coffee and sober up."

The bartender set the cup on the table with a sympathetic smile.

"Almos' forgot." Robert handed Terry a rumpled paper bag. "Here're your cos'umes."

Terry reached into the bag and pulled out a green felt tunic with matching peaked cap. She stuffed the costume back inside and thrust the bag at Robert. "I told you, I don't do little elf outfits."

"Come on, Ter," I said. "For Robert?"

"For François?" said Robert. "For the li'l—*hick*—chil'ren?"

"Oh for Christ's sake." Terry grabbed the bag from Robert. "I'll be a damn elf. But I'm having a drink first."

In the elevator, Robert swayed on his feet, humming *Good King Wenceslas* while wringing Armagnac out of his ermine collar.

Terry brushed off the velvet coat. "You've got peanut salt everywhere."

"You need to take a nap," I told him. "And brush your teeth and gargle about ten times. And spray yourself with cologne. Better the kids should think Santa's a dandy than a drunk."

"Sorry I succumbed, girls. But I promise it'll be the las' time."

"Has Reba heard about François?" I asked him.

He put his hand over his mouth. "Ugh! No."

"Don't you think someone should let her know? After all, he *was* her lover."

"For five minutes." Robert shuddered. "To think–*hick*–I was conceived while her derriere was being imprinted with an airplane sink. Wonder if she carries an indentation on her cheeksh to this day, like a… like a mark of shame."

Terry raised an eyebrow at me. "Don't think I want to find out, do you?"

The elevator doors opened and we dragged Robert down the hallway. Teetering in front of the door, he pulled the brass key out of his pocket and attempted to jam it into the keyhole. He missed on three occasions, striking the key on the metal face-plate. The third time, it shot out a bolt of static electricity, blue sparks crackling through the air.

"Yahhh!" Robert dropped the key. "Not again!"

Terry bent over to pick up the key, turning it over in her palm. "Still warm," she said, then unlocked the door. "Go get some rest, Robert. We'll be back in an hour."

Robert tottered over to the bed and collapsed like a building visited by the wrecking ball. The room shook.

"Can't sleep on my back," he murmured, and then he was out cold.

I looked at him lying on his stomach spread-eagle and shook my head. "They just don't make Santas the way they used to."

Terry took Robert's laptop from the nightstand. "We need to borrow this so we can do the search on Steve Petty."

"Okay, but first we have to break the bad news to Reba."

We left Robert there sawing logs and knocked at Reba's room.

There was shuffling on the other side of the door, accompanied by melodic moaning. Reba opened, dressed in a pink silk dressing gown and matching turban. She wore an ice pack over her eyes in the shape of a harlequin mask, giving her the look of a Mardi Gras reveler the day after.

"Yes, dears?"

"How're you doing?" I asked her.

"I feel as if my head has been cleaved in two. The only thing holding it together is this turban."

"We'll come back," Terry said.

"Nonsense." Reba motioned us inside. "If I'm going to die, I wouldn't want to go without bidding adieu to my darling nieces."

"The thing is," I said, entering her room. "Something's happened, and it's not likely to make you feel any better."

"Don't be silly. Nothing could surpass the humiliation and degradation I've experienced in the past twenty-four hours. Any bad news you could bring me would be trifling by comparison."

Reba shuffled over to the bed and draped herself across the pillows arrayed against the headboard. "Fire away."

"Robert's had an email from a lawyer in Paris—" Terry began.

"Damn the luck!" Reba said. "I knew it!"

"How could she know?" I whispered to Terry, and she shrugged back at me. "Apparently he was rather elderly," I said to Reba. "We can't know for certain that your billboard caused his heart attack."

She shoved the eye pack up on her forehead, blinking. "Excuse me? Did you say something about his heart?"

"She's not getting it," Terry said.

I tried to soften the blow. "We're very sorry to tell you, but your lover...Robert's natural father, François Gautier... died of cardiac arrest."

"I thought you were going to say he was on his way here!"

"No, actually he expired sort of suddenly. So I guess there won't be any opportunity for that."

"Opportunity?" Reba jumped up from the bed. "I was dreading it like the Plague! You're quite sure he's dead?"

Terry shot me a baffled look. "Well, I hope so. He was cremated."

"Robert got an email from the guy's landlady," I explained. "She's sending the ashes and some of his personal belongings. He fessed up to being the one on the airplane, only seconds before he died."

"Hallelujah!" Reba threw her arms in the air and danced in a joyous circle.

I guess we'd misread the situation.

"So you're happy about this?" Terry asked her.

"Happy?" Reba ripped the turban off her head. "I'm delirious! Can you imagine what Eli would have thought if the man had insinuated himself as a daddy-come-lately? How could we have stood before the rabbi with this between us?" She tossed the turban across the room, bouncing it off the bed, and shimmied into the bathroom.

"It's a Christmas miracle!" she sang.

nineteen

*W*e left Reba to her private celebration and went back to our room to don the costumes. I tried mine on in the bathroom, away from Terry's mocking eyes. I pulled on the green tights and felt tunic, and slipped my feet into the Aladdin-style slippers with jingle bells sewn onto the toes. They tinkled as I walked back into the room to model the ensemble for Terry.

She took one look at me and howled, falling down on the bed.

"Well, you're going to look the same," I said.

"I'm not wearing that stupid thing!"

"Terry, you promised!"

"No, I lied."

"You would lie to a drunk man in mourning?"

She grinned. "Yup."

"You *have* to do this!"

"Why?"

"'Tis the damn season, that's why!"

"I don't know why I should make an ass out of myself just because it's Christmas."

I put my hands on my green felt hips. "Oh, far be it from me to suggest you should be unselfish one night out of the year."

She made a face. "You're a real pain, you know that?"

"At least I keep my promises to drunks."

"All right. Give it here."

I tossed the other costume onto the bed. She shucked off her jeans and T-shirt, pulling the kelly-green tights over her skinny legs and topping it off with the tunic. She turned around in front of the full-length armoire mirror.

"I look like the Jolly Green Beanpole."

"Oh, what do we care? We'll never see any of these people again. Now let's poke around and see if we can't find a clue to the missing bride. Why don't you take the bathroom?"

Terry saluted and disappeared into the bathroom while I searched the main room. I lifted the eiderdown coverlet, checking under the bed. Nothing, not even a dust bunny. The armoire was empty except for our clothes hanging from the rod and our duffel crumpled on the floor. I checked underneath and ran my hand across the top. Again, nothing.

Suddenly Terry came running back into the room, all excited.

"I don't believe it. It's her engagement ring. The one in the picture."

The green stone in her hand was a jawbreaker, set in platinum and surrounded by small, brilliant diamonds.

"Where'd you find it?"

"In the toilet tank." She removed her silver skull ring and slipped the engagement ring onto her left hand.

"Did you wash it off?"

"Yes, I washed it, you freaking germaphobe."

"What on earth made you look in the tank?"

"I used to hide my drugs in there." She held the ring up to the overhead light, flashing sparks on the walls. "You know, in the bad old days."

"Is it really a diamond? I've never seen a green one."

"They have blue ones. The Hope Diamond is blue."

I thought about the bauble's former owner, who'd been so pleased to display it in the photo. "Did she forget it when she left? Or did she deliberately leave it there, maybe as a clue?"

"I doubt it," Terry said. "That was too much of a statement, leaving it in the toilet. She's trying to send a message."

"I guess we hand it over to Petty now, huh?"

"Why?"

"The wife doesn't seem to want it any more than she wants him. When you break off an engagement, you usually return the ring."

"But when you break off an engagement, you usually inform the fiancé. And they were married, not engaged."

Just then something drew me to the window—a sense of being watched. I looked out at the harbor, still in the twilight. Then I noticed a golf cart at the bottom of the hill. Leaning out of the cart was a woman with a bobbed blond hairdo, aiming a pair of binoculars up at our room.

"Don't look now, but Psycho-Doris is spying on us."

"Holy schneikes." Terry rushed to the balcony, leaning out over the rail. "Yoo hoo! Psycho-Doris! Having a nice day?"

The binoculars withdrew and the golf cart wheeled out into the street, screeching around a corner. She was gone.

"We need to find out who the hell that woman is," Terry said. "And why she's so interested in Petty."

I felt a chill go up my back. "She seems to be interested in us now, too."

We did an online search and found that the Internet was littered with stories about Steven Petty of Orange County. There he was, beaming from the home page of his real estate company, Petty Investments. In a hard hat, breaking ground on a new office park. Leading a group of agents in a money cheer from the top of a company cubicle. Pumping his fist after a birdie on the eighth green.

"Hello," Terry said. "Petty's *invested* in diamonds."

"What?"

"It's right here. Petty Investments bought a controlling interest in a Namibian diamond mine that had been inactive for nearly sixty years. Paid ten million for it." Terry waggled the ring on her hand. "Did this stone come from his mine?"

"Probably."

"Then why did he make such a big deal about what he paid for it?"

"Just because he owns it, doesn't mean he can raid the company store anytime he wants."

She read further. "Says it was closed down after miners experienced strange symptoms back in the Fifties."

"Maybe it was carbon monoxide poisoning or something. It must be gone now if they've reopened the mine."

Next we found an article on the mystery woman.

She was indeed a blast from Christmases past—Paige Petty, the former Mrs. Steven. The Pettys' marriage had ended in divorce three years previously, their private turmoil going public when it hit the front page of the *Orange County Register*. Paige crashed her Lexus through the living room window of Steven's bachelor pad during their separation. She copped to misdemeanor reckless driving and was given a one-year suspended sentence with probation.

The couple's wedding photo was archived with the article. Paige appeared in a white lace gown, fresh-faced and pretty, with sparkling eyes and a million dollar smile. Steven was a nerd in a shiny tux, with a bush of unruly hair. In more recent photos, Paige looked haggard, older than her years, steadily packing on the pounds. Whereas Steven had come into his own, going from pencil-neck geek to slick real estate magnate in tailored suits and expensive haircuts. Apparently, he'd put the old nag out to pasture and found a pretty little filly to complete his transformation.

"A classic case of trophy wife-itis," Terry groaned. "He's finally successful in his forties, so he dumps his first wife like a steaming turd."

"He used to be a runt, but now the slight build is working for him. And the gray in his hair makes him distinguished. He's grown into his looks."

"And she's grown into a muumuu."

"Nice, Ter."

"But true."

"I feel sorry for her. Maybe we should stop calling her Psycho-Doris."

"Uh-uh. However she got that way, we have to remember that she has a borderline personality. She's on record as being violent."

How full of promise Paige had once been. How unlike the dissipated and dangerous loose cannon she'd become.

"Did she follow Petty and his new wife here to harass them?" I wondered aloud. "And that's why the wife ran out, because she saw Psycho-D tailing them in the golf cart everywhere they went?"

"It would do it for me."

"She was on probation after the car-crashing incident. What do you want to bet that this constitutes a violation?"

"A one-year suspended sentence, handed down three years ago. She's in the clear. Anyway, she wasn't charged with stalking."

"I think she's resorted to it now."

The phone rang. When I picked up, I was surprised to hear Whitehorse on the line.

"Good news, bad news," she said, after the barest preliminaries.

"I'll take good."

"Our man Beaver is a fugitive. A two-time loser who skipped on an assault charge. I could arrest him right now on the bench warrant."

"Whitehorse says Beaver has an outstanding warrant!" I whispered to Terry, then put the phone back to my ear. "So he's a skip?"

"Yeah, on the assault charge. But he did seven years in Lompoc when he was younger."

I whistled. "What for?"

"Aggravated rape."

"Aggravated?"

"Tortured and mutilated his victim."

I swallowed hard. "Oh."

"And there's another interesting detail. He's a pro-so-pag-no-sic." She pronounced the word slowly, syllable by syllable.

"A what?"

"It's a rare neurological disorder, also known as 'face blindness' because people who have it can't recognize faces. They have perfect eyesight otherwise, but they can't distinguish human features. They compensate by memorizing other physical characteristics or the sound of voices."

"I've never heard of it before."

"Neither had I, but there it is on his sheet. His lawyer argued for dismissal on the grounds that he accidentally assaulted the wrong woman."

"You're joking!"

"Can you imagine that? 'It was an honest mistake, your honor. My client actually meant to hurt someone *else.*' "

"Please tell me that didn't fly."

"Nope. That's why he was set to go to trial."

"So you're going to arrest him now?"

"That's the bad news."

My heart sank. "He's gone?"

"We have an APB out on him."

Terry hopped up and down, waving her hands. *"What?"*

I motioned for her to wait. "Let me ask you this, Deputy Whitehorse. Do you think it's possible he went after the wrong woman in this instance? That his intended victim was someone other than Nikki Edwards? I ask because Nikki herself had no idea why someone would want to harm her."

"I don't care who he wanted to kill, I care about who he did kill."

Whitehorse had a point. But if Beaver had killed the wrong person, he could still be after the right one. Another innocent woman might be in danger. However, I suspected this theory was too far afield to engage her attention just now. She had to concentrate on finding the hairy bastard, and the chances were good he'd be caught in the dragnet before he could cause any more mayhem.

"Meanwhile, we've made an interesting discovery." I started to tell her about the ring and Petty's wacky ex-wife, but she was anxious to get off the phone.

"Give me a call tomorrow. If we pick him up, I can give you all the time you need."

"Okay, good luck."

"Take care of yourselves," she said, hanging up.

"You, too," I told the dial tone.

twenty

$\mathcal{A}$ half-hour later we were headed out to the Casino Christmas party. There were no reindeer to do the honors, so Terry drove the golf cart. Robert was perched on the bumper seat facing backward, relatively sober and cheerful, the inflamed blood vessels giving him that *just back from the North Pole* look—perfect for the evening's role.

Reba declined to attend. Her migraine having lifted, she claimed to be ravenous for buffalo steak and cabernet. She made herself reservations at *Le Metropole*, never looking so radiant as when she passed us in the lobby on the way out.

"The black widow strikes again," Robert said, watching her go.

We walked up the stairs to the Casino ballroom. It was large and round, with a ceiling that arched fifty feet above our heads, Art Deco Tiffany chandeliers casting a warm glow on the polished wooden floors below. Banquet tables were lined against the floor-to-ceiling windows, piled high with red and green cookies, crescents dusted with powdered sugar, cakes, peppermint canes, and rum balls piled up like tiny cannon fodder.

Now you're talking, I thought. *A feast fit for an elf.*

We were corralled by an earnest woman with gray ringlets bouncing next to her face. "Hi, I'm Danette from the Chamber of Commerce. You must be Santa and the elves!"

Robert saluted. "Claus. Reporting for duty."

Danette noticed his donut. "What's that for?"

"Scraped my backside coming down a chimney," he said confidentially. "Occupational hazard."

"I get it." She slapped his arm playfully. "Now, let me explain how this works. Santa will sit on the throne and receive the children. Elves are in charge of making sure the kids are entertained in line, then escorted up to the throne and helped onto Santa's lap. Okay?"

"Sounds easy enough," Terry said.

"Enjoy!" Danette hurried off to greet the arriving guests.

A gold throne sat atop a raised stage, the red carpet leading up to the platform thronged with rugrats. Fingers up their noses, faces caked with cookie sugar, a couple of toddlers looking like they were wearing loaded diapers. Suddenly one of the kids spotted Robert.

"Thantaaaaaa!"

The rest of them squealed and jumped, almost wetting themselves with excitement.

Robert gawked at them, the blood draining from his face. "I'm not sure I'm up to this." He spun on his heel and began power-waddling back to the exit.

Terry and I chased after him.

"No you don't, big guy." Terry grabbed his left arm and I took his right. We whirled him around in a circle and aimed him back at the squealing kids. Terry pulled while I pushed.

"You'll be fine," I said. "Just ask them if they've been good boys or girls, then tell them they can have anything they want for Christmas."

"Anything?" Robert looked around at me, terrified. "Anything at all? But what if they don't get what they want? They'll rip me to pieces!"

"You're not going to be there to deal with the fallout if they don't get what they want. Their parents will."

"Still, there's a lot more of them than there is of me. What if they turn into an angry mob?"

"They won't." Terry yanked on his arm. "Come on, it's only for an hour."

"One hour and one hundred squirming, snotty, larval human beings!"

"Suck it up, Robert!" she yelled at him.

"All right, already!" Robert stopped and hiked up the red pants, girding his loins. "Here goes nothing." He took a deep breath and strode up the red carpet through the knee-high crowd, waving like the Pope on parade.

The cheer went up: "Yay! Thanta Clausth! Yay!"

Robert lumbered up the stairs to the throne, tossing his donut onto the crimson cushion. He plopped down on top of it, firing up his most Clausian demeanor. "Santa's lap is open for business!"

At that moment I noticed a photographer standing to the side of the crowd. It was David, holding a camera and grinning in our direction.

"Oh, no." I pointed him out to Terry.

"No one will see us, huh, genius?"

David approached as Terry scooted discreetly away.

"Hi!" I chirped at him. "Welcome to Santa Land!"

He snapped a picture, the flash causing me temporary blindness. He bent over next to my ear and whispered, "You have no idea how sexy you are in that outfit."

I shaded my eyes. "Um, thanks. But you blinded me. I can't see my way to Santa's throne."

He took me by the shoulders and angled me in the right direction. "Straight ahead." He gave my arms a squeeze that sent electricity straight down the front of my chest.

Yikes! An elf with erect nipples—what would Mrs. Claus say?

I stumbled up the aisle, using the long line of kids as guideposts. Terry sidled up next to me, smirking. "That guy David is totally hot for you."

"I worry about a guy who's hot for Peter Pan, don't you?"

"There are kinkier things."

At the head of the line was an eager five-year-old clutching a teddy bear, bouncing from one foot to the other in his Buster Brown shoes. He lifted his heart-shaped face up to me, eyes filled with hope and magnified to twice their size by the glasses perched on his nose.

"I sure hope Santa can get me some new video games," he said.

"Of course he can." I gave the little tyke a pat on the head.

"Or else I'm gonna pee on him."

Oh dear.

I crouched down in front of the kid. "Santa's got the largest inventory of video games in the northern hemisphere. You hold it in, and you'll get you what you want, I promise."

"Otay!"

I stood up and grabbed his hand, his palm sticking to mine with some sort of sugary muck, and we started toward the stage. Suddenly, he dug his heels in the carpet.

"Grand Theft Auto," he said.

I looked down at him. "What, sweetheart?"

"*I want Grand Theft Auto!*"

I glanced back at all the kids in line, eagerly awaiting their turn. "Okay, he'll get you Grand Theft whatever. Let's get going." I tugged on the kid's hand, but he pulled me back once again.

"Yes, honey?"

"It's rated M for Mature," he told me.

"Oh well, then you're probably not old enough to—"

"*I WANT GRAND THEFT AUTO! I WAAAAANT IT!*"

The parents threw me worried glances. No doubt they were wondering if I'd pinched the little guy or something. I got down in his sniveling face again.

"You can have the X-rated version if you want, just get your butt up there, okay?"

He nodded, wiping his nose on his sleeve, and finally let me lead him up to the platform.

Robert hollered from his throne: "Ho, ho, ho! Come sit on Santa's lap!"

"No."

Robert was momentarily flummoxed, but he recovered quickly. "Come along. Santa won't bite you!"

"I'm staying right here." The kid looked at Robert's pants legs as if they concealed poisonous snakes. "Can you hear me up there? Or do you got fat in your ears, too?"

"Ho, ho, ho! Sit here and have a nice talk with Santa," Robert rumbled in a jolly voice, slapping his leg.

The kid stepped up to inspect Robert's cotton beard. "I'm in Montessori. I know you're not real."

"Well, aren't you the smart young man." Robert signaled for me to lift the nipper to his knee.

When I grabbed the kid under the armpits and hoisted him in the air, he screamed like a banshee, kicking his feet wildly. I took a few blows to the shins before I dropped him back down to the platform.

"Okay," I said. "Just this once, you may address Santa from a distance."

The kid glared up at Robert. "Redheads are thought to be descended from Neanderthal man in central Europe."

"I don't think so," Robert said with a faux belly laugh.

"Look it up, tubby."

"Ho, ho, ho! Good one, young man. Now, tell Santa, what do you want for Christmas?"

The kid gave a superior nod. "Are so. Neanderthal man." He reached up and yanked off Robert's fake white beard, revealing the natural red one underneath. "Santa's a Neanderthal! Santa's a Neanderthal!" The kid waved the fake beard in the air.

Terry bounded up the stairs to Robert's rescue. "That's enough of that, mister." She ripped the cotton beard out of the kid's hand, tossing it back to Robert. "You're getting switches for Christmas!" She grabbed him by the arm and pulled him, screaming and twisting, away from the throne.

"Next!" she shouted at the line below.

"You hurting me!" the kid wailed.

"I haven't *begun* to put a hurt on you." She shoved him in my direction.

He stumbled over and slammed into my thighs, then pushed

off and yanked back a stumpy leg to kick me square in the shin.

"Yeow!" As I was doubled over in pain, he clubbed me on the top of the head with his little fists.

"You're a redhead, too," he yelled. "Neanderthal elf!"

"Hey!" I shielded my head with my arms. "Back off, dirt devil!"

He stomped my foot.

"Ow!" I screamed, my toes starting to throb.

"You got a fat butt!" a kid yelled from below the platform, yanking on the hem of my tunic.

I whirled around on him. "No I don't!"

"Fat butt, fat butt!"

"Well, you're a pygmy! How do you like that? Pygmy, pygmy!"

"You're a girl with a fat butt!" another boy chimed in. "There are no girl elfs!"

A little girl slugged him in the gut. "Are so!"

"Nuh-uh!" He whacked the little girl. "Real elfs don't have fat butts!"

"You're a stupid doody-head!"

Then all hell broke loose as the entire crowd of kids rushed the platform, yelling and shoving and biting. Midget fists flew. Baby Nikes cut the air. There were screams for *Mama* and big open-mouthed *Waaaaahhhhs!*

Terry and I waded into the crowd, pulling the little monsters off each other, getting scratched and pounded and bruised all over.

How could Robert have been so right? And we so wrong? 'Angry mob' didn't begin to describe this crowd. 'Miniature hooligans' was more like it. The future of American hockey, right here.

"I picked a hell of a day to stop drinking," Robert announced, watching two tots as they rolled around on the platform, locked in a death grip. "Ho ho ho...*horreur!*"

Where's David? I thought. *We could use another pair of hands, here.*

I searched for him in the mayhem, but either he'd been trampled to death under the pitter-patter of little feet, or the bastard had cut and run.

twenty-one

$\mathcal{E}$ventually things calmed down in Santa Land, with moms and dads bringing their authority to bear, backed up by threats of spanking and no more cookies. The kids went through the ritual without further violence, leaving the throne full of the empty promises of a hung-over Santa. When the last supplicant rolled off his knee, Robert yanked the cap from his head.

"You can find me in the hotel bar if you need me." He toddled toward the front door, unsnapping the black belt as he went.

Terry shrugged at me. "We tried."

"I guess it wasn't the best idea, forcing him into this right after his biological father died."

"Probably not. I'll go along. Maybe I can talk the bartender into watering down his drinks."

"Okay, I'm outta here, too."

"Um, I think someone wants to talk to you." She grinned and gestured behind me, then skipped out the door after Robert.

I turned and saw David standing there, an amused look on his face. He'd appeared out of nowhere.

"That went well," he said.

"Yes. Remind me to have my ovaries removed. Where the hell were you?"

"I had to take care of something."

"Had to take care of your own hide, is more like it." I held out my arms for his inspection. "Look at these bruises!"

He took both of my hands in his, turning them over. Then he bent forward and kissed the underside of my forearms. "Better?"

My knees melted.

He laughed and pulled me to him, slipping an arm around my shoulders. "Want to see what I've been working on? The mural's just around the corner."

"Can I go dressed like this?"

"Don't worry. We'll be in the dark."

"Oh." I mentally rubbed my palms together. *The dark.*

David led me down the sweeping staircase and out a side door. The fresh air cleared my sinuses of the smell of kiddie sweat, and the waves lapping gently against the rocks began to soothe my nerves.

"Come on. It's over there." I followed him to the back of the Casino, where he pulled a white candle from his back pocket.

"What's that for?"

"You really should see the mural by candlelight. It brings out the iridescence of the tiles."

We looked up past the scaffolding at a tile fresco covering an area ten feet by twenty. It depicted an enchanting underwater scene—a mermaid surrounded by fish and kelp. She was Botticelli beautiful with the sly humor of the Mona Lisa, her red hair flowing out into the blue water like the tentacles of an exotic sea organism. Her breasts were bare, the svelte torso curving down into a shimmering green tail below the cleft between her legs. A frisky little sea horse floated alongside her like a devoted pet.

"Gorgeous, isn't she?"

I nodded dumbly as David grabbed onto the scaffolding and started to climb. "Come on. You need to see her close up."

I followed him, careful not to slip in my elf shoes, and we

hoisted ourselves over the top rail onto the wooden platform. He handed me a matchbook, cupping his hand around the candle.

I struck a match and lit the wick. David aimed the candle at the mural, and suddenly thousands of specks of gold and silvery blue flickered into vibrancy. Streaks of light sliced through the water, illuminating the magical submarine world.

David held the candle up at arm's length, shining it directly into the mermaid's eyes. Jade specked with gold, they appeared to be looking straight into mine, tracking me as I moved from side to side.

"It's an interesting optical effect," he said. "Wherever you go, her eyes seem to follow you."

"When was this made?"

"It was designed as by John Gabriel Beckman in the late Twenties. He didn't have time to finish it before the Casino opened, so at first it was painted directly on the wall. It took a few more years before the tile was installed."

"Kind of risqué for that era, wasn't it?"

"It was a pretty free-wheeling time. People weren't offended by the sight of an idealized human form."

"I'll say she's idealized. Nobody's that beautiful in real life."

He turned the flame toward me, gazing at my profile. I pretended not to notice, staring up at the mermaid instead.

"You're that beautiful," he said.

The blood rushed up my neck. I started to deny it, but then thought, *Why blow the moment?*

"You don't believe me?" he asked.

"I don't see any freckles on her, that's for sure."

"I'm an artist. I study faces for a living. Every day that I worked on her, I thought to myself, 'If I ever found a woman who looked like that...' "

"If you ever did?"

"I'd beg her to make love to me."

I turned and looked deep into his eyes. "And if she said no?"

Because maybe, just maybe, she already had two sort-of boyfriends?

"Then I'd settle for one kiss."

One kiss was very close to zero, when you thought about it.

He moved closer. "Well, a very long kiss."

My hand went out and blocked his chest. "I have a sort of boyfriend."

He calmly removed my hand, squeezed it and let it fall to the side. "Please don't think I'm a pervert, but I'm finding you irresistible in that little elf suit."

"I won't think you're a pervert if you won't think I am."

"Why would I think you are?"

"Because you remind me of Jesus, and you have to admit it's kind of perverted to have impure thoughts about him."

He burst out laughing. "Are you Catholic?"

"Episcopalian, but I can still go to hell. Theoretically."

"Why do you say you have a *sort of* boyfriend? That's like saying you have a sort of cat."

"How so?"

"If you have a cat, there's no two ways about it. You have to feed it and clean the litter box. It's always in the back of your mind. Gotta get home and feed the cat, gotta pick up some treats, gotta give it some fresh water. The cat will *die* without your attention. So if you say you 'sort of' have a boyfriend, I can only assume you're not really concerned with his care and feeding."

"I *do* care for them. I do."

Oops.

He gave me a wise look. "Them? You have two?"

"N-not really, no," I stammered. "One is more of a fantasy, actually. He's never around. They keep him busy at the FBI."

His eyes widened in surprise. "The FBI?"

I cocked my head. "You look worried. Are you a fugitive or something?"

"Not that I know of."

"Do *you* have a cat?"

"Lost him in the divorce."

"Oh. So, no wife, either."

"No, and you don't have a boyfriend."

"Maybe I don't," I said, my breath coming quicker. "Tonight."

He blew out the candle and dropped it to the platform. I felt his arms go around me in the darkness. He pressed me into his chest, my face fitting perfectly into the side of his neck. After a few wordless moments, I tilted back my head and he kissed me. Strong, smooth mouth. Lips that were unlikely to leave mine during the whole act of love, I knew.

At least I wanted to know. I reached up around his neck and pulled him down, arching my back until I was no longer supporting my own weight. He lowered me to the platform with one arm while he clung to the metal railing with the other. And true to my prediction, his lips never left mine the whole time.

I wrapped one green leg around him, and we both laughed when the jingle bell tinkled.

We kissed—long and slow and hypnotic. After what seemed like an eternity, he pulled away and looked down at me. "Want to come to my place?"

"I shouldn't."

"I didn't ask if you should. I asked if you wanted to."

My head nodded. Damn thing always seemed to have a mind of its own.

David raised himself up again using the rail, lifting me by the hand. We were so focused on each other and what we were going to do next, that we didn't see the figure below.

David started to climb over the rail, and that's when I saw a man in a black ski mask at the base of the scaffolding, raising a gun.

I grabbed David's ankle and pulled. *"Down!"*

He collapsed into me and we rolled up against the Casino wall as a gunshot rang out. Bits of tile and plaster rained down on us, my arm burning from the melted candle wax. David and I clutched each other, our hearts pounding. Then we heard the shooter running away around the side of the Casino.

"You okay?" David asked breathlessly.

"I think so."

"Good. Stay here."

Before I could protest, he'd swung his leg over the railing and was rappelling down the side of the scaffolding.

"David, no! What are you doing?"

He hit the ground and took off in pursuit of the gunman.

"Shit!" I jumped to my feet and climbed over the top. My foot slipped on the way down and I fell, grasping the rails over my head, legs flailing. "Damn elf shoes!"

I regained my footing and scrambled down the bars hand over hand. I dropped the remaining three feet to the ground, toe bells tinkling. I had no thought for how ridiculous it may seem for an elf, her romantic tryst interrupted by a gunshot, to be churning up the street in pursuit of the shooter.

My only thought was for David.

He was an unarmed artist in pursuit of a potential killer. I didn't know how much good Santa's little helper was going to do in this situation. I only knew I couldn't let him face it alone.

I saw the shooter moving in and out of the shadows, broad-shouldered and bow-legged, scampering like an ungainly primate. He wore a mask, but he couldn't hide his freaky body.

The Ape-man.

"David, stop!"

But he kept on running.

The restaurants and bistros were on my right, the harbor to my left. Beaver sprinted down a dock, coming in and out of view as he passed under the lamps, his footsteps echoing like explosions off the water. David leapt onto the dock, trailing him tightly down the wooden boards.

When Beaver reached the end of the dock, he turned and aimed the gun.

"David!" I screamed.

Another shot rang out.

David hit the dock face-first. Beaver dove into the harbor, splashing out to sea. I spotted his black mask floating in the water next to the pilings as I raced to where David lay, crouching down beside him.

"Are you all right?" I ran my hands over his body. "Were you hit?"

He slowly pushed himself up to his hands and knees, shaking his head. Tears of relief streamed from my eyes at seeing him alive and unharmed.

"I banged the crap out of my head when I threw myself down."

We looked out to see Beaver moving farther and farther away from shore. Then a powerboat sped up to him, cutting its engine.

"Is it the law?" I asked David, wiping away my tears.

"I don't think so."

The driver secured a small ladder on the side of the boat. Beaver paddled over to it and climbed aboard.

"It must be an accomplice." I strained to see Beaver's rescuer, but the boat was too far away. It spun around, weaving in and out of the anchored boats as it headed out to sea, the taillights leaving streaks of red in its wake. "Was he shooting at you or at me?"

"Both of us, maybe."

"Why, because we identified him?"

"Who knows?"

I heard a siren wailing. The cavalry was on its way.

Whitehorse was first on the scene, still in uniform. We related the sequence of events to her as we walked back to the Casino. She climbed the scaffolding with us, and David pointed out the hole in the mural. Fortunately, the bullet had missed the mermaid, though several tiles to her right had been demolished.

"You're sure it was Beaver who shot at you?" She probed the depth of the hole with her fingertip.

"Absolutely," David said.

I confirmed with a nod.

"And you gave chase?" she asked him.

"I followed him down to the dock. He ran to the end and took another shot at me. I went down. Then he dove off and swam to a boat."

"Make of the boat?"

"I'm not that into them, I wouldn't know."

"It was small, a powerboat," I told her. "White. Or possibly yellow."

"And you couldn't tell anything about the pilot?"

"No, sorry."

"Man? Woman?"

"I just couldn't say."

She clicked on her radio. "Whitehorse to harbor patrol, over."

A man's voice, "I read you, over."

"Any sign of the boat?"

"Negative."

"Have you been to the south shore, over?"

"That's a ten-four, over."

"The Coast Guard has been alerted. Be on the lookout for them."

"Roger. Out."

"Anything else we can do to help?" David asked, as we scaled back down to the ground.

Whitehorse shook her head. "He's probably on his way to Mexico. Dang it all, our prime suspect for the Edwards murder."

"You'll catch him," I said.

She gave me the once-over. "You might want to try a different outfit next time you're in a gunfight. Elves make good targets."

"I'll keep it in mind."

We said goodnight to her and walked back to the St. Lauren, keeping our heads low to avoid eye contact with the curious bystanders, who were gathered in wary clumps along the street.

David took my hand in his. "Thanks for coming after me."

My body shivered at the feel of his warm, smooth palm. "One stupid turn deserves another," I said.

"You think it was stupid to chase him unarmed?"

"Nah, you could have always beaten him to death with your gum eraser."

"Hey, these hands are lethal weapons." He dragged me into the shadows and placed his hands on my shoulders, then ran them slowly down the sides of my body, grazing my breasts on the way.

"Okay, okay." I licked my lower lip. "They're deadly."

He smiled at my reaction, sliding his hands back up. When I was actually on the verge of drooling, he swept my hair away from my shoulder and leaned in to kiss me on the side of the neck.

Take me! A voice screamed in my head.

"He tried to gun down my mermaid girl," David murmured near my ear. "I had to go after him."

"I guess that makes you... *my hero.*"

He laughed as his arms went around my waist, pulling me closer. "I'd love to see your room."

I went stupid all of a sudden. "My room? Why do you want to see that?"

"Kerry," he whispered. "I want to be alone with you."

"Oh, right. But we wouldn't be alone. You're forgetting Terry."

He bent down and pressed his full lips against mine. Then his tongue went between my teeth, forcing open my mouth.

I dug my nails into the back of his neck. He groaned and drove his tongue deeper. I raked my fingers through his long hair, pulling back on his head, causing him to become so excited him that he reached down and swept me up in his arms. He began marching toward the hotel entrance, with me kicking my legs.

"Seriously, Terry will be in the room."

"She can go out for a drink." His voice was husky.

"Let me down!"

"Uh-uh."

I finally succeeded in wriggling out of his arms, landing on my feet in front of him. "Tomorrow, okay? Tonight has been too crazy."

I was actually touched by the look of frustration in his face.

"Okay," he said at last. "I'll call you."

"Thanks for understanding."

We stood there, neither of us anxious to part.

"You going to be all right walking home?" I asked him.

"I think the criminal element on the island was pretty much eliminated tonight."

"Still, be careful."

"Always."

He kissed me on the tip of the nose. Then he waved goodbye and started back down the hill, adjusting his pants.

As I watched him go, my heart began a flutter of anxiety. Suddenly, I had the feeling that I'd never see my gentle artist again. I wanted to call him back, to spend the night with him. I wanted to hold and protect him.

That's just the adrenaline talking, I chided myself. *Calm down, Kerry. You'll both be alive to ring in the new year.*

twenty-two

$\mathcal{A}$ crowd had gathered in the lobby as word spread about the latest crime spree. Guests milled about, looking stricken and excited at the same time. Most of them had traveled here specifically to get away from the crime, congestion, and general horrors of life across the water. They weren't exactly happy to learn that these social ills had followed them here.

After answering a few questions from rattled vacationers, I took the elevator up to our room. I wondered why I hadn't seen Terry among the looky-loos down by the dock, but that mystery was soon explained. Her elf suit lay on the bed next to a note on hotel stationery: *In lobby bar with Petty. Come join us. Don't mention ring!*

She was sharing a drink with none other than Steven Petty. I shrugged out of my tunic and dressed in jeans and a sweater. I was on my way out when I noticed the exotic ring sitting on the bedside table.

That's casual treatment for such an expensive bauble, I thought.

The toilet tank had worked just fine as a hidey-hole, so back the ring went. I lifted the porcelain lid and tossed it into the water, watching it sink to the bottom.

Another marriage down the tubes.

I went downstairs and found Terry nursing an Amstel Light, Petty sipping a high ball. He stood when I entered the bar, quite the old-fashioned gentleman.

I took a seat at their table. "Did you hear what happened?"

"We heard shots," Terry said.

"So you didn't actually see me running down the perpetrator in my elf outfit?"

"Missed that part," she said, laughing.

Petty gave me a surprised look. "Are you... okay?"

"All in a day's work," I assured him.

"Thank goodness for that. I was just telling your sister that I want to hire you."

"Oh? What can we do for you?" I asked, having already guessed the answer.

"I want you to find my wife."

Be careful what you wish for, I beamed to Terry telepathically.

"Mr. Petty was just about to give me some background," Terry explained.

I couldn't wait to hear what he had to say for himself. "Yes. Please do fill us in."

Whereupon Steven Petty launched into his story, starting with the rancorous divorce from Paige, better known to us as Psycho-Doris. They'd been married straight out of U.C. San Diego, he said. Paige had put him through night school, where he specialized in real estate law. After graduation, he began investing the dowry he'd received from her rich father, eventually making his mark in Orange County real estate.

But while the investments thrived, the marriage disintegrated. The couple had no children. Paige couldn't conceive and she wouldn't discuss adoption. They tried the usual fertility treatments, even *in vitro*, but nothing seemed to work. The situation became a big stressor in their marriage, ultimately driving Paige to drink. Between the alcohol and the hormones wreaking havoc on her system, the once vivacious woman became unstable and increasingly manic.

She blamed Steven, even though tests revealed that he wasn't the source of the problem. When the doctor suggested surrogacy, Paige went over the edge into full-blown paranoia. She accused the doctor of giving her drugs to inhibit conception, and of conspiring with her husband to keep her childless so that Petty could marry a younger woman.

Fearful of a lawsuit, the doctor refused to treat Paige any longer, which only increased her suspicion. To top things off, Steven's close friendship with a young female colleague turned romantic as he sought solace from the erratic mood swings of his wife. The thing Paige had most feared, she brought upon herself. Steven filed for divorce and made plans to marry his new lover.

"So the new girlfriend was Anna?" I said.

He shook his head. "No, Ruth."

"When does Anna come into it?"

"I'm getting to that."

Petty related what we already knew about the nasty breakup, the car through the front window of his condominium, Paige's arrest. It wasn't the only incident, he assured us; there were others just as bad. But whenever he filed a complaint, Paige was able to put one over on the officers, playing the faithful wife who'd been wronged by the very man she'd helped to make a success.

The judge gave her a suspended sentence on the window-crashing incident. He apparently bought into her story that her handbag had become entangled with her feet, causing the car to accelerate by accident.

Then Petty and his fiancé got smart. They started recording Paige's abusive phone calls. She screeched, she cursed, she threatened to cut off Ruth's breasts with a knife. In the face of this evidence, Paige was no longer able to pawn herself off as the innocent victim. She was ordered to undergo psychiatric evaluation, and Petty was awarded a restraining order against her. But it was too late to save his new relationship. The fiancé was so traumatized, so fearful of his ex, that she called off the engagement altogether.

"And when did you meet your present wife, Anna?" I asked, taking notes on my steno pad.

"Only a couple months ago. It was a whirlwind romance. We fell in love and got engaged immediately."

"And how was Paige behaving in the interim?"

"Fine. I didn't have much contact with her, but whenever I did, it was completely civilized. She was on medication, which I thought was helping. She'd lost fifteen pounds and was feeling good about herself again. She'd even started dating. I was actually happy for her. *And* relieved."

"Then why did she come here to wreck your honeymoon?" Terry asked him. "Or could that be a coincidence?"

"No coincidence," he said. "I realize now it was all an act. Maybe she had been hoping for a reconciliation, and hearing about the marriage set her off again."

"How do you suppose she got wind of your honeymoon plans?" I asked.

"I have no idea."

"Was your new bride aware of the problems you had with her?"

"I didn't want to dwell on the past, but I'd told her some of it."

"Did she know you had a restraining order against Paige?"

"No."

Terry gave him a curious look. "Why didn't you enforce it?"

"I'd feel like a fool, running to the police to tattle on her. Besides, she stayed the legally mandated distance away. Two hundred yards."

"But Anna wasn't covered by the order, was she?"

Petty frowned at her. "What do you mean?"

"Paige wouldn't have been breaking the law if she approached your current wife. Especially if she took no overtly hostile action toward her. She could walk right up to her and have a conversation without fear of arrest."

"I hadn't thought of that," he admitted.

It was time for the tough questions.

"Is Paige capable of violence?" I asked him.

Petty turned away to face the window. "In spite of all the craziness, I never really believed she could hurt anyone. Now, I'm not so sure. If the worst has happened... I mean, if Anna hasn't gone off somewhere, but was actually the victim of...?" His voice trailed off and he closed his eyes. "I'd be responsible for that, wouldn't I? My ex-wife, my stubborn refusal to leave the island, my *fault.*"

I paused before the next question, giving him a chance to pull himself together.

"Did you print a notice of your engagement in the newspaper?"

He opened his eyes tiredly. "Anna wanted to, but I talked her out of it."

"Send out any announcements?"

"No."

"So nobody knew to send you wedding presents?"

"We didn't need anything. I could buy Anna anything she wanted." His voice quavered. "All I wanted was to spend the rest of my life with her."

"Then why were you so angry?" Terry said.

"When we saw you on the glass-bottom boat, you were practically cursing her."

He nodded, as if only now remembering the incident. "I... I can't explain what I was feeling. Anger because she skipped out. Fear that she'd been the victim of foul play. Guilt on top of everything else." He pressed his fingertips into his forehead. "I should have left as soon as I found out Paige had followed us. But you have to understand; the woman had made me miserable for years! She'd already destroyed one relationship, and here she was, doing it again. I had to draw the line somewhere." His lower lip twitched with the effort not to cry. "I can't lose Anna. I can't."

Terry gave him an empathetic smile that was pure bunk. "Don't worry, we'll find her. And if we can't persuade her to come back, at least you'll be assured that she's okay. Right, boss?" she said to me.

I wasn't sure what she was up to, but I went along. "Right."

"Mind if we see that picture of her again?" Terry asked. "I want to be sure I'll recognize her."

Petty obliged her by pulling out the wallet photo we'd seen earlier in the day. Terry knew full well what the woman looked like, but she had another reason for asking.

"I didn't notice the ring before," she said. "It's so beautiful. What is it, an emerald?"

He gazed longingly at the photo. "A green diamond."

"Really? I didn't know there was such a thing."

"Yes, they have them in green, blue, pink—brown's the most common color—and white."

From the rapt expression on his face, I began to wonder if it was the bride or her ring Petty was so eager to locate.

"But most diamonds are white, aren't they?" I asked.

"No, most are actually colorless. White diamonds are more opaque, with less brilliance. But they're in very high demand, just like the colored ones."

Terry smiled at me. "Learn something new every day, huh? I'll bet Anna was wild about that ring."

"She ought to be. She picked it out herself at Tiffany's."

"Tiffany's?" I asked innocently. "But I understand you have your own diamond mine."

His face went hard and he sat back in his chair. "Been checking up on me, have you?"

"Yes, we have."

"Well, you don't get stones like that from an old, washed-out Namibian mine."

"No? Then why did you pay ten million dollars for it?"

"Our other investments were doing so well, we needed a loser for tax purposes."

"We read that the mine was closed down because the workers were becoming sick," Terry said. "What caused it? Gas or something?"

He gave a careless shrug. "It was probably an early outbreak of AIDS. Nobody knew what it was at the time. They assumed the symptoms were due to something underground."

"AIDS?" Terry said, surprised. "Way back then?"

"Researchers think it's been around for a long time in a less virulent form. It took decades for it to rise to the level of a deadly epidemic." He waved a hand as if swishing away imaginary viruses. "Anyway, the mine was a loser, like I said. We'll get some industrial grade stones out of it, but it's not going to produce consumer quality gems." He took the wallet back. "Nothing like *that*."

Terry snagged the bill, signing the drinks to our room. "We charge three hundred dollars a day, plus expenses."

"A bargain, if you can find her," Petty said, standing. "If that's all…?"

I held up a hand. "One more thing?"

"Yes?"

"We can reach you at the Motel Six?"

"No, I've moved to the Sunspot Motel."

Terry glanced at me.

The same place that Beaver had occupied.

"It's a little nicer than the Motel Six," he said. "Let me know when you find something."

Once he'd taken himself out of the lounge, I looked over at Terry. "What's up with the motel hopping?"

"Got me. But no way is The Sunspot nicer than the Motel Six. If anything, it's probably seedier."

"Maybe his investments aren't doing as well as he claims."

Terry picked up Petty's glass and rattled the cubes. "He sure knows a lot about ice for someone who's only in it for a tax write-off."

I sat there a moment, turning the interview over in my mind. "Exactly how much of his story should we believe?"

"Around seventy percent, I'd say. He's definitely holding back."

"Then why did we take the job? As a rule, don't we try to avoid working for sleazy liars?"

"Because I'm concerned about his wife."

"Even if she's alive, she's *not* going back to that man," I said. "I don't care what he says. He *didn't* tell her about the situation with Paige. He thought he could finesse it."

"Let's just hope it wasn't Anna who got finessed."

twenty-three

"*R̶innnnng… Rinnnnng… Rinnnnng*"

"Stop them! Stop the sleigh bells. I'll do anything. Just make them stop!" I shouted in my sleep.

"It's the phone, moron." Terry picked up the receiver from the nightstand and listened for a second, then hung up.

I cracked open an eyelid. "Who was that?"

She jumped out of the king bed, throwing back the covers. "It was our wake-up call. Rise and shine!"

I pulled the blanket up over my head. "Are you insane? It's six o'clock!"

"Sorry, forgot to tell you with all the excitement last night, but François' ashes are coming special delivery this morning. I said we'd go with Robert to the airport to pick 'em up."

"Good Lord. Can't he go by himself?"

"You want him to recover his father's ashes alone?" She slugged me through the covers. "Selfish beast."

"But what about finding Anna?"

"We're just going to have to balance the job with our family obligations, okay? It'll only take an hour."

I groaned.

"I'll shower first. That way you can spend fifteen minutes more in bed."

"Most generous."

"'Tis the season."

She padded into the bathroom and I got a few more winks. Soon I was awakened by the sound of the hair dryer. I lay there thinking about the previous night—the thrill of kissing David mixed up with the terror of being shot at, the crushing disappointment when the most likely suspect for Nikki's murder had escaped by boat.

At least the authorities knew who he was. They'd find him and lock him up for good. That thought gave me some comfort.

Now we needed to track down Anna Petty.

Compared to what had gone before, it seemed like child's play. But we'd spent two hours the previous night calling hotels with no results. They hadn't seen the missing woman and furthermore, they informed us, the sheriff's department had already contacted them. Had Anna Petty stowed away on a private boat and gone back to the mainland?

When we were showered and dressed, Terry and I went next door to collect Robert. He answered the door holding Reba's ice pack over his eyes.

"Morning!" Terry said, obnoxiously cheerful. "Ready to roll?"

"Ready to *hurl*." He closed the door behind him, moaning. "Mumsy's not coming, although she said she'd try to make it to the funeral."

I led the way to the elevator. "Funeral?"

"Yes, the burial at sea. I've booked a boat for three o'clock. We'll pop some champagne for a toast, then sprinkle *pater* to the wind. I think he'd like that."

"Sure he would." Terry punched the call button, giving me a dubious look. "Who wouldn't?"

Who the hell knew what the man would have liked? Who knew anything about him? The email said that the ashes would be accompanied by some of François' personal affects. Maybe that would give us a clue as to his character.

"Did you do any research?" I asked Robert. "Do you know what films François directed?"

His face turned a deeper shade of red. "No, I seem to have lost my computer. I thought perhaps I'd left it in the bar, but the management can't locate it."

"Sorry, dude," Terry said. "We took it. We needed to do a check on someone."

"I should have known it was lifted by you little gremlins." He wagged a finger at us. "Never mind, there'll be plenty of time for research after we pick up the cremains."

$\mathcal{W}e$ *sat in* the island's dinky airport lounge, which consisted of vinyl benches and an arrival/departure board. Tourists whiled away their time reading magazines or James Patterson paperbacks.

Finally, a courier pushed a luggage cart into the lounge, carrying a sign with Robert's name on it.

Robert shot up from his seat. "Over here!"

The luggage cart was piled with six gray feature film cans along with a brass urn—François' final resting vessel. Sitting on top of the cans was a white plastic case that looked suspiciously like a dog kennel.

The courier held out a clipboard for Robert. He signed where instructed, at the same time trying to see inside the carrying case.

"Uh, what's in the crate?"

The taciturn young man grabbed the pen and the clipboard back from Robert. "Jacques," he answered, raising a thick Gallic brow.

"Jacques?"

"The dog of the deceased monsieur," the courier replied. "Bonne chance." With that, he spun on his heel and exited the lounge without another word.

Robert was aghast. "A dog! Well, they might have bothered

to inquire whether I was a dog person before sending him over here. What were they thinking?"

Peeking inside the kennel, I saw a mat of tight yellowed curls. "I think Jacques may be a poodle."

Robert's dismay turned to disgust. "A *poodle?*"

"That's what it looks like."

"Fabulous. This is just what I need. Why don't I hang a sign around my neck that says 'Beverly Hills Fop'? Oh, why in the name of God did they saddle me with this creature?"

"They probably had no choice," Terry said. "No surviving relatives."

"They don't have dog pounds in Paris?" Robert said. "No humane society? No sausage factories?"

I smacked him. "Meanie!"

"Well, it's hardly the kind of inheritance I was expecting from a great film director."

"You ought to be sorry. He's an innocent animal. Besides, François had no other children, right?"

Robert shook his head.

"And didn't you say you'd want to know if you had any interesting family members? Jacques here is your half-brother."

"When I said 'interesting,' I really had in mind someone who was fluent in English."

"Give the poor thing half a chance," I said.

We all leaned over to peer into the wire mesh.

"Jacques?" Robert spoke to the fur-bound hide. "Bonjour, Monsieur le Poodle!"

"Um, he's not moving," Terry said.

Robert's eyes widened hopefully. "Perhaps he died on the trip over. Imploded in the cargo hold due to depressurization, or something."

Terry poked a finger between the wires. "Hey, pooch! Welcome to America!" Her finger made contact with the dog's haunch and an ominous growl rumbled inside.

She withdrew her hand quickly. "He's alive, all right. But he might be a little nasty-tempered."

"I'm sure he's perfectly nice," I said. "He's probably jetlagged."

Robert sniffed at the kennel door with nostrils flared. "Do you smell that?"

Terry took a whiff. "Guess he needs a little freshening up after the trip."

"Lovely. Just lovely!" Robert said. "A smelly, bad-natured dog and a can of ashes. Can't wait to see what other treats are in store for us here."

We wheeled Robert's inheritance out to the golf cart in the parking lot. I volunteered to sit with Jacques on the trip back to the hotel.

"Fine. I'd better ride with Dad on my lap." Robert shoved the kennel onto the bumper seat with me. Then he leaned over with a grunt to lift one of the round cans.

"What's that?" Terry asked. "You think it's one of his films?"

"Yes, it must be," Robert said excitedly. "At last, the *oeuvre* of the man whose genes I share!" He read the handwritten label, and then his face collapsed. "*Ooh là là, Les Girls*?"

"I'm sure it's a very good film," I said, taking the rusty can from him.

"Dad was a hack!" Robert buried his face in his hands.

Terry exploded with laughter. "What is it, pornography?"

"It's probably some hideous Fifties' kitsch, with mademoiselles doing the Mambo in chinos," Robert groaned.

Terry plinked the urn with her fingernail. "About those ashes. You know, sometimes they have bits of bones and stuff in them when they don't get the person incinerated all the way."

"Thank you so much for that information." Robert shook the urn. "Papa, can you hear me?" he sang.

Sure enough, something clanked inside. "What do you suppose it is?" he asked. "A bit of femur? Or perhaps a tooth?"

I was at my limit with these two. "Would everybody stop being so morbid and bummed out? You know, we have a lot to be grateful for this holiday season."

"Yes, so much to be grateful for!" Terry sang her own ditty: "All I want for Christmas is a dead man's molar!" She busted up laughing again, as Robert stole another forlorn glance at the dog carrier.

"Why, oh why didn't he take his dog with him into the after-life?" he said. "The pharaohs did it."

Something told me this particular pet would have been left outside the pyramid walls at burial time. But I was determined to be positive.

"Better a poodle than a stick in the eye. N'est-ce pas?"

twenty-four

$\mathcal{J}$acques didn't get any livelier or friendlier on the trip back to the hotel. Terry tossed her jacket over the kennel and sneaked it through the lobby up to Robert's room, then dumped it in the middle of the floor. The three of us stood there, each one waiting for the others to make a move. More ardent growling came from the case. It was deep and ominous-sounding for such a small animal.

"Does he do anything other than growl?" Robert said.

"Maybe when he gets outside he'll be in a better mood." I reached down to pop the latch, ignoring the sound of evil canine intent coming from within. I flipped the door open as quickly as I could and jumped back.

No growling now. Only silence.

What would he do? Charge out of the kennel with teeth bared? Rip into one of our calves and infect us with French rabies? We stood there like the townspeople in some old western, gathered in front of the saloon to await the gunslinger in black.

And then… a whisper of movement… a shuffling noise.

One yellowish-white paw emerged from the kennel, its claws overgrown and curling over the toes, the pink pedicure chipped away. The sinewy leg made its way slowly out the door, showing a straggly pompom of fur just above the gray ankle flesh. Then came the head—a small skull with an overgrown afro wobbling on top like a ball of dirty soapsuds. Jacques wore a pink rhinestone collar, cracked with age and missing a few stones. His black button nose twitched at the tip of his snout, and his lip was curled up in a snarl, revealing his completely empty, pink and black gums.

"He's got no teeth!" Terry yelled.

"Grrrrrrrrrrrr," said Jacques.

"Say something nice to him!" I hissed.

"Hey, boy," she said. "I mean, hey *garçon.* Good *garçon!"*

Robert put on a desperately playful tone, clapping his hands. "Come on out, Jacques. Let's have a look at you. There's a good boy!"

Another paw ventured outside, complete with matching hairball. Jacques limped slowly over the lip of the kennel, growling all the while. When at last his hind feet had emerged, we saw a tail with a pompom like a slushy snowball jammed between his scrawny legs. He glared up at us with filmy eyes.

"I think he has cataracts," I said.

"And arthritis," said Robert.

"And a really bad haircut," Terry said.

Jacques balanced precariously on his rickety legs, shivering like a victim of the DT's.

"He looks like some decrepit old drag queen," Robert said with a revolted grimace.

"Oh, you guys! He's just a slightly over-the-hill, poor little doggie." I reached out to pet him. "Nice doggie…"

"Arf!" He snapped at my finger.

"Ouch!"

"Did he bite you?" Terry grabbed for my hand.

"Not really." I pressed on the finger pad. "He didn't break the skin. Just sort of gummed me."

Terry crossed her arms, scowling at Jacques. "Why don't we find a veterinarian and have him put down? They can cremate him and we'll throw him in the drink with François."

"That's so cruel!" I said.

"Well, what do you suggest? He's not going to get along with our dogs. He's too mean. And he's way too old to give away for adoption. If we put him in a shelter, he'll be the first one to get the needle."

"What did we say about this being the season? Can we show some compassion for a dog who's literally on his last legs? A little kindness in his final days?"

"Get a load of St. Kerry of Assisi," Robert muttered.

"*Somebody* around here has to do the right thing," I said, stomping toward the door. "C'mon, Jacques. You probably need to go outside, right?"

Then, as if I'd caused him to remember his over-encumbered bladder, Jacques lifted his hind leg and let loose on the carpet. Everyone jumped back as hot pee sprayed the floor.

"Jesus!" Terry yelled. "He's not housebroken?"

"He just got off the plane!" I said. "What's he supposed to do?"

"Take him outside, quickly!" Robert snatched up the phone. "Hello, housekeeping? We've had an accident. Send someone immediately with industrial strength carpet cleaner. There's a twenty-dollar tip in it!"

"C'mon, Terry. I'm sure he needs to do number two." I reached onto the top shelf of the closet and grabbed the plastic laundry bag for poop-scooping.

"He's not on a leash, and I'm not gonna try to hook him up," she said. "I don't want to get near the gums of death."

"Forget the leash, then." I threw open the door and Jacques took his cue, hobbling over the threshold.

Terry followed us into the hallway. "Maybe he'll dash out in front of a golf cart and get creamed."

We watched as Jacques made his painful way down the carpet runner.

"I wouldn't bet on it," I said. "That guy's not dashing anywhere."

Jacques teetered off the elevator and into the lobby, clicking toward the entrance on his unclipped nails. A bellboy saw him coming and opened the door. Jacques brazened his way past without acknowledging the gesture, his attitude pure canine snob.

"Does Avalon have a leash law?" Terry asked the guy.

"I think so," he said.

"If we're caught, will they confiscate the dog?"

"Nah, they'll just write you a ticket. You'll have to pay a fine."

"I'd pay a small fortune for somebody to run over him."

I slugged her in the back. "Be nice."

Outside, Jacques stopped on the front porch and sniffed the air. Then all at once he took off running down the street, his fop-top buoyed on the winter breeze like a nimbus drifting through the sky.

"Hey, look at him go!" Terry marveled. "Maybe it's the ocean air."

"Yeah, I'll bet he was just stiff from being in that cage. He's getting loosened up."

We jogged after him, wondering what accounted for this sudden burst of energy. Jacques pranced down Beacon Street, tongue flying, drawn forward by some mysterious instinct, or perhaps by a scent undetectable to our human nostrils. *Clippity clippity clip* went his nails on the cobblestones. He bounded around the corner at Metropole Avenue.

"Where's he going?" Terry said.

"I don't know!"

Jacques was some distance from the shoreline, but he was getting out of range and I feared he might actually run into traffic on the main drag. I picked up my pace, and amazingly, so did Jacques.

"Terry, he's not slowing down!"

She overtook me easily—always the better runner—but she was too far behind to catch up to him. He'd gone from decrepit dog on his last legs to downhill racer in no time flat. Suddenly, I had a view of impending disaster on the street below.

A golf cart loaded with passengers was traveling east on Crescent Avenue. Another golf cart was entering the same intersection headed west. I screamed in horror as Jacques ran directly into the road between them.

"Jacques, *no!*"

The two drivers spotted the poodle at the same instant, swerving in opposite directions as if they'd just entered a roundabout. They yelled curses, their air horns blowing, as the carts behind them screeched to a stop. Terry pulled up short, narrowly avoiding being hit by a circling cart. Jacques slipped through the snarled traffic, doubled back across the street, and pounced up on the sidewalk headed east.

Terry and I waved apologetically to the drivers and raced after him. He turned left on Whittley Avenue, whipping around the feet of a middle-aged couple in shorts, causing the two of them to crash into each other. The woman bounced off her husband and landed on her butt on the sidewalk.

"Put that animal on a leash!" the husband shouted.

"Sorry about that!" Terry called to him, but there was no time to stop and help.

"Catch him!" I hollered. "Catch him before he kills someone!"

I rounded the corner at Whittley to see Jacques' pompom bobbing up the cobblestone street as he trotted along, his nose straight up in the air. Then without warning, he pulled a one-eighty, darting inside an open storefront door.

"He went in there!" Terry skidded to a stop, catching her breath.

Jacques had disappeared into a bakery. We ran inside to find him sitting on his haunches in front of a glass display case, panting heavily, his nostrils quivering. The case was full of fresh-baked croissants.

"He was after the croissants!" Terry cried.

"We almost got killed for baked goods? Bad Jacques! Bad *garçon.*"

And then to my shock, Jacques made a loud hacking noise and keeled over on his side. He lay there with his tongue trailing the linoleum, legs stiff as twigs, his chest stilled. His eyes were open and glazed like Krispy Kremes.

"Omigod!" Terry ran to Jacques, kneeling on the floor. "Is he dead?" She pressed her finger to his carotid artery to feel for a pulse.

I threw a couple of dollars on the counter. "I need an emergency croissant!"

The saleslady plunged a gloved hand into the display case, snatching one off the aluminum tray. I fell to my knees beside the moribund pooch, waving the warm roll under his wee black nose.

"Hey, Jacques! Here's a nice fresh croissant for you, boy!"

A crowd of concerned citizens gathered around us.

"What's wrong with the little doggie?"

"Did he have a heart attack?"

"Is there a vet in the house?"

"Come on, breathe!" A woman in flowered shorts snorted in and out through her nose to demonstrate.

Endless seconds passed as I waited for a sign of life, feeling terrible for the way we had treated poor Jacques, the hard-hearted things we'd said about him. Had he made the trip across the wide Atlantic only to die here on a cold bakery floor?

I saw a flicker of movement—a barely perceptible twitching of his snout. Then Jacques retracted his tongue and snapped the croissant out of my hand.

"He's alive!" someone said.

"Praise the Lord!" a black woman sang. "It's a Christmas miracle!"

The bystanders hugged each other tearfully, sniffling and laughing with relief.

I picked Jacques up off the floor. He growled, but I was in no danger as long as his mouth was clamped down on the croissant. Holding him up in the air like a baby saved from a house fire, I took a bow.

The crowd applauded wildly.

"Never underestimate the power of pastry," I said modestly.

Terry went back to the lady behind the counter. "Better give us a few for the road. It may be the only thing keeping him alive."

"On the house." The saleslady wiped her eye with a sleeve. "I'm just so happy he made it."

As she waited for the road croissants, Terry stared at the strange little dog with the roll hanging out of his mouth. "He can't chew it, you know."

"Maybe he holds it there until it melts," I said.

"We'll buy a blender and grind them up for him. That way he can enjoy pre-digested pastries."

After thanking the saleslady, Terry opened the door for us. "C'mon, Jacques. Let's see if we can find a nice patch of grass for you to do your business in."

I exited with Jacques in my arms. Once outside, my eye was caught by a woman leaving a market carrying a full bag of groceries. She was dressed in dirty, wrinkled clothes, her dark hair unkempt. Large black sunglasses sat askew on her sunburnt nose, and she had a sandwich shoved halfway into her mouth, chomping down on it as ravenously as Jacques had the croissant. We stared at each other, and before I'd even registered her identity, my feet started chasing her. They'd known who she was before I did—Steven Petty's runaway bride.

"Anna!" I shouted. "Hey, Anna! We need to talk to you!"

Her eyes widened in fear, then she dropped the grocery bag and ran. Canned goods, power bars, and a home pregnancy test spilled out onto the street.

"Anna, please!" Terry called. "Your husband's very worried about you!"

The woman kept running, but she appeared tired and weak, dragging her feet on the sidewalk. She spotted an unlocked mountain bike leaning against a street sign and jumped onto the seat, tossing away her half-eaten sandwich.

As fate would have it, the sandwich was a ham and cheese croissant.

"She's getting away!" Terry said.

Jacques whimpered, scrambling in my arms to be let down. I set him on the sidewalk and he dropped the croissant from his mouth, lunging for Anna's more interesting meat-filled one.

I had a sudden inspiration: Jacques had picked up the bakery scent from two whole blocks away, hadn't he? Maybe with the right incentive, he could track the woman who'd been eating this very sandwich.

I snatched up the ham and cheese croissant, waving it in front of his face. "Go, Jacques! Follow the lady! She's got more of these!"

Sure enough, Jacques sprinted off in Anna's direction. Anna looked over her shoulder and saw him coming, then churned the pedals with all her might, disappearing down a cross street.

Jacques stopped on the spot where Anna had stolen the bike. He sniffed the ground, vibrating like a hound on the hunt, then pointed in the direction of the departing bicycle.

"Terry, I think we may have a tracking dog on our hands!"

"Can he lead us to her?"

"He has an incredible sense of smell. He got the scent off her sandwich and gave chase."

"But we'll never catch her on foot!"

At that moment a golf cart pulled up to the curb. A man and a woman alighted from inside. Terry turned to me, waving her fingers. "Give me your license!"

"What for?"

"Just *give* it!"

She grabbed the wallet from my hand and ran to the couple, flipping it open to the investigator's license.

"We need to commandeer your cart! Official police business!"

They started to protest, but Terry had already leapt into the driver's seat. "Come on!" she shouted at me.

The woman passenger was perplexed and a little frightened. "What are you doing?"

"Pursuing a bicycle thief!" Terry told her. "You want to take a bite out of crime or what?"

The husband shrugged and tossed Terry the keys.

"Thanks, crime-stoppers!"

I jumped into the front seat next to Terry, with Jacques in my arms. "Be back soon!"

And we took off in pursuit of the runaway bride.

twenty-five

*A*t each intersection, I set Jacques down on the street, where he'd spin in a tight circle, picking up the scent. After he pointed, I scooped him back up and we sped off in the direction he'd indicated. Eventually we came to a dirt road leading up the side of a bluff. Jacques whimpered again, his nose aimed straight up the hill.

"Do we dare take the golf cart up there?" I said.

"That's where she is." Terry stomped the gas pedal. "Let's go!"

We bumped up the rutted path for a few minutes until we came upon the stolen mountain bike, abandoned by the side of the road.

"That's the good news," Terry said. "She's on foot. She'll be that much easier to track. So far our bloodhound hasn't led us astray."

I set Jacques down next to the bike. "Where is she, boy?"

He snuffled at the ground, barked once, then took off through a stretch of grass toward a stand of trees. Terry gassed the cart, angling off the path to follow Jacques across the plain.

He ducked inside the thicket.

We parked the cart outside and went in on foot, picking our way through gnarled roots, fallen branches, and piles of dead leaves. It appeared that Jacques had located a campsite. A blanket lay next to a cold fire. Empty tin cans were strewn about, their outsides charred.

Jacques circled the blanket, then plopped down on his haunches, triumphant. He looked up at us as if to say: *Mission accomplished.*

"Good Jacques!" I scratched him behind the ears.

Terry folded her arms, laughing. "Who'd have thought that little poufball had the instincts of a K-9?" She looked around the area. "No wonder they couldn't locate Anna in the hotels. She was camping out up here. Looks like she didn't come back, though."

"Maybe she dropped the bike to throw us off the scent, then hid and went down the mountain after we'd passed her."

"Wouldn't Jacques have noticed?"

"Not if she retraced her own steps."

"You think she's clever enough to do that?"

"We don't really know anything about her, do we?" I said. "She could be a career Girl Scout. Remember, she left the ring in the toilet tank as a sort of bread crumb."

"But when we followed the bread crumb, she ran away from us."

"That was because we mentioned her husband. Obviously it wasn't the right approach."

While poking around the encampment, we came across a blue vinyl overnight bag containing toothpaste, sun block, and other sundries. We walked the perimeter, checking behind every tree.

"She's definitely not here," Terry said finally.

"Nope." I went to retrieve the dog, but he wasn't there. "Hey, where's Jacques?"

"He's gone?"

"*Damn.*" I pounded a tree trunk with my fist. "I should have been watching him."

"Maybe he tracked her back down the hill."

We heard distant barking and ran out of the trees to see Jacques bounding through the grass like a fluff-covered wildebeest, cresting a rise a hundred yards away.

"There he is!" I said. "He can really move when he's motivated, can't he?"

"We'd better go after him." Terry ran to the cart, jumping into the driver's seat. "He may have picked up her trail."

I got in next to her and we took off after Jacques, urging the cart up the side of the hill. When we got to the top, I grabbed Terry's arm, gasping. Down below us, not a half-mile away, was a herd of grazing buffalo. They were still as statues, a half-ton of meat on each set of hooves, heads turning lazily in our direction.

"I've never seen buffalo in person before." Terry eased up on the gas pedal. "They're pretty scary."

Jacques was running toward the herd like a lost lamb returning to the fold.

"He's headed straight for them! He won't go all the way, will he?" Even as I said it, my heart was filled with dread.

Terry tried to reassure me. "Nah, he's just curious. Wants a better look, is all."

"I'm sure you're right. He probably never saw any buffaloes in Paris."

"Doubtful."

Up and down Jacques bobbed on the plain, bearing down on the herd. He had too much of a lead for us to catch up to him. Even if we tried, the tall grass would probably clog the undercarriage of the cart, and the engine might frighten the cows or threaten the bulls.

"I don't think we can go out there," I said. "This thing is like a glorified lawnmower without the blade. The grass will jam the axle."

"I was just thinking the same thing."

I cupped my hands to my mouth. "Jacques! Come back, Jacques!"

But my words were lost in the wind. It was eerily quiet as we sat there on the grassy hill, waiting for Jacques to come to his senses and turn around. A breeze wafted to us from the herd, redolent of stockyards. The stillness combined with the altitude made me feel like I was suspended in a hot air balloon.

Jacques was no longer visible but I could see the grasses bending as he moved inexorably toward the buffalo. "Terry, he's not stopping. This is bad."

"I know."

"Do you think they'll stomp him?"

She gave a fatalistic shrug. "Wouldn't you, if you were a buffalo?"

I had to admit that, yes, if I were a bison, I would be sorely tempted to stomp the life out of that annoying creature. "We can't just sit here while he gets squashed, can we?"

"What do you want to do? Go running up to them and say, 'Don't mind us, enormous hairy wild animals. We'll just grab this poodle and go'?"

Another minute passed, Terry drumming her fingers on the steering wheel, me tapping my foot on the floorboard. Had Jacques been revived by pastry only to meet his end up here on this desolate bluff?

Soon we heard the faint sound of barking—a series of tinny little yaps cutting the air—followed by deep, irritated lowing. *A warning moo?*

"Is he trying to herd them?" Terry said. "What's he playing at now, border collie?"

"Shhh! Listen."

We could just make out the sounds coming across the plain.

"Arf arf!"

"Mooooo."

"Arf-arf-arf!"

"*Moooooooooo.*"

"*Arf-arf-arf-arf-arf-ar—*"

Then there came a pitiful squeak, like a mouse caught in a trap, followed by an ominous silence.

No more yapping. No more mooing.

I looked over at Terry. "They stomped him."

She lowered her head. "Too bad. I was getting kind of attached to him."

"Me too." A tear stung the corner of my eye. "What do we do now?"

"I guess we go back to the hotel and give Robert the bad news."

She eased the golf cart down the other side of the hill, pain etched on her face. We drove back silently in the direction we'd come from.

"You think Robert's gonna blame us for what happened?" Terry said at last.

"He'd be right to. It is our fault."

"Our fault the dog has no common sense?"

Her defensiveness didn't fool me for a minute. She felt just as bad as I did.

"We're going to have to live with this on our conscience, Ter."

"Times like this, I wish I didn't have a conscience," she said, and then glanced into the rearview mirror. "Hey, what's that?"

"What?"

"It looks like smoke on the horizon."

I spun in my seat, squinting against the sun. "Could it be a grass fire?"

"Yeah, maybe Jacques sent up sparks as he ran."

I became aware of the earth moving beneath us, rocking the golf cart. "Hey, Terry. Stop!"

She let up on the accelerator. "What's the matter?"

"Do you feel that?"

Now that we were stationary, the sensation was even more pronounced. The cart was swaying as if from a low-grade temblor.

Terry looked down at her feet, undulating on the floor of the cart. "Earthquake?"

"It's a long friggin' earthquake, if it is."

There was a low rumbling, like thunder. I looked up and saw nothing but a few wisps of white against the powder blue sky. No angry gray rain clouds were hulking overhead. Then my gaze traveled back down to the ground, where the puff of white smoke had morphed into a roiling spume of dust. The dust cloud was moving directly toward us, the rumbling increasing in volume behind it.

I felt a shock of cold horror as I realized what was happening.

"Stampede!" I yelled.

"Holy shit!" Terry grabbed the wheel and pounded the gas pedal to the floor. "Jacques, you poufy mother! What did you do?"

"He spooked 'em!" I peeked in the mirror. *"Go! Go! Go!"*

Terry's eyes were big as hubcaps. "Let's make a break for it! Dump the cart and run to the trees!"

"No! They're too far away!"

Not only that, but the herd was on a trajectory that would take them between the trees and us. We'd be trampled for sure.

"Stay in the car!" I said. "They might go around us!"

"I'd rather run for it!"

"They're catching up! Go faster!"

"This thing won't go past twenty!" She glanced in the mirror again. "They're coming straight for us! We're dead!"

"Just *drive*!"

"God is my co-pilot, God is my copilot!" she chanted, squinching her eyes shut.

"Terry, open your eyes!"

"I don't want to see myself die!"

I grabbed the wheel to keep the cart going straight. If we rode at an angle, we'd be broadsided for sure. Our spines took a pounding as we bumped over the rough terrain, but that was hardly our biggest concern at the moment. I hazarded a look and saw the herd advancing at much faster than twenty miles an hour.

More like seventy.

They emerged from the dust cloud with their outsized heads down, necks humped, nostrils blowing like steam whistles. There was no way they were going around us; they were coming straight on. They looked like the mounts of the headless horsemen, about to trample us right down to hell.

"We're goners!" I wailed.

"It's our karma!" Terry cried. "We should never have eaten those buffalo steaks!"

"It wasn't *my* idea! I was going to have a Caesar salad!"

"Oh, yeah! You say that *now!*"

"Terry," I yelled over the noise of the rampaging herd. "I forgive you for everything!"

"What the hell is that supposed to mean!"

"It means we're about to die, so I'm taking this opportunity to forgive you for all your transgressions!"

"*My* transgressions! What about *yours?*"

"There's no time for that!"

"The hell there isn't!"

"Trust me, there's not!"

A ditch yawned open before us, a deep fissure in the ground that had been hidden by the tall grass. Terry saw it the same time I did and we both screamed.

"*Ahhhhhhhhhhhhhhhhhhhhh!*"

The cart plowed into the hole, the front bumper slamming into the opposite side, the back bumper lodging into the wall behind us. We were wedged in the crevice, suspended above a hole that narrowed into a fathomless crack below.

"We're stuck!" Terry tried to scramble out of the cart and it rocked precariously, threatening to come loose.

"No, stay inside!" I pulled her back in. "They might jump over."

The ground shook like the precursor to a volcanic eruption. The buffalo would be on us in seconds. If they had the sense to leap over the ditch, we might survive. If they stumbled over the edge and plunged down on top of us...

We were a couple of dead redheads.

We clung to each other, sweat streaming down our foreheads to mingle with the tears.

"I'm sorry I'm always so bitchy," I sobbed.

"I'm sorry I've caused you so much grief!"

Bits of earth crumbled away from the wall, the cart slipping down a few inches. Terry and I gasped, holding each other tighter.

"You haven't caused me grief," I said. "You're the best sister a girl could ever have!"

"No, you're the best. I've always been jealous of you."

"I've always envied *you*. You're fun and daring and you live life to the fullest."

"Yeah, but while you've been busy keeping a roof over our heads, I've been irresponsible and selfish, always getting us in trouble!"

My life flashed before my eyes in glorious Technicolor, starting with my earliest memory. I was in the crib, my face jammed between the bars, and Terry was sitting on my back, yanking on my baby fine hair while I bawled my little heart out.

Then I flashed forward to the second grade. I got up to write on the blackboard and my fellow students began laughing—horrible, mocking laughter that seared my very soul. I reached over my shoulder and pulled a sign off my back.

It said, *"Not wearing underpants"* in Terry's handwriting.

"Kerry, I'm scared!" she yelled, snapping me back to the present.

"Me, too!"

Then everything went black, the sun blotted out by the huge beasts leaping overhead. We heard the buffalo snorting and mooing in open panic, saw their undersides as they soared overhead like hairy dirigibles, felt the booming of their tonnage as they hit the ground on the other side. Over and over they leapt, each carrying a potential death sentence for the frail humans below. One slip of the hoof and we were cooked.

It felt like years of sheer, unrelenting torture. Never knowing when the end would come, our lives snuffed out before we were thirty. And then—

All of a sudden, the roaring ceased.

The whole thing was over.

The buffalo had somehow had the presence of mind to jump the ditch, even as they charged in fear. Every last bull, cow, and calf had cleared the divide, those blessed beasts of the field.

Slowly, Terry and I released each other, wiping dust from our eyelashes. We sat there for a moment, completely stunned at having survived. Then we both started cheering at once.

"We're alive! We're alive! It's a Christmas miracle!"

Eventually, we stopped and peered at the top of the ditch.

"Okay," Terry said. "Now, how do we get out of here?"

$\mathcal{T}$here's only one way to get out of a golf cart balanced over a bottomless pit, and that's *very carefully*. Terry went first, rocking the cart as she did. She stuck her fingers into the cracks in the earth, toeing the outcroppings of rock and pulling herself up by dangling roots like a mountain climber. Within minutes, she was up and out.

"It's easy!" she shouted at me.

I contemplated my situation. If the ground gave way and the cart fell, I would be crushed like the contents of a tin can. I made a move toward the earthen wall and felt the cart slipping in response.

"Pull me up!" I called to Terry.

"How? It's too far!"

"Take off your shirt and hold it down to me."

"It'll rip!"

"Just do it!"

After a few moments, her T-shirt flopped over the side of the ditch, tied in knots. She lay on the ground with her arms extended, the cloth hanging just above my head.

I braced my left foot on the running board of the cart, and slowly stretched up, closing my hands around the T-shirt.

"Use your feet against the wall!"

I poked my right toe into a crack and pushed off the cart with my left foot. The dirt suddenly collapsed under the front bumper. The cart plummeted to the base of the ditch, its front fender crumpling below.

"Omigod!" I shouted at Terry. "I just missed crashing!"

"Don't look down! Pull yourself up!"

My foot slipped and my face slammed into the dirt. Scraping my feet against the wall, I struggled to get a purchase with my toes. The sound of ripping cotton made my pulse race.

"It's tearing!" I yelled.

Terry reached down and grabbed my wrists, grunting.

I kicked off a rock at the same time she yanked upward with all her strength, then my upper body finally cleared the ledge. She released my arms, falling back into the grass and kicking her legs in the air. "We did it!"

I rested there on my stomach, my legs hanging down in the hole. My fingers were buried in the dirt up to the first knuckle. I breathed in the smell of the earth, luxuriating in the scratchy feel of grass against my face.

I looked over at her, lying on her back in her jeans and black bra, her silver navel ring glinting in the sun.

"Terry?" I said.

"Yeah?"

"Bad move commandeering that cart."

She propped herself up on one elbow. "What happened to 'Wish I were so adventurous?'"

"The moment's passed. Now we're back to *what the hell were you thinking?*"

She chuckled. "It's like sex in a fox hole, huh?"

"It was actually kind of fun." I hauled myself all the way out of the ditch. "In retrospect."

"You know what I was thinking? Next year we should go to Pamplona and run with the bulls."

I crawled over to her on my hands and knees. "Yeah, I'll be

right behind you." I collapsed on the ground. "In Portugal."

We lay there for another moment, just being alive. Then I remembered what had brought us here. "We have to go back and search for Jacques."

Terry gave me a baffled face. "Honey, they *screwed* the pooch."

"I meant look for his *body*. We should give him a decent burial. It's the least we can do."

"You're right." She rose to her feet, wiping off her jeans, and wandered over to the hole to check out the crushed golf cart. "Guess we're going on foot." She reached down and picked up a piece of torn cloth. "I loved this shirt," she said sadly.

"We'll get you another one. C'mon, let's go find Jacques."

The buffalo had settled at the other end of the island. They were hanging out and chewing their cud, blissfully unaware that they'd almost sent two terrified humans to their reward. It was just as if they'd been out for a little exercise, a mid-day stampede to get the blood moving.

I had no doubt that Jacques had been the cause of their panic. Maybe he'd never have seen a herd of buffalo before, but it was just as certain they had never been confronted with a malicious little puffball, barking his head off and nipping at their ankles. No wonder they freaked. If I'd never seen a mangy poodle before in my life, I'd freak, too.

The ground was pitted with holes gouged by the herd's furious hooves. Dust hung in the air like ash from a Krakatoa blow. When we arrived at the spot where the buffalo had been grazing peacefully only a half-hour before, we saw something sparkling in a streak of sunlight that had penetrated the dust.

Terry bent down to pick up a pink dog collar, the name *Jacques* etched on the tag. Torn almost in two, it hung together by a thin shred of leather.

We stared at it for a moment, then Terry stuffed the collar into her back pocket.

"Wherever he is now," she said, lifting her face skyward. "I hope he has fresh croissants to eat."

"And teeth to chew them with."

We searched a wide area but couldn't find Jacques anywhere. He had probably been ground into the topsoil to fertilize the next generation of prairie grass. Or perhaps he was stuck like bubblegum to the bottom of someone's hoof.

"What do we do now?" she asked.

I studied the horizon, pondering it. "Now we find Steven Petty and let him know that Anna's alive."

"Good idea. And we'll tell him he has to pay for the golf cart."

"Will he go for that?"

"Damn straight he will. Or else."

This threat was coming from a shirtless woman with dirt between her teeth. Steven Petty, meet your doom.

Terry was clearly enjoying the attention she got in her bra as we hiked back to the center of town. I got a few looks, too, with my bruised body, dusty hair, and tattered clothes. I ducked into a T-shirt shop, and walked out a few minutes later carrying a tank top featuring a saucy redheaded mermaid on the front. I found Terry leaning against a wall, smoking.

"Where'd you get that cigarette?"

She flicked the ash, grinning. "Bumming stuff is easy when you're not wearing clothes."

"Don't even think about starting up again. You want lung cancer?"

"Like I'm going to get a chance to die from disease." She stubbed it out and pulled the tank over her head. "Sweet, a mermaid! I *love* mermaids."

I almost told her about my romantic encounter with David, but decided against it. Terry was John Boatwright's biggest fan, and I doubted she would take the news well. She once said that if she were straight, she'd go for Boatwright in a second. I argued that since she was *not* straight, her opinion had limited validity. Then she accused me of being a homophobe, and I retaliated by calling her a pushy dyke, and afterward came a champion round of bitch slapping. Best not to repeat that cycle.

We wound up at the Sunspot Motel. The manager was a surfer dude past his prime, probably forty but much older looking, with receding hair in a blond ponytail. His tanned skin was the color and texture of cured tobacco leaves, proving the good life has its costs.

I handed him our card and inquired after Steven Petty. He glanced at the card, then looked up again, grinning. "Hey, I know you. You're those twins everybody's talking about."

Terry did a head wag. "Well, they ain't talking about the Olsens."

"Mr. Petty's golfing," the guy told us. "I saw him leave this morning with his clubs."

"He should have married a caddy," I said, rolling my eyes. "He'd have never-ending bliss."

"Hey, were you working here when that guy Beaver was staying in your motel?" Terry asked him.

The manager made a face. "What a pig. It took the cleaning crew two whole hours in his room before Mr. Petty could move in. Stuck me with the bill, too. Paid with a stolen credit card."

"Yo, back up. Steven Petty has *his* room?"

"Yeah, he asked for it this morning. Said he wanted a room closer to the office."

I exchanged a startled look with Terry. "Did he specify the actual room number?"

"I think he did."

"How did he know it was available?"

"Beats me. Maybe he saw housekeeping in there. He couldn't have heard about the guy biting it, they hadn't found him yet."

"Huh?" Terry said.

"You didn't hear?" Ghoulish pleasure gleamed in the surfer dude's eyes. "The guy washed up on shore this morning with his throat cut."

The two of us gasped.

"Serves him right," he said. "Bastard murdered that nice scuba instructor."

"You're talking about Ben Kirch?" I asked, just to be sure. "Also known as Beaver?"

"Uh-huh, but he used a false name when he checked in. The sheriffs told me his real one."

"And you're sure it wasn't a drowning or something else?"

"Yeah. I heard it was a pretty ugly scene, but I didn't get a chance to go look. Couldn't leave the desk."

What was this strange new development? Who had a reason to murder Beaver?

"Won't the officers want to get inside that room?" Terry asked. "To look for evidence?"

"They went through it last night around midnight, after the shooting at the Casino. Released it to us this morning."

"Do us a favor and let Mr. Petty know we were here," I said, heading for the door. "But don't tell him about the conversation we just had. Tell him we have good news about his wife."

"I'm sure he'll be happy to hear that." He waved our card at us. "See ya when I see ya."

Once out in the parking lot, Terry and I stood and stared at the door of room number three, now occupied by our sneaky new employer, Steven Petty.

"So who killed Beaver?" I wondered aloud.

"I don't know." She chewed her lower lip. "But somebody killed him for a reason."

"Boy, you are one super sleuth!" I put on an English accent: "Someone killed him for a reason, Watson. That is what we in the detective business call a *motive!* "

"What I mean, smartass, is this changes everything. We have to dump the lone gunman theory. This is what we in the detective business call a *conspiracy.*"

"How do you figure that?"

"The person who picked him up in the boat killed him. That means he's in league with someone who double-crossed him. And our darling client Steven Petty is involved in some way that we don't understand yet."

She had a point, but I spotted a hole in her theory. "It couldn't have been Petty on the boat because he was in the hotel with you at the time, having drinks."

Terry looked over at Beaver's old haunt. "You're telling me

it's a coincidence that Steven requested this room?"

"Probably not." We started walking down to the main drag. "Let's go to the sheriff's office and see if we can get the scoop on Beaver's demise. That might tell us something. And we can make a report on the golf cart while we're there."

"What?" She stopped and stared at me. "You want to turn us in?"

"Terry, we can't commandeer a golf cart, wreck it, and then just walk away. That's vehicular theft and leaving the scene of an accident. I'm pretty sure those are felonies. And you know what that means."

She kicked at some gravel, pouting. "Yeah, Paris Hilton time for me."

"More like John Gotti time. Besides, you heard the clerk. Everyone knows who we are. All they have to say is two red-headed twins stole their cart and *boom*! We're busted."

"Okay, but let me do the part about the stampede."

"Why?"

"You'll take all the drama out of it. It'll be—*We were driving in the cart and got run over by buffalo.* No build-up, no suspense. If we're going to gain their sympathy, we have to convey the extreme bodily danger we were in. I'm the one to do it. *I'm* the storyteller. You have more of a journalistic style."

"Meaning I'd only confuse them with the facts?"

"Bor-ing," she said with utter disdain for the truth.

When we got to the station, Deputy Whitehorse was talking to someone in her office. She spotted us in the hallway and came to the door, giving us a one-word greeting: "Wait."

She closed the door and carried on with her meeting for another ten minutes. Afterward, two men left her office, glancing at us as they passed—baldish, fortyish, completely unremarkable. Neither tourists nor law enforcement personnel, I thought. Maybe land management bureaucrats or something.

Whitehorse motioned us to the chairs in front of her plain oak desk. Above her head hung a dreamcatcher, a macramé hoop braided with colored beads and feathers. It was the only personal touch in a room that was otherwise spare, functional, and scrupulously neat. A tan vinyl couch bumped up against gray file cabinets. The American flag sat in one corner.

Whitehorse leaned forward on her desk. "What's up, girls?"

"We heard about Beaver," I said. "Another one dead in the water?"

"Yep."

"Any leads on his killer?"

She pressed her lips together, shaking her head.

"In other words, you're not going to share," Terry said.

"Can't." That was all Whitehorse offered.

"We just found out that Steven Petty moved into Beaver's room at the Sunspot Motel," I told her.

She confirmed with a nod.

"So what the hell is going on?" Terry demanded. "Who killed him?"

"I realize this is frustrating for you, but there are some things I'm not at liberty to discuss. You'll just have to live with that for now." She stood as if to dismiss us.

I waved her back down. "That's not the only reason we're here. We need to report that we, uh, commandeered a golf cart. And it's sort of wrecked."

She squinted at me. "You *what?*"

"Commandeered a golf cart?" My voice went high and querulous. "See, Steven Petty hired us to locate his missing wife. We saw her coming out of a store and we chased her up on the bluff."

"In a commandeered golf cart," she repeated dully.

I gave her a sheepish grin. "Uh-huh."

"And what did you do with this commandeered cart?"

"Accidentally drove it into a hole in the ground?" I squeaked.

"Are you asking me or telling me!"

Terry grunted. "See, this is why I wanted to tell the story! How about a little context, huh?" She turned to Whitehorse. "Anna Petty ran away, and for some reason she's hiding out in the hills, desperate and alone. So fearful of someone or something that she'd rather risk death from exposure and other dangers than come in from the cold."

"What 'other dangers'?"

"I'm glad you asked, because we found out the hard way. There are buffaloes up on that plain—"

"Tame as cattle," Whitehorse interjected.

"Sure, very tame. *Until* they encounter a poodle!"

Whitehorse burst out laughing. I slouched in my seat, covering my eyes.

"You laugh now," Terry said. "But how funny will it be when we slap you with a big hairy lawsuit?"

"On what grounds?" Whitehorse guffawed. "And how the heck does a poodle come into this?"

"Our precious family pet was trampled by your so-called 'tame' buffalo!"

"You took a dog around the buffalo? Why would you do something stupid like that?"

Terry crossed her arms. "Have you been listening or not? We were tracking the girl—"

"With a *poodle*?"

"Not just any poodle, an investigative poodle with the instincts of your finest K-9 breed. Imported from Paris."

"Oh yeah. I've heard a lot about those Parisian poodle trackers. They're world famous, like the Mexican attack Chihuahuas."

"So anyway, we were in town and we saw the missing woman—you know, the one who had so far eluded all of your crack law enforcement personnel…"

Whitehorse squinted at her. "And?"

"We chased her. And then Jacques… uh, that would be Jacques, the poodle…"

"I figured."

"Jacques tracked Anna to the top of the bluff with his amazing nose, and then he got wind of the buffalo and he went over to see what they were, because they don't have buffaloes in Paris— "

Whitehorse arched an eyebrow.

"Well, they don't. And somehow when he went near 'em, the buffalo got spooked." Terry jumped up from her seat and mimed driving the cart. "And before we knew it, they'd stampeded! They were coming straight for us, hundreds of 'em!" She quaked in fear, looking over her shoulder. "And there was dust in our eyes and we couldn't see a thing." She swiped at her eyes before gripping the imaginary wheel again. "And when we were seconds away from being trampled to death, I threw my body over Kerry's in an attempt to spare her life—"

Whitehorse looked over at me. I gave her a quick shake of the head and mouthed the words "not true," but The Terry Show went on without pause.

"And even though we were in the most *extreme* bodily danger imaginable, I still managed to forgive Kerry in our last moments. You know, for all the abuse I've taken from her over the years—"

Whitehorse looked over at me. Again, I shook my head.

"And then, and then—"

Terry drew a big breath, and I took advantage to jump in.

"And then she drove the cart straight into a hole in the ground and the buffalo jumped over us, after which we climbed out of the hole and the cart crashed at the bottom of the crevice. End of story."

Terry plopped down in her chair. "Thanks for the 'big finish'. I'm trembling all over with emotion."

"Sounds like a happy ending anyway," Whitehorse said. "Except for the cart."

"Not so fast." Terry pulled out the tattered dog collar and tossed it on her desk.

Whitehorse stared at the torn piece of bejeweled leather. "Jacques?"

"Our beloved, irreplaceable family pet!"

Everyone observed a moment of silence, heads down. Terry covered her eyes, faking a sob. She peeped out from behind her hand at the same instant Whitehorse glanced over at her, then the two of them looked down again.

"I'm very sorry about your poodle."

"Well, *sorry* won't cut it in a court of law!" Terry slapped her armrests. "There's absolutely no signage up there warning of stampedes! What kind of *Jurassic Park* death trap are you running here? Stocking the place with monsters that lie in wait for unsuspecting tourists!"

It was a standoff—Terry maintaining her indignant posture, Whitehorse calmly evaluating her sanity, me, mentally cursing Terry for her antics. If there was a law against criminal stupidity, we were headed for the gas chamber for sure. Then, unexpectedly, Whitehorse offered a compromise.

"I'll make you girls a deal. If you agree not to sue, I'll talk to the rental company about the cart. I'll tell them you *thought* you were doing the right thing and ask them not to press charges. But you're going to have to make restitution."

"Deal!" Terry said, gloating at me.

I tried not to show my relief. "I'm pretty sure our insurance will cover the accident. We'll hit up Steven Petty for the deductible."

Whitehorse put her hands behind her head, leaning back in the chair. "So Anna Petty is camping out on the bluff? That's why we didn't find her in any of the rooms."

"We may have scared her off," I said. "But at least now you know you're not looking for a dead body."

"Not yet."

"What do you mean by that?" Terry asked.

"Let's just say I'm glad she's all right. But I need you to hold off on telling Petty you found her."

"Why?"

"No comment."

"Are you aware that his ex-wife is here on the island?" Terry asked her.

Whitehorse didn't reply, nor did she convey surprise.

"She's a total psycho bitch," Terry went on. "She followed him and Anna here to deep-six their honeymoon. She's under a restraining order, but Petty says she's stayed the mandated distance away and that's why he hasn't filed a complaint with you."

"She's all over the place," I added. "Driving like a maniac, yelling and cursing at him. Steven thought Paige might have been the reason his bride disappeared in the first place. In fact, he thought his ex-wife might have *disappeared* her."

"Don't worry, we'll bring the woman in unharmed."

"Oh, sure," Terry said. "Now that we've found her, you swoop in and take the glory."

Whitehorse gave her a shrug. "That's life."

"This puts us in an awkward position," I said. "We have to tell Petty something. What do we say to him?"

"Wait a couple of hours." Whitehorse looked at her watch. "Then you can give him the whole play-by-play. Poodle tracker, killer buffaloes, the works."

"Okay," Terry said. "We'll do things your way. But as soon as you can tell us something, you will?"

"Guaranteed."

Terry got up and retrieved the frayed dog collar from the desk. "Come on, Ker. It's time to give Robert the bad news."

twenty-seven

_J_erry and I trudged up the stairs at the St. Lauren rather than taking the elevator, doing unconscious penance for poor little Jacques. We stood outside Robert's room for a moment, gathering our courage. Then I took a deep breath and rapped on the door.

"Entrez!" Robert called from inside.

The door was locked. I knocked again.

"Coming, coming…"

He opened the door wearing a dressing gown of quilted maroon satin, holding an armload of wet towels.

"Girls, hi! Thought you were housekeeping."

Terry held out the collar to him, her head bowed. "We're sorry, Robert, but there's something we have to tell you."

"Ah, Jacques' collar." Robert took it from her, inspecting the damage. Then he tossed it into the trash can next to the door. "It must have been run over or something. No worries, we'll get him another."

Terry glanced sideways at me. "Um, actually it's not that simple. See, we took Jacques up in the hills and we… sort of lost him."

"Yes, I thought it was something like that. How else could he have gotten so dusty? But we've had our bubble bath now, and we're all clean and fresh and sweet smelling, aren't we boy?"

A head poked out of the towels in Robert's arms.

"Arf!" Jacques said.

Terry and I leapt backward. *"He's alive!"* we screamed.

Jacques' head pouf was slicked back on his head, giving him a suave, continental look.

"What on earth is wrong with you two?" Robert asked us.

"Well, ob-obviously," Terry stammered, gaping at the dog. "We thought he was dead!"

"He's an urban creature, Terry. He knows his way around traffic. I must say, I'm rather impressed with the little fellow. Imagine finding his way back to the hotel when he'd only been here once! It's like something out of *The Incredible Journey*, though not nearly so dramatic as going cross-country." Robert buffed Jacques' head with the towel. "You're a smart boy, aren't you? A very smart boy!"

"Arf!" Jacques replied.

"I think I'm falling for him, after all." Robert leaned down to rub noses with Jacques.

Jacques responded by giving Robert a tongue kiss, flush on the lips.

No! He's got poodle pyorrhea! I almost yelled, but caught myself just in time. I poked Terry in the arm, indicating that she should close her mouth. She blinked and pulled herself together.

"We'll go now and let you guys get coiffed." I pushed Terry down the hallway before she could mention the stampede. I saw no point in telling Robert how close we'd brought his new best friend to the brink.

"Speaking of which," Robert said. "Could you let me borrow some nail polish and files and whatnot? Jacques needs his paws tended to. And I don't suppose you have a hair pick and spray?"

"Uh, no," I said. "We only have straightener."

"Oh, that wouldn't do!" Robert fluffed Jacques' pouf with his fingertips. "We want our hair nice and curly, don't we?"

"Arf!"

"Okay, I'll drop everything over. Would you like blue or raspberry polish?"

"Blue would be more appropriate for a boy, no?"

"Actually, it's powder blue."

"Bring them both and I'll see which one he prefers."

"Okay, 'bye guys."

I shoved Terry again. She stumbled forward with all the grace of a reanimated zombie.

Robert stuck his head back out the door. "Are we still on for the burial at sea?"

"Sure," I said. "When is it?"

"Three o'clock. Give you plenty of time to clean up. And we'll have dinner at Le Metropole afterward."

"Oh goody," I said. "Can't wait to rip into another buffalo steak."

"*Ta!*" Robert called.

"*Arf!*" said Jacques.

Slam went the door.

When we reached our own room, Terry's face had gone pale. "Another Christmas miracle?" she whispered.

"It's gotta be."

"Holy buffalo," she said.

twenty-eight

erry took a shower while I lay on the bed, contemplating the events of the last two days. With all the bizarre goings-on, it was almost possible to forget that everything had begun with the murder of an innocent young woman.

The fact that we'd done nothing to prevent Nikki's death was preying on my mind. If only she'd let us stay the night, there might have been a happier outcome.

Whitehorse was right—it *was* frustrating being left out of the case at this point, forced to wait for a resolution brought about by others.

Well, she couldn't stop me from thinking about it.

I tried to put it together from the beginning: Nikki had been stalked by Beaver, an itinerant worker who'd known her long ago on the mainland. Then the day after Nikki conveyed her suspicions, she was killed and dumped in the bay. After that, Steven Petty charged onto the scene, ostensibly believing the dead woman to be his new bride. When the body turned out to be Nikki's instead, he got sick over the side of the boat.

That was sort of a strange reaction, now that I thought about it. Was it seeing the disfigured corpse that had upset him so? Or was it relief that the body wasn't his bride's?

If it was relief, then why had he sounded so angry with her? And why *had* she run away in the first place? Why had she seemed so frightened when we encountered her?

Now there was the added element of Beaver's partner in crime, as demanded by our conspiracy theory. Did this mean he hadn't been motivated by pure depravity, but was in someone's employ? Maybe one of the Pettys had taken out a hit on Nikki.

This jumble of thoughts was getting me nowhere. I needed to organize myself. I got up and retrieved the steno pad from my shoulder bag. It was time for the famous… (drum roll)… case diagram!

I drew a circle in the center of the page, writing *Nikki Edwards—Victim* inside. On the radiating lines, I wrote: *Beaver—Dead Suspect, Steven Petty—Creepy Client, Anna Petty—Runaway Bride, Paige Petty—Crazy Ex-Wife.*

Next I added lines for *Diamond Ring, Diamond Mine.* I hesitated before adding *David Solomon.* After I wrote down his name, I immediately started to erase it again. Of what importance was our little romantic subplot?

My subconscious nudged me again: *David's involved with the main plot, like it or not. He identified Beaver, had a prior relationship with him, was even shot at by him…*

This caused a flutter in my stomach, as did the memory of something David had said: "These hands are lethal weapons."

Nah.

He was kidding around, right? He's no killer. He's just what he appears to be—an easy-going, laid-back artist who gets moony over mermaids. My sudden paranoia was probably resistance, the tossing up of psychological roadblocks. I was madly attracted to him, but I didn't need another man in my life right now. Especially not one who lived a two-hour ferry ride away.

My hand, however, had a mind of its own. It traced the letters of David's name over and over again, until the pencil almost went through the paper. Slowly, I drew an arc between his name and Beaver's, placing a big question mark underneath.

And who else was involved, however peripherally?

I remembered our trip to the sheriff's office and the two men who'd been meeting with Whitehorse. They wore coats and ties, and leather shoes. Very odd attire—even conspicuous—in a vacation spot such as Catalina. I dubbed them the Men in Black and gave them a line. Whitehorse and Young had referred to some other "parties" they were expecting the night of our attack. If those parties were the Men in Black, their arrival had been anticipated before any of this went down, so they were probably irrelevant. I left them there, just in case.

Whitehorse got a line of her own.

She had asked us to hold off on talking to Petty, implying that Anna was in danger from her husband. From what I'd seen, Anna had more to fear from Paige Petty than from Steven, but the deputy hadn't bought into that theory.

As much as I was coming to like her, I'd noticed Whitehorse had one glaring fault—besides her almost complete lack of humor—and that was a tendency to get stuck on one idea, closing her mind to other possibilities. She'd done it with us, only letting us off the hook as suspects after David had corroborated Beaver's existence. And when I'd speculated that Beaver's inability to recognize faces could have a bearing on the case, she'd refused to listen.

But if he *had* killed the wrong woman, who would have been the right one?

The answer hit me like a ton of bricks.

Anna, the new Mrs. Petty. She was the intended target.

She looked a lot like Nikki. Though bedraggled and dirty when I'd seen her, she still bore a striking resemblance to the actual murder victim—a wholesome brunette, pretty, twenty-something.

And who had a motive to kill a pretty young brunette?

Paige Petty, that's who. The pathologically jealous ex-wife.

What if Paige had hired Beaver to kill her rival, but he'd killed the wrong girl by mistake? How would Paige Petty even know a low-life like Beaver?

There was one way to find out. I flipped open the laptop

and logged onto the Petty Investments page, scrolling through the various businesses under the main company's umbrella. I ran across Petty Real Estate, Petty Industrial Diamonds, and... Hello?

Petty Construction.

Beaver had been a laborer—someone who knew his way around cement and scaffolding. I found the number to the main office and called from my cell phone. A tipsy young receptionist answered, the sounds of an office party going on in the background.

"Petty Construction, happy holidays! How may I direct your call?"

"Hello, I'm calling from McAfee Builders here in Los Angeles, wondering if I could get a referral on a construction worker?"

"On Christmas eve?"

"It's an emergency job for a church. Their roof caved in and destroyed the crèche. Heck of a thing."

"Oh, how terrible. I'll put you through to our personnel manager."

I listened to a Muzak version of *Jingle Bell Rock*, grinding my teeth.

Would somebody please write some new Christmas songs before I open my wrists?

Finally, an officious-sounding woman picked up the line.

"Julie Farnsworth," she said, as sober as the day is long. Julie hadn't been throwing back nog with her colleagues. "I'm so sorry to hear about your church's manger scene."

"Yes, it was a real mess. The baby Jesus was all covered with plaster and insulating material." I clicked on the personnel button, searching for Julie's picture. There she was, smiling from behind her desk. She was somewhere in her thirties, with brown hair in a short flip and eyeglasses on a chain. Her title was "Personnel Manager," but she could easily pass for a librarian or a third-grade teacher.

"How may I help you?" she asked.

"I'm calling for a referral for one of your former workers, Ben Kirch."

"And when did he work for us?"

"Um, I believe it was last year."

"Project?"

"Gosh, I don't know."

A pause. "He didn't give you the name of the project he worked on?"

"Yes, but I can't read his writing. These construction workers don't always have the best penmanship," I complained, just one beleaguered office gal to another.

She chuckled at that. "Hold, please. I'll see what I can find."

More Christmas Muzak. Somebody was conspiring around the fire. Sounded like my life.

Julie Farnsworth came back on the line, clearing her throat. "I'm sorry, but I don't have any information on that particular individual."

"Really? You mean you can't give him a recommendation? Or you can't confirm that he worked for you?"

Another pause while she mulled it over. "I can't say any more. I'm sorry."

This was sounding like a non-denial denial. Had she been instructed not to talk about Beaver? The man was a convicted felon. Maybe they feared exposure, some sort of liability for having him on the job.

"Let me ask it this way," I said cagily. "If you were building a shelter for the blessed baby Jesus, would you hire this man to do it?"

"No, I certainly would not."

I clicked back to the home page and noticed the address in the upper left-hand corner. The company was located in Tarzana, Nikki's old neighborhood. I decided to take a flyer. "By the way, Nikki asked me to wish you a merry Christmas."

"Nikki Edwards?" Julie said, brightening. "Oh how nice. Are you a friend of hers?"

Eureka!

"Yes, ma'am. I am."

"Well, she can probably tell you anything you want to know about the person you mentioned. She used to be a project manager for us, as I'm sure you know. One of the best."

"So I hear."

Before she could ask me why I hadn't gone directly to the source, I rushed her off the phone. "Gotta go shore up that manger scene, Julie. Thank you so much."

"Good luck with it. And give my best to Nikki."

"I sure will."

Now I had another hunch I wanted to follow. After searching online for another two minutes, I found an article from the *Orange County Register* that proved it to be correct.

I am so good, I scare myself.

I started scribbling on my diagram, drawing arcs between Steven and Nikki and Beaver and Paige. Every last one of them hailed from the same stinking cesspool, Petty Investments. I felt a growing sense of elation as I watched my hand sketch a picture of a large, sparkling diamond ring in the margin.

The diamond was the Maguffin, the thing that tied it all together. It was the oldest one in the book—whoring after treasure, killing for it, dying for it. Maybe it was just too obvious for me to have seen it before.

Terry came out of the shower moments later, a towel wrapped around her head. She peered inside the armoire. "What do you wear to a funeral at sea?"

"I don't know. Anything you can coordinate with a life jacket."

"Black jeans, black top?"

"Works for me."

She pulled out a black lace blouse with a satin collar, completely see-through. "Problem is, I don't have another black bra. Don't think I want to wear the same one I wore to the stampede."

"Wear it without a bra."

"How risqué!" she said in mock horror.

"The guy was French. I'm sure it's all right."

She pulled on a fresh pair of black jeans over her pink thong, then slipped into a black camisole to wear under the blouse. "French funeral or no, I don't want to freeze my boys off."

She began to towel dry her hair and her eyes met mine in the mirror.

"Okay," she said. "Spit it out."

"What?"

"The canary." She pointed to my steno pad. "You've got your little diagram out and you're looking very pleased with yourself. What's up, pussycat?"

I waved the pad in the air. "While you were showering, I did some crack investigating."

She tossed the wet towel onto the bathroom floor, and grabbed a hairbrush from the vanity counter. "What'd you find out?"

"I just checked with Petty Construction, and guess what? Ben Kirch was one of their workers."

She dropped to the bed, agog. "So Petty knows the killer!"

"It's a real possibility. Guess who else worked there as a project manager? Nikki Edwards. The personnel manager said she headed up a job that Beaver worked on."

Terry hit the mattress with her brush. "Stop it!"

"No," I said with a cocky grin. "I will not stop it."

"How'd you figure that out?"

"I called the company to see if Beaver had worked there. If he had, there'd be a chance he knew one or both of the Pettys. I noticed the company address was in Tarzana, so I took a chance and asked if the woman knew Nikki. She totally spilled the beans."

Terry ran the brush through her long wet tresses. "What does this mean, oh wise one?"

"I think Paige Petty hired Beaver to kill Nikki. It was a hit."

"Paige? Why not Steven? He didn't say he knew her when she turned up dead. That shows guilty knowledge."

"Not necessarily. The guy's a major weasel. He might have been afraid of being implicated, without being directly responsible himself."

"Hmmm."

"I told you about Beaver being a prospo... propas... one of those people who can't recognize faces? What if Beaver was hired to do the deed, but he killed the wrong girl? He murdered Nikki in place of the new bride!"

"How could he make such a stupid mistake?"

"Did he strike you as a rocket scientist?"

"No, but if he worked with Nikki, he'd have to know who she was. You said they used voices to identify people."

"He could have seen her out with Steven and naturally assumed she was the new wife. Came up behind her when she was alone again and knocked her out before she could say anything."

"But why would Nikki be seeing Petty in the first place?"

"They're former colleagues, they could have had business to discuss. Or they may have been lovers at one time. The man likes his brunettes. And remember Max, the next-door neighbor? He said he saw her leaving with a man the night she was killed. That could have been Steven Petty."

"Yeah, but Max said he was a 'beach bum.' "

"Golf bum, beach bum. What's the difference to a cranky old man?"

Terry flopped on the bed, staring at the ceiling. "But what if you're right and the alleged beach bum *was* Steven Petty. He could have taken her out and killed her himself."

"I'm telling you, I've been over and over this in my mind, and as much as I think Steven Petty's an untrustworthy snake, no one here has a motive for murder except Paige."

"Jealousy?"

"Yes, but something else, too."

I dragged her over to the desk and fiddled with the touchpad to reveal the online article. It was an account of the court proceedings when Paige was brought up on stalking charges. The AP photographer had snapped her going up the courthouse steps wearing a tweed Chanel suit with green velvet lapels, a hand through her lawyer's arm.

"Check out Paige's right hand." I enlarged the photo.

Paige was sporting the large green stone, a perfect complement to her suit.

Terry slapped the desk. "Omigod! It's the hopeless diamond!"

"Steven told us Anna picked it out at Tiffany's as an engagement ring, but it had obviously belonged to Paige at one time. He took it back, or maybe he even got it as part of their divorce settlement. And then he gave it to his new bride to rub salt in Paige's wounds. *That*, my dear Watson, is what we call a motive. Where there's jealousy and greed, murder can't be far behind."

She studied the photo. "It's compelling, I have to admit."

"Big of you."

"But wait a sec. We can't let Petty off the hook just yet. Remember, he checked into Beaver's motel right after Anna disappeared, then he requested Beaver's very room after the guy was killed." Terry picked up the diagram and wrote *Sunspot Motel* next to Petty's name, drawing a straight line to Beaver.

"Maybe he was doing his own investigation. When he heard Beaver was the suspect, he decided to get close to him and see what he could find out."

"If he was doing his own investigation, why hire us?"

"So he can continue to look like the injured party, the poor guy whose wife ran out on him because he played a round of golf."

"You're saying there was another reason?"

"Yes. The reason was Paige. We didn't appreciate the extent of the problem, but Petty did. Or should have."

"What do you mean?"

"Petty *knew* his ex-wife had followed them here. And he knew Paige wanted that diamond back. Yet he flaunted his new wife with the ring on her finger. I think his whole life has become one long exercise in taunting his ex. He *enjoys* her suffering. But when Anna disappeared, he feared the worst. That was the reason for his guilty reaction, throwing up over the side of the boat. He realized he'd driven Paige to murder. He just didn't know, until he saw Nikki's body, that she had killed the wrong girl."

I waited for my props.

"I'll say it again. Compelling, but not totally convincing." She pulled out a tube of cherry gloss and ran it over her lips.

I stuck by my guns. "We'll just see about that, won't we?"

"I've got five bucks on Steven," Terry said, digging out her wallet.

"You're on. I'll take Paige." I handed her a five-spot.

Terry opened the end table drawer and stuck the two five-dollar bills inside the Gideon Bible for safekeeping. "Whitehorse is on my side. Obviously, she suspects Petty. That's why she said not to tell him we found Anna."

"She said not to tell him for a couple of hours," I reminded her.

Terry picked up her studded leather watch, snapping it on her wrist. "It's been an hour and a half."

"Okay, let's go find him on the golf course."

She gave me a surprised look. "You don't want to shower first?"

"Nah, I'll just want to take another shower after talking to Petty."

"Good point." She pulled her damp hair into a ponytail. "Is Whitehorse gonna be pissed that we kept investigating?"

"Yuh-huh. Especially if we crack the case."

"Tough beans."

"Word up," I said, heading for the door. "Now here's the tack I think we should take with Petty..."

twenty-nine

$\mathcal{T}$he golf club was a short ride up the bluff. It looked like it had been built for Jay Gatsby's personal use, complete with an ocean view and a luxuriously manicured course dotted with palm trees and evergreens. As we approached the Spanish-style clubhouse, we spied a deer scampering across the first green.

Steven Petty was seated in the bar, talking to a sixty-year-old man who looked like he might own Connecticut. A captain of industry, no doubt. Petty was dressed in a baby-blue golf shirt and checked pants, a pair of reflector shades atop his head. A gold Rolex gleamed on his tanned wrist.

He spotted us and raised a finger to indicate we should wait.

We stood by the doors as he made his apologies to the older man and slipped him a business card. The man tapped the card on his highball glass before stuffing it in his pants pocket, giving Petty a hail-fellow handshake and clapping him on the shoulder as if he were the son he'd never had.

Terry whispered to me, "You know it's highly unethical, what we're about to do."

"Suddenly you're concerned about ethics? Anyway, what's more important, telling the truth or saving a woman's life?"

"I'm *with* you. I'm just saying he could nail us for this if he wanted to."

"Don't worry. He won't want to."

Petty did a little bow as he got up from the table, then made his way over to us.

"Ladies," he said, holding open the door to the back patio. "Let's talk outside."

The patio was empty of customers. We took a seat at a wrought iron table away from the clubhouse. A waiter approached our table.

"Iced tea all around," Petty told him.

As the waiter left to get our drinks, Petty suddenly noticed my appearance. "What on earth happened to you?"

"Buffalo stampede."

"Beg pardon?"

"It's a long story that I'll be happy to tell you about. But first, you should know that we found Anna."

He gasped. "Alive?"

"Yes."

Petty pulled out a handkerchief, wiping his brow. "Thank God," he murmured.

"We tracked her up onto the bluff," Terry informed him. "She was camping out there, in hiding."

"But in heaven's name *why?* Did she tell you?" His confusion might have fooled someone unschooled in his lying ways, but not us.

I hewed to the script Terry and I had worked out on the way over. "She's afraid of your ex-wife. She's convinced Paige is after something and will stop nothing to get it."

"What on earth could be so important?" He appeared startled. "You mean *me?* Paige wants me back?"

Nice try, Stevie, I thought. *But you're hardly God's gift.*

"No. She wants her ring. The big green diamond."

"But it's not hers. It's Anna's! Has the woman gone completely around the bend?"

"Stow it," Terry said. "We know the ring originally belonged to Paige. Anna didn't shop for it at Tiffany's."

He was about to sputter another denial when the waiter arrived with three tall glasses garnished with lemon wedges and sprigs of mint. Once the waiter had gone, Petty picked up a sugar packet, shaking it delicately between his fingers.

"I couldn't tell you the truth about the ring." He ripped open the sugar packet. "You'd think I was a cad."

Terry stifled a laugh.

"Mr. Petty." I leaned over the table, forcing him to look me in the eye. "Whether or not you are a cad is irrelevant. We don't care. What's important is that you hired us under false pretenses. How are we supposed to do our job if you're not honest with us?"

He tapped some sugar into his glass, folded the edges down *just so*, and replaced the half-used packet into a ceramic swan container. He stirred his tea. "Anna's let her imagination run away with her. We fought over a golf game and then she left. *That's* the truth."

I sat back in my chair, shaking my head. "That's not what she told us. She said Paige followed you on your honeymoon specifically to get her ring back. And you *knew* it was happening."

Petty removed his spoon and brought the tea to his lips. "Anna must be under some kind of psychological duress. I've never told anyone this, but she's prone to panic attacks." He watched for our reaction over the rim of his glass.

A lie for every occasion. Now the new wife was mentally unstable, too.

"Have you ever witnessed her having a panic attack?" Terry asked him.

"On our first date. I thought it was a case of the jitters. She got very flushed and excused herself. Twenty minutes later I sent a waitress into the bathroom, afraid that she might be ill. The waitress came back and reported that Anna was in a stall, breathing into a paper bag." He used a napkin to dab at the corners of his mouth. "I guess I didn't let myself think about the implications of this. She was… she *is* so beautiful, I didn't want to believe there could be a problem. I should have said something, but when she came back to the table, she was smiling and radiant as ever. I simply forgot about it."

"Was she ever treated for this condition?"

"Not that I'm aware of, and for that I blame myself. Perhaps if I'd seen to it that she got the help she needed, none of this would have happened. But I assure you; Paige has no right to that ring. I paid through the nose for it. It was mine to do with as I pleased. It pleased me to give it to my love."

Terry slipped me a sardonic smile. *It pleased me to give it to my love? Was he writing song lyrics?*

She turned back to him. "Where did you pay through the nose for it? Not Tiffany's."

"No, I traded Paige for it. I gave her the title to a property worth a million dollars."

Terry and I frowned at each other.

"Why?" I said.

"Because I wanted the best for Anna!"

"What she means is," Terry said, "yesterday you said the ring was worth a hundred thousand. Now suddenly it's worth a million. That's a lot of appreciation in one day." Petty averted his eyes, but she pressed on. "What's the ring really worth? And let's try the truth this time."

Petty hesitated. Then, finally, he coughed up an answer. "It may bring as much as four million."

I gawked at him. "What the heck? I mean, it's beautiful and everything, but—"

"Because of its provenance. It's not just a beautiful stone. It was a crown jewel."

Petty's gaze focused on a point between us. With most people, the avoidance of eye contact would indicate lying. But Petty normally looked straight into your pupils when confabulating, so as to convince you of his utmost sincerity. Maybe his off-center gaze meant that he was now telling the truth.

"A crown jew-el." I drew out the words skeptically. "Whose crown?"

"A king from the Persian Raj in India. The one who built the Taj Mahal."

"Sounds like something out of *Indiana Jones*."

Petty huffed. "It's a world-class treasure, not a matinee fantasy."

It was really hard to say what was or was not fantasy with this guy. The more time I spent with him, the more I wanted to crawl under a tarp to escape the hail of bullcrap. But what if he wasn't lying this time? What if the ring *was* more valuable than we'd known? That would certainly increase its potential as a motive for murder.

"Did Paige know that the stone was worth four times what you paid for it in trade?" Terry asked him.

"Yes, she was willing enough to make the exchange. Real estate is more liquid than a stone, however rare and valuable. You never know what's going to happen at auction. So much depends on the state of the world, the price of oil, currency exchanges—"

"But if Paige made the exchange willingly, why would she be here trying to get the ring back?"

He traced a bit of condensation down the iced tea glass with his finger.

"Well?" I prompted him.

"There may have been a little problem with the property I gave her."

Terry cocked her head. "*May* have been a problem?"

"A second mortgage."

"For how much?"

"Seven hundred and fifty."

The math was ridiculously easy, even for me. "So she gave you a four million dollar ring in exchange for property worth two hundred-fifty thousand?"

"Is it my problem she didn't do her due diligence?"

Terry aimed an accusing finger at him. "You cheated her!"

Terry McAfee, staunch defender of all female victims. No matter that Paige was a dangerous loon, Terry was now firmly on her side.

"Paige is no babe in the woods," Petty snapped. "She was every bit as involved in the real estate business as I was."

I didn't know my way around real estate, but I was sure he'd found some way to hide the liability from Paige. And now she was fighting mad. Maybe even killing mad.

"I hope it was worth it," I said. "You've lost your 'great love' because of this."

Petty gave me sorrowful eyes. "Do you think Anna could be persuaded to give the diamond back? Especially if it meant Paige would be out of our lives forever?"

Not a chance. Anna had already made her feelings clear. She'd left the ring in the toilet tank, showing how much she valued world-class treasures with strings attached. It was still in our possession, and we planned to use it as a bargaining chip between these two losers, Paige and Steven Petty.

"Hard to say if Anna would come back." Terry rubbed her chin thoughtfully. "I'm sure she didn't appreciate being deceived."

Petty sighed as if to say, *Women can be so troublesome.*

"But it might be worth a try," I said, rallying to the cause. "What did you have in mind?"

"Could you talk to Anna for me and see if she'll give up the ring?" Tears clung to his lower lashes. "I feel like such a fool, I don't know if I could bear to face her right now."

Perfect. He was playing right into our hands.

Terry pretended to consider it. "Okay," she said finally, "if you'll promise to keep your part of the bargain this time. No tricks, no hidden liabilities."

Petty sat up straighter in his chair. "If Paige will promise to stop her harassment, I'll meet her and return the ring. And I'll buy Anna whatever she wants at Tiffany's or anywhere else, if only she'll consent to having me back."

"Um, there is one more thing, Mr. Petty."

I told him about the golf cart and the stampede. I said we needed another five hundred dollars to cover the deductible for the wreck.

"You may be the most incompetent investigators I've ever met in my life," he sniffed. "Very well, add it to my bill."

It was a good thing he said that, because I no longer felt bad about lying our asses off to him. And I felt a whole lot better about what we were planning to do next.

"We need you to settle now," Terry told him. "No offense, but your credit's no good with us."

Petty pulled out a silver money clip, peeling off hundreds with the expression of someone passing a kidney stone. Terry ripped them out of his hand, just as the older man Petty had been chatting with earlier strolled out of the clubhouse door.

"Hide it!" Petty whispered.

Terry licked her finger and held the up the bills showily, counting them one by one. The captain of industry blanched and hurried away from the patio.

"See you tomorrow, Gregory!" Petty called after him. "I'll bring that prospectus with me!"

Something told me Petty's business proposal would no longer be welcome.

The man gave a brusque wave without looking back. He had witnessed his Boy Wonder handing a wad of cash to two dubious-looking redheaded twins, and what was he to make of that? Were we call girls? Drug dealers? Not part of their country club set, that was for sure. Petty watched in despair as his mark jumped into a cart and drove away.

"Well done." He sneered at Terry. "Very discreet."

Terry ignored his tone, stuffing the bills into her breast pocket. "I wouldn't worry about it. There's one born every minute, right?"

Petty glared at her, his face darkening.

I made an attempt at mollifying him. "Your troubles will soon be over and you can get back to business. If Anna's willing to go along, we'll do the exchange tonight. Do you know how to reach Paige?"

"She'll have her cell phone."

"Don't talk to her until we get back to you. No sense in getting her all worked up until we have the ring."

"All right." He stood and walked away.

"Mr. Petty?" Terry called. "The tea?"

He returned and peeled another ten off his wad, tossing it on the table. "You're welcome."

Terry smiled sweetly. "Thanks ever so much."

He climbed into a golf cart and took off down the drive. Once he was out of sight, Terry gave me a high-five.

I only wished I shared her enthusiasm. "You think this is going to work?"

"It's *already* working. He took the bait. Now all we have to do is arrange the meet, confront Paige and Steven together, and then figure out who's guilty. Afterward, we'll take the information to Whitehorse."

"It's feeling riskier now. What if Paige flies off the handle?"

"I'm not worried about some out-of-shape housewife."

"But what if she brings a gun? You don't have to be in shape to pull a trigger."

Terry scoffed. "Where would she get a gun?"

"This is America, hello?"

"You probably have to pass through a metal detector to get on the ferry. Listen, we're not going to set her off. We're just going to see if we can fake her out, get her to give something away. Then we'll know which one of them is going up the river, and which one of us is five bucks richer."

"But what if *you're* right and Steven's the killer? What if he brings a nine iron to club us to death?"

"Are you saying you want to scratch the plan?"

I did, sort of. But not at the price of being the one to wimp out. "There's more at stake now. Someone in their position probably wouldn't kill for a hundred-thousand dollar diamond, but one worth four million—?"

"Do *not* tell me you believed that Raj shit."

"Not for a second."

"Thank God you haven't gone completely soft-skulled."

"No, the guy's pathological. The lies pour out of his mouth before he even knows what he's said. But whatever its 'provenance,' the diamond is worth more—maybe a lot more—than we thought."

"Not buying it, sorry. He never would have let go of it in the first place if it was that valuable, not even to give to his 'great love'." She paused, sizing me up. "So? Are we doing it or not?"

"Of course. It was my idea."

"And it's a good one," she said, punching me on the arm. "There's no reason for either of them to kill us. They're both getting what they want. Paige will have her ring, and Steven will believe that Anna's coming home. We'll solve the case and there'll be one less murdering a-hole in the world."

"One thing I don't know…"

"Yeah?"

"Exactly how to trick the murderer into giving him or herself away."

"We'll do what we always do."

"Which is what?"

"Improvise." She smiled confidently and checked her watch. "Time for the funeral. You ready to send François down to Davy Jones' locker?"

I gave her a salute. "Ready when you are, matey."

thirty

*W*hen we arrived at the waterfront, we found Robert standing in a sleek black power boat with a white interior. He was receiving driving instructions from a nervous-looking rental agent. It was cool out, so I suspected the sweat stains on the man's shirt were due to putting the expensive craft into the hands of my cousin. Robert hardly even drove a car, let alone piloting a boat.

Robert was outfitted in a navy blazer with gold braid epaulets, white pants, and white deck shoes. His red hair curled out from beneath a jaunty, black-billed captain's hat. Jacques wore a navy dog's sweater with a pattern of yellow sailboats, his pompadour mashed down under a miniature yachting cap like Robert's. The brass funerary urn sat on a bench, swaddled in a monogrammed hotel towel.

"Hello, girls! Be with you in a moment." Robert situated his donut in the captain's seat and plopped himself down. "All right, now I push it this way to give it gas." He mimed moving the throttle south. "And pushing it up cuts the power."

"That's it," the rental agent said uneasily. "Has either of you driven a boat by any chance?" he asked Terry and me.

Terry held up a hand. "I have. Friend of mine used to pick up, um, packages from vessels at sea. I went with him a couple of times."

"Not to worry, old man! I've got it figured out," Robert assured him. "But it can't hurt to have an old salt aboard to advise me, eh?"

Terry, an old salt?

"Where's Reba?" I asked him.

"Not coming. She said she'd buried enough men, thank you very much. But she asked us to save her some champagne."

Jacques laid his head on his paws and yawned.

"The poodle's suffering from *ennui*," I said. "Better get this show on the road."

Terry and I climbed aboard. The rental agent jumped off the boat, removed the rope from the piling and tossed it to us.

"Have a good funeral," he said as we floated away from the dock.

"Life jackets, everyone. Remember the Titanic!" Robert pushed down the throttle and we were on our way.

I gave Terry a worried glance. "I wish he hadn't said that."

"Don't sweat it. We can't have two disasters in one day. It would be statistically impossible, even for us."

Nevertheless, Terry and I followed the captain's orders. After slipping on a life jacket, I lifted the lid on an ice chest and found several bottles of Cristal champagne chilling inside. "Looks like François is going in high style."

"Keep that stuff away from Robert," Terry said. "I don't want him loaded behind the wheel."

"Relax. If he gets tanked, you can take over. You're an old salt, remember?"

"Cheerio!" Robert waved jovially to the occupants of the other boats as we passed. He kept the engine at an even five miles per hour, his arm resting on the hull, looking relaxed and in command. Jacques jumped off the bench and made his way up to the front of the boat, sitting at Robert's feet.

"Arf!" Jacques said.

"Ahoy, matey!" Robert grinned down at him. "Want to sit in the captain's seat?"

Jacques panted affirmatively.

Robert stood and tossed his donut aside. With one hand guiding the wheel, he reached down to scoop up the dog, placing him in the captain's chair. Jacques sat with his tongue hanging out of his toothless mouth, his button nose quivering in the breeze.

"Get a picture, get a picture!" Robert called to Terry.

Terry retrieved the camera from her backpack.

"Wait." I grabbed the urn from its place atop the storage bins, handing it to Robert. "I'll steer, you pose."

He let me take the wheel while he grinned for Terry, hoisting the urn like a bowling trophy.

"Smile!" Terry braced her legs against the side of the boat to steady herself and clicked off a few shots.

Robert handed the funerary urn back to me and returned to the wheel. We were now on the open sea, having moved out of the protected waters of the harbor. The sun shone bright in the clear blue sky, the wind blowing chilly and crisp. Terry tapped me on the shoulder and pointed to a family of dolphins.

"Nice way to go," she said.

"I wouldn't mind it myself."

Robert pushed up on the throttle and the boat slowed to a stop. He waved an arm at the view. "It's a gorgeous day for a send-off, don't you think? Let's open the champagne."

"Thought you were off the sauce," Terry said.

"Just one little toast, then I'm turning over a crackling dry new leaf."

Terry acquiesced, pulling a bottle from the ice chest. Robert opened his Louis Vuitton tote and extracted three champagne flutes, along with a small crystal bowl wrapped in chamois cloth. Terry popped the cork and soon the champagne was flowing, the glasses and dog bowl filled with bubbly.

Robert set the bowl on the captain's seat. Jacques went straight for it, lapping the champagne every bit as eagerly as he had gummed the croissant. Then Robert took a glass from Terry, and the three of us lifted our flutes in a toast.

"To François Gautier, master of the French cinema and protector of feeble dogs!" Robert shouted into the ocean breeze.

We clinked the burnished vase, and I added my own toast. "Thank you for giving us our beloved Cousin Robert. May you be rewarded for it in the next life!"

Clink.

It was Terry's turn. "Only next time around, you might want to stay out of airplane bathrooms. And beware of bodacious American redheads."

Robert wagged a finger at the urn. "And always pack condoms in your shaving kit."

We laughed and sipped. I looked over to see how Jacques was coping. He was running in a circle around the glass bowl.

"Hey look! The champagne made Jacques frisky."

Robert chuckled. "He's really rather cute, isn't he?"

"He's a pistol," Terry agreed. "I wonder if he's too old to teach some new tricks."

"Yeah," I said. "Maybe we could teach him to drive the boat, ha ha."

No sooner were the words out of my mouth, than Jacques reared up on his two hind legs, horsey-style. Then he came back down again, his freshly manicured paws landing right on top of the throttle.

"No!" I screamed, but it was wasted breath.

The boat lurched forward, knocking Terry and me on our asses. Robert stumbled back to the stern, his arms pinwheeling in air. A wave smacked the hull, rocking us sideways. Robert's momentum took him right over the edge and into the drink, his champagne flute arcing away through the air. The crystal bowl rolled off the captain's seat, shattering against the starboard hull, while the metal urn went clanging across the deck, losing the lid and disgorging its contents. The ashes were whipped up by the wind, swirling around like a miniature tornado of death.

Terry retrieved the lid, recapping the urn before all of François's remains could be scattered to the winds, then stuffed it inside a coil of fiber rope. I crawled to the front of the boat, bouncing up every time the boat hit a wave, slamming back down again on my wrists and kneecaps. I looked over my shoulder to see Robert bobbing in the water, waving his yachting cap. He seemed to be shouting something, but the noise of the motor drowned him out.

"Turn it off!" Terry yelled from the stern.

"What do you think I'm trying to do?"

I reached up and pushed the throttle so hard and fast that the boat screamed to a stop, slamming me into the hull. I crumpled to the deck, seeing stars.

Terry ran to my side. "Are you okay?"

"R-Robert," I said, holding up the inflated donut. "He doesn't have a life preserver!"

She scanned the water, a hand shading her eyes. "Yes, he does! I see a blue life jacket out there!"

I squinted back over the wake, trying to spot Robert through the sparks on my retinas. "That's not a life jacket, that's his belly. He's being buoyed by his stomach."

Sure enough, Robert was floating on his back, his girth rising above the waves like an oversized dumpling. He waved to us with the soggy captain's hat.

"Your forehead's turning purple." Terry fished a handful of ice out of the chest and wrapped in a towel for me. I held it against my head to numb the pain, while she took the wheel and spun us in a circle.

Wait a minute. I didn't see Jacques anywhere on the boat. Where was that little troublemaker?

"Where's Jacques?" I called to Terry.

"He's not on deck?"

I held onto the windshield for balance, scanning the interior of the boat. Then I dashed to the stern, checking behind the ice chest and under the extra life jackets. When I didn't see him, there was only one conclusion to draw.

"Poodle overboard!" I yelled.

"Oh no," Terry said.

I peered out over the water, hoping to see Jacques floating by means of his poufs, the same way Robert had by his stomach. But who was I kidding? He'd sink like a wet sheep, the water-logged fur dragging him straight down to the bottom.

"What do we do?" I cried.

"We have to save Robert," Terry said, angling the boat toward him. "Jacques is a hundred and fifty in human years, he's had a full life."

"Poor little Jacques." Had he crossed the wide Atlantic, been revived by pastry and miraculously spared in the stampede, only to drown here in Avalon Bay?

"At least he's with François, now," Terry said.

Once she pulled up beside Robert, I grabbed the ladder and affixed it to the side of the boat.

"Swim for it, Robert!" I called to him.

He rolled over on his stomach and paddled toward us, and then launched himself up the ladder. Terry and I each grabbed a handful of wet shirt, hauling him aboard with a flood of salt water. It drained from his pants and squished out of his deck shoes.

"What on earth happened?" he asked with a shiver.

We sat him down on the bench with one final *squish*. He twisted his captain's hat, wringing it out.

"We're sorry," Terry said. "Jacques jumped on the throttle, then he went overboard when the boat took off."

Robert's eyes bugged. "Did you look for him?"

"We thought we should pick you up first."

"Are there any binoculars on board?"

"Good idea!" I found a pair under the steering wheel and lifted them up to my face. I quickly adjusted the focus and...

Wonder of wonders—there was Jacques! Paddling back toward shore.

"I've got him! There he is!"

"Where?" Robert snatched the binocs from me. "Ah, I see him! Why, that amazing little pooch! He'll be swimming the English Channel next!"

"Or taking the gold in the doggie Olympics!" Terry cheered. Then suddenly, her smile faltered.

"Uh-oh!" She dove for the captain's chair, maxing out the throttle. I was thrown off balance again and my butt slammed to the bench.

"What's going on?" I could still see the white afro bobbing above the waves. Little Jacques was paddling toward shore as if his life depended on it.

Then I saw why.

A large gray dorsal fin was knifing through the water, heading straight for the frantically sculling poodle.

"Shark!" I screamed. "It's headed straight for Jacques!"

"What?" Robert said. "Where?"

But I'd lost him. "I don't see him anymore!"

"Who?" Terry shouted. "The shark?"

"No, Jacques!"

Terry slowed the boat and the three of us scrambled to the bow, desperate for a sign of the dog.

"He was right there!"

Before us lay only an empty stretch of water. Just like that—*poof!*—Jacques had vanished. We watched with heavy hearts as the monster's dorsal fin made an abrupt turn, gliding back toward the open water, no doubt with a curly mammalian treat in its gullet.

Terry and Robert were crestfallen.

"Not everyone can have nine lives," I offered as solace.

We floated wordlessly for a moment. Then Robert picked up the urn and tipped the remaining ashes out of the back. At one point I thought I saw a gold-filled tooth drifting on the waves, but my eyes may have been playing tricks on me.

"Will someone say a prayer?" Robert's voice was choked with emotion.

The three of us pressed our hands together, heads down.

"God bless François and Jacques," Terry prayed. "May they find their way peacefully into the ecosystem of this beautiful island."

"Amen," I said.

"Amen," said Robert.

"Arf!" someone yapped from the deck of a yacht.

We looked up to see a woman in a bikini top and sarong with wet hair. She was waving to us with one arm, while in the other she held a bundled-up beach towel. And poking out the end of the towel was a little white snout.

"Ahoy there!" the woman shouted. "Are you by any chance missing a poodle?"

thirty-one

*W*ould it be redundant to say, *It's a Christmas miracle?*

It felt more like Christmas in *The Twilight Zone.* I was beginning to think these yuletide wonders were proof that we'd entered a parallel dimension where poodles and fat men were impervious to injury and death.

I was tempted to get a gun and shoot Jacques to test my new theory, but then I thought—*Nah.* The bullet would probably bounce off his magic hide and hit me right in the middle of the forehead. I was already sporting a walnut-sized lump just above my right eye. The Nintendo kid's words had been prophetic. With my brow swollen to twice its normal size, I definitely resembled a Neanderthal babe.

Terry and Robert went to get Jacques combed out—salt water is *hell* on your permanent, apparently—then I went to bed with Reba's harlequin ice pack on my face. I was just about to doze off when the phone rang. I answered, expecting it to be Terry.

"Hey. What's up?"

"Kerry? It's David."

"Oh, hi." I yanked the ice pack off of my face as if he could somehow see me through the line. "How are you?"

"Better than you, sounds like. I heard about the stampede and the funeral at sea."

"Yeah, we've really been through it today. Who have you been talking to?"

"Your sister. At least I *think* it's your sister. She looks a bit like you, says her name is Terry."

"That would be her."

"I saw her going into the beauty supply store with your cousin Robert."

"They were shopping for a hair pick for the poodle."

He laughed. "She also said you found the missing bride."

"We caught a glimpse of her. She was all strung out and paranoid. Turns out she's been camping on top of the bluff."

"Why was she hiding out?"

"We have an idea, but I can't share it with you."

"Can't tell me?" he said in a wounded tone.

Oh, why not tell him? David had nothing to do with the crimes, I realized now. I had only doubted him because anyone and everyone was suspect until we'd narrowed it down to the two most likely culprits.

"Okay, if you promise not to repeat it."

"Who would I tell? All right, I promise."

I told him about our Maguffin, the extravagant diamond ring.

"I think Steven Petty's ex-wife is out to get the ring back. She hired Beaver to do it, and he killed Nikki in the process."

"But why kill the scuba instructor? She didn't have the ring, did she?"

"I believe he did it by mistake. On the other hand, Terry thinks Steven is the one who killed Nikki. We're going to try to solve the mystery tonight."

"Tonight? You're not going to do anything *stup*—uh, dangerous, are you?"

He was going to say stupid but thought better of it. Well, I'd called him stupid for chasing after Beaver. Fair is fair.

"It may be stupid," I countered, "but it's the only way to get to the truth."

"Isn't that the sheriff's job?"

"Maybe, but it's *our* case."

"So who has this ring now?"

"We do," I said, then cringed down to my toes. Telling David we were investigating was one thing. Blurting out our ace in the hole was another.

"How did you get it?"

"She left it in our hotel room."

"Why?"

"Because she hates the man she married and she wanted to make a statement. He deliberately put the ring on her finger to get his sadistic kicks from the ex-wife's reaction. Anna didn't like being used that way, so she split."

"It all sounds very complicated."

"The ways of the heart usually are."

"Speaking of…"

I hesitated. "Yes?"

"You up to getting together?"

Not looking like this, I wasn't. I checked myself out in the armoire mirror. I'd showered, but hadn't blow-dried my hair. It stuck out of my head like copper wiring, complemented by the blue lump over my eye. "Actually, I'm whipped. How about tomorrow?"

"Tomorrow I'm going to L.A. for supplies."

I tried to sound casual. "When will you be back?"

"After New Year's."

"We'll be gone then."

There was a momentary silence.

"You know, I get to the mainland every couple of months."

"Really? You want my number?"

Way to play hard to get, Kerry.

"Meet me for coffee now. I can't wait that long."

Aha, so two can play at not playing hard to get.

"All right," I said. "Where?"

He named a café near the famous pastry shop where Jacques had gone apoplectic.

"Be there in fifteen."

I hung up and threw on some sunglasses to cover my shiner, stuffing my disastrous hair under a bright pink baseball cap.

Oh, well, I thought. *Some days you're a mermaid. Others, you're the Creature From the Black Lagoon.*

The elevator took forever to get to my floor, or so it seemed. I was on the verge of taking the stairs down to the lobby when it finally arrived. It was filled to the limit with older women, all of them holding rolled-up copies of the L.A. Times.

"She's a dead ringer for Greer Garson, if you ask me," one of them said, as I squeezed onto the elevator car.

"No, no," said another. "Lucille Ball in her showgirl days."

"With Ingrid Bergman's class."

"I hear she's slept with everyone who's anyone," a voice said from the back, and they all snickered.

When the door pinged open, the women jostled to get out, shoving me to the back of the elevator. *Where's the friggin' fire?* I thought.

When at last I entered the lobby, I saw a whole crowd of gals of a certain age, waving newspapers at a glamorous woman seated at the far side of lobby, and begging for her autograph.

Guess who?

Aunt Reba was holding court from a spot near the window. She was resplendent in a cap-sleeved, red designer suit, her hennaed hair styled perfectly. She sat on a stuffed chair with legs crossed, bobbing her upper foot coquettishly. And heaven only knows where she got them, but she was wearing the fabled *fruit shoes.*

"No, I never worked as an actress," she told the captivated group. "Although they certainly tried to get me in front of the camera. I was more of a behind the scenes kind of inspiration, *if you know what I mean.*" She winked and her adoring public twittered in glee.

One of the women from the elevator thrust a newspaper at her. "Did you know Cary Grant?"

Reba dashed a signature over her front-page photo. "*Know?*

In the Biblical sense?" The audience erupted into giggles. "No, but ask me about Richard Burton."

The woman's eyes widened. "What *about* Richard Burton?"

Reba shook her head, returning the paper. "No, I shouldn't. Not while Liz is still kicking. It would be tacky."

I elbowed my way through the crowd to the front door, where I had to ask an elderly man to step aside in order to exit.

"She's a corker, ain't she?" he said, nodding at Reba.

"The corkiest," I agreed.

Leave it to Reba to turn a major calamity into minor celebrity.

The waiter at the café brought me an iced cappuccino, and I settled in to wait, watching the tourists as they wandered in and out of the souvenir shops. I felt my body gearing up for David's appearance the way an athlete's does for a race. Tense and tingly, so ready to go I was about to explode. Absorbed in my own thoughts, I didn't even notice the woman until she was standing right beside me.

It was Anna Petty, the runaway bride.

She wore sunglasses under a white sailor's cap, and she looked pitifully scrawny inside her dirty, oversized T-shirt.

"Would you like a coffee?" I asked, trying not to appear shocked.

"No, thanks." Anna kept her gaze moving at all times across the crowded street, like a government mole making a secret drop. "I have to talk fast. Don't say anything, just listen."

"Okay."

She sat down at the table. "My husband wants to kill me."

"Why?" I asked.

She pressed a finger to her lips. "Not until I've had my say." She paused, waiting for me to acknowledge her instructions. "I was too stupid to see it, too impressed with his money. He swept me off my feet, took me to nice restaurants, bought me things. But it was all so fast; I should have known something was wrong. It was all part of his plan."

This was sounding like crazy talk. I began to wonder if Steven

Petty were actually some kind of psycho magnet. So far, he was two for two.

"I know it sounds whack," she said, as if reading my mind. "I thought he really cared for me, but it was always about somebody else."

"Who?"

"The girl who was killed, Nikki Edwards."

I choked on my coffee. "Why do you say that?"

"I saw them together, kissing."

"You did? When?"

"Our first night here, when Steven thought I was asleep. I went out on the balcony and looked down. They were going at it hot and heavy, right there on the street."

"He told everyone you left because he played a round of golf on your honeymoon."

"Not true. I saw them, and that's when I understood—the quick courtship, the marriage. It had all been a set-up. I think he came here intending to kill her, using me as cover."

Anna gave me a searching look. In spite of my doubts, I nodded to indicate a willingness to continue listening.

"It was brilliant, really." She gave a harsh laugh. "Who would suspect a groom on his honeymoon? But he must have realized he would have to kill me, too, once I had seen them kissing, because I could place him with the murdered girl."

"That's such an elaborate scheme," I said. "If he wanted to kill Nikki, why not just do it? Why go to all the trouble of marrying you?"

"I told you, for cover. Once the deed was done and we were back home, he was probably planning to dump me. Or maybe I was scheduled to become the victim of a tragic accident."

This wasn't meshing with my theory of the case, so I tried to pin her down on the details. "He said you packed your bags and were gone when he came back to the hotel at six in the evening."

She shook her head. "At six o'clock, we were just getting started. He'd brought some champagne with him and we made love in our honeymoon suite. We went at it for hours."

Maybe I'd let Terry have the king bed for the rest of the trip.

"Finally, I pretended to be asleep because I couldn't take it anymore. He was on Viagra or something—insatiable, and so cold. It was like he was trying to get his money's worth before the clock ran out.

"When he thought I was asleep, he snuck into the bathroom and made a call on his cell phone. Then he got dressed and left. I went out on the balcony to see where he was going, and that's when I saw them together."

"What did you think at the time?"

"I couldn't believe my eyes. She had been our van driver, that's all I knew. Had he passed her some sort of signal? What kind of creep picks up a woman on his honeymoon?"

What kind of creep, indeed? A murdering one?

I still didn't think so.

"Then I heard the girl was killed," Anna went on, "and I realized I'd sensed something funny between them on the drive. But I wouldn't let myself acknowledge it. I'd only been married a few hours, for pity's sake."

"I don't know if you're aware of this," I said, "but it's almost certain Steven and Nikki did have a prior relationship. She worked at Petty Construction once. He could have been meeting her to discuss business."

She snorted. "That was really some business-like kiss, let me tell you."

"Is it possible that she kissed him, rather than the other way around? Maybe she's an ex-girlfriend."

"His hands were all over her," Anna said in disgust. "And if he didn't want to run into an ex-girlfriend, why did he insist on having our honeymoon here?"

"He said you were the one that—"

"I wanted to go to Vegas." She reacted to my surprise with a shrug. "I like to play Keno."

"Okay. What did you do afterward?"

"I grabbed a few things. I was going to check into a motel until I could figure out what to do. I went outside and hid in the shadows, watching them for a while. Finally, he went back inside. After he'd been in the room for a few seconds, he came running out on the balcony with his cell phone. I was right beneath him. I could hear him leaving me a voicemail."

"What did he say?"

She took a deep breath. "He said, 'I screwed the bitch.' "

Wait a minute. Wasn't that what we'd heard the man saying on Nikki's phone the night she was killed? *No, not quite.*

"Are you sure it wasn't, 'You're going to pay for this, bitch?'"

"I was upset, but I know what I heard."

"And you're certain the message was for you?"

"I'd left my phone behind in my hurry. But I know he was taunting me, telling me he'd been with the van driver."

"But he would have heard your phone ringing in the room, right? He'd know he wasn't reaching you."

"I'd turned down the ringer volume while we were making love."

"The reason I'm asking... the tone, the words... It's like a call someone made to Nikki the very next night."

"That proves he killed her!"

"I'm sorry, but it doesn't."

"But who else could have?"

"A man named Beaver, a laborer who had also worked with Nikki. My sister and I saw him lurking outside her apartment. Then he broke into our room—your former suite at the hotel—and attacked us. He was found floating in the harbor this morning with his throat cut." I waited a moment for this to sink in. It was a lot of information to absorb.

"There's really no question he killed her," I continued. "The only question is whether he did it on his own, or on behalf of someone else. And whether that someone else killed him afterward."

She didn't want to hear any of this. "But I saw them kissing!"

"Even so, it's not indicative of murder."

"I'm not taking that chance."

"Anna, you're in more danger from some weirdo out here in the open than you would be from your husband. Believe me, there are too many people who know about you now, including the sheriff."

She pulled off the sunglasses. "You have to believe me." Her large hazel eyes were beautiful, despite being sunken and bloodshot, and they were pleading with me. Perhaps she'd had an abusive boyfriend or husband in the past that had caused her to project these fears onto Petty.

"Why don't you ask your parents to come get you if you're afraid?" I asked her.

"What parents?"

"I mean, your mother. I overheard Steven telling the sheriff's deputies that he had a nightmare of a mother-in-law."

"My parents are dead. He was lying."

"What do you know about his ex-wife, Paige?"

"What?" Anna blew out a sigh. "He said he'd never been married. I believed him. I didn't see any signs of an ex." She sat up suddenly. "Oh, wait a minute! Is she a heavy-set blonde?"

"That's her."

"I asked him why that woman was following us around, and he acted like he didn't know her. He said she was probably some menopausal maniac who'd mistaken him for someone else."

I suppressed a laugh. "She's definitely a maniac, but there's no mistake. She's here because she wants the green stone he gave you. It may be worth more than you think."

Anna rolled her eyes. "She's welcome to it. Can you say 'ostentatious'? I hated that thing."

"That's why you left it in the toilet?"

"Along with my so-called marriage. I asked Steven for a simple band. I said platinum would be good, but white gold was okay. He *made* me wear that rock."

"Did he give you a reason?"

"He said we needed something glorious to symbolize our love."

The line was such vintage Petty, I couldn't help cracking up this time. "Sorry," I said. "Insensitive."

She rested her forehead on her hand. "I was such a chump. I fell for it, hook, line, and sinker. I wanted to believe we were madly in love."

"The Pettys had a very public split three years ago. It was major gossip at the time. You never heard about it?"

"I'd only been in Newport for a year. I didn't think to check into Steven's background, and when would I have done it? We were together twenty-four seven. I even quit my job. He was so generous, and when he started talking marriage..." She lowered her head. "I thought I'd hit easy street. I wasn't about to look that in the mouth."

"So you're not attached to the ring."

"Hell, no. I don't want any reminder of him."

"Good, because I believe that his ex-wife is the one who hired Beaver to do the killing. But in order to be sure, we need to use that ring."

"Use it how?"

I told her about the exchange planned for that evening. As she listened, she began to giggle. The giggling turned into laughter, which escalated into a full-on bout of hysteria. The girl was coming unglued.

"People are staring," I whispered, hoping she'd get herself under control.

She took a series of deep breaths, eventually calming herself down.

"Listen, Anna. Why don't you go to the sheriff's office? You'll be safe there."

"Not until he's caught, I won't be."

"Are you still camping on the bluff?"

"No, I found another hideout. I'll leave the island as soon as I know the coast is clear."

"How can I reach you to let you know how things turn out?"

"You can't, but I will know. There is one thing you can do for me until then."

"What?"

"Tell Steven I'm gone. Tell him you found out I left on a private boat and went back home."

I stared at her for a moment. She was my age, my size, my

general background—but with a radically different life history. For whatever reason, she'd cast Petty in the role of murderer, instead of mere jerk. But it made no difference, really. Either way, in my opinion, she was better off without him.

"I guess I can do that."

"Thank you," she whispered, squeezing my hand.

Just then I remembered why I was there in the first place. David was twenty minutes late, according to my watch. I glanced up the street and saw group of people talking in front of a curio shop, one of them a tall man with dark hair. I thought for a second it was David, but then a woman moved to one side, allowing me to see the man's face. I realized I'd been mistaken. When I turned back to speak to Anna, she was gone—slipped away into the crowd.

I didn't get the chance to ask how she'd found me.

When David hadn't shown after another half-hour, I didn't know whether to be pissed off or worried. I settled on emotional detachment until I had more information. Maybe he couldn't get away from work. To be fair, I'd never given him my cell phone number, and the cell phone was with Terry, anyway.

I tried to get my arms around this new scenario—Steven Petty kissing Nikki and threatening her afterward. How much of what Anna said could be credited?

The whole thing is so confusing, I thought as I tromped up the hill to the hotel. Not only could I not see the forest for the trees, I was literally lost in the woods.

When I arrived, Reba was no longer in the St. Lauren's lobby signing autographs, telling tall tales out of school. But a few of her fans lingered, chatting about her in excited tones.

"Isn't she gorgeous?"

"Fabulous."

"I can't wait till her tell-all book comes out."

"Me, too. You can *keep* Jackie Collins."

Reba was writing a book? God bless us, every one.

I rode with a carload of her groupies up to my floor. As I approached the room, I heard the faint sound of voices inside. *Probably the TV,* I thought, as I swung open the door and...

Found myself staring down the barrel of a gun.

"Kerry McAfee," Deputy Whitehorse said. "You're under arrest."

thirty-two

$\mathcal{M}$y shock was compounded when I walked in and saw the other occupant of the room. David was seated at the desk, hands cuffed behind the Queen Anne chair.

"If I'm under arrest, why is he the one in handcuffs?"

"I found him breaking into your room."

I gave David a palms-up. *What gives?*

"I was held up at the job," he said. "I figured you would have left the café, so I came here to meet you. Like you told me to, remember?"

I hadn't asked David to meet me here, but evidently he wanted me to back him up. I'd have wanted the same, I guess, if mistaken for a cat burglar. But why couldn't he have waited until I returned?

"He said you offered to leave the door open?" Whitehorse prompted me.

David's face held the promise of an explanation. I decided to trust him on a provisional basis.

"That's right. I must have forgotten."

Whitehorse appeared skeptical, but she went ahead and

unlocked David's cuffs. Afterward she walked back to me, spun me around, and slapped the cuffs on my wrists.

"What are you doing?" I yelled.

"Arresting you, like I said."

"For what?"

"Impersonating an officer. You flashed a badge and commandeered a golf cart under false pretenses."

I whirled around. "Are you kidding?"

She shook her head.

"We told you about taking the golf cart. Why didn't you arrest us then?"

"I didn't know you did it under false color of authority. We got that from the complainants."

"Then how do you know it wasn't my sister who did it?"

Whitehorse flashed a smile. "Because she swore it was you."

Dammit, Terry.

All our lives, she'd set me up to take the rap for her baby felonies: Barbie dolls shorn and maimed, windows broken with carelessly aimed baseballs, holes burnt in the carpet by pot seeds. Now she was setting me up for her adult felonies, as well.

"She's down at the station," Whitehorse said as she marched me to the door. "You'll come, too, and we'll straighten this all out."

"Straighten what out?"

"Who did the impersonating and who was the accomplice. They'll carry pretty much the same penalty, anyway."

I dug in my heels. "I want my lawyer."

"Your sister already called him." Whitehorse held open the door. "Are you staying?" she asked David.

"No, he's not." I was willing to get him off the hook for burglary, but not to provide him sanctuary afterward. "I'll catch up with you later, David."

"Good luck with..." He waved his hand as if he were at a loss for words.

Out in the hallway, he threw me a look of regret as he pushed through the stairwell door. I heard his feet clattering down the metal stairs.

I had averted my eyes, not wanting to meet his. I was busy replaying the night before in my mind, remembering how desperately David had tried to get me upstairs under the pretext of mad passion. When that didn't work, he lured me out today so he could break in.

Had all of it been a manipulation? I thought uneasily. *What reason could he have to burglarize our room? What was he looking for?*

Then it came to me.

The ring, stupid.

thirty-three

he sun was setting as Whitehorse loaded me into the back of her cruiser. She got in and the two of us watched David shuffling back down the hill, his head hanging low. Once he was out of sight, she eyed me in the rearview mirror.

"You're not really under arrest," she said.

"Hello!" I wriggled my shoulders. "I am handcuffed and locked in the back of a police vehicle. What do *you* call it?"

"I didn't want your boyfriend to suspect the real reason I was there."

"And what is that?"

"There are some folks from Homeland Security who want to speak to you."

"Homeland Security?!"

My mind instantly provided me with a series of flash-photos: Men in suits. Balding men, fortyish, overdressed for the locale. Land Management bureaucrats? Try, *The Men in Black*.

"Yes, Homeland Security," Whitehorse said. "How well do you know David Solomon?"

"Not... that well, apparently."

"Did you know his name is actually Mohammed?"

I could only stare back at her reflection, completely tongue-tied. Was this some kind of joke? I saw no mirth in her intense black eyes.

"Didn't think so." Whitehorse put the cruiser in gear and started down the street, passing David on the way. Somehow I refrained from gawking at him.

"Will you please tell me what this is all about?" I was beginning to feel dizzy.

"You seem to be dating a terrorist."

Forget dizzy. A wave of nausea washed right through me. I bent forward in my seat, trying to catch my breath. "Jesus."

"No, his name is Qamar. Qamar Mohammed."

When I was relatively sure I was not going to blow chunks, I sat up again. "I just met him! And I never would have met him if you hadn't brought us in to work with him on the sketch!"

"I know, but they may ask you to continue the relationship in order to get information."

"Homeland Security wants me to *spy*?" I asked incredulously.

"Yeah. I told them I thought you'd be willing."

"Based on what!"

"Based on the fact that I'll arrest you for the golf cart theft if you don't."

"Great." I laughed. "There's nothing like a free choice."

"Call it your patriotic duty." Whitehorse paused for a moment. "You weren't suspicious of him at all?"

Instinct told me to evade the question. "Were you?"

"No," she admitted.

Could I be such a lousy judge of character? Had I been swept off my feet by a jerk with a hidden agenda, just as Anna had been? I'd always taken pride in my finely calibrated creep-o-meter, but it seemed to have fritzed out in the electrical storm of my desire.

"You had him in custody!" I protested. "You could have charged him with breaking and entering, holding him for the counterterrorism people or whoever."

"I had orders not to interfere with him. When I caught him breaking in, I had no choice but to apprehend him. But I would have found an excuse to let him go."

"And I conveniently provided that excuse."

"Right."

I sat there a moment, my thoughts slowly coming back into focus. "They must want him to lead them to his handler or something. Otherwise, they'd just pick him up and interrogate him right now. They're not shy about that. They could 'render' him to some secret prison in Germany and beat it out of him."

"You're probably right." We drove in silence for a while, then she said, "Uh, if it's not too personal, did you sleep with him?"

Oh, not too personal at all.

"We didn't get that far," I told her.

Thank God for small favors. Sleeping with the enemy was bad enough. Sleeping with Public Enemy Number One could land you in really deep doo doo.

"So you don't know if he was circumcised or not?"

"No. I think that little detail might have tipped me off."

She smiled at me in the mirror. "So to speak."

Wonderful. Now she gets a sense of humor.

Terry was in the holding cell at the station, still under the impression that she was under arrest. She jumped up from the bench, clutching the mesh wire. "You didn't say anything to them, did you?"

I shook my head. "Nothing they didn't already know."

"I called Eli. He's on his way."

"You can tell her," Whitehorse said to me.

Terry shot her a murderous look. "Tell me what?"

"We're not really under arrest," I said.

She cackled sardonically. "Oh, sure. I've heard that one before."

"For real, Ter. It's not about the golf cart. It's about David."

She blinked. "Your David?"

I cleared my throat. "I wouldn't call him *my* David..."

"David Solomon is not who he appears to be," Whitehorse told her.

"Then who is he?"

"His name is Qamar Mohammed. He's an international terrorist."

Terry released the wire, stumbling backward. "Are you serious?" She looked at me. "Is she serious?"

I nodded. "Homeland Security wants to talk to me about him."

"Then why all of this?" Terry said. "Why the handcuffs and the holding cell?"

"It was for your own protection," Whitehorse said. "Apparently this Qamar dude is one ruthless son of a bitch."

"Oh." Terry gave me a look full of pity. "That's a real bummer. Huh, sis?"

thirty-four

$\mathcal{I}$ was seated in the break room at the sheriff's department, facing the Men in Black across the lunch table. The two of them were living, breathing clichés. Dark suits, narrow ties, lightly starched shirts. Their names so all-American I couldn't even recall them. Smith and Jones? Johnson and Jackson? White and Off-White?

Rather than ask my interrogators to reintroduce themselves, I nicknamed them Bland and Blander.

I don't know what I'd expected. Something sexier, I guess. But my first clue should have been the term "Homeland Security." It conjured up *The Little House on the Prairie*, not hot-looking spies slaloming downhill in pursuit of the bad guys. Who said global intrigue was always glamorous?

Ian Fleming, that's who.

But I had to admit these dull boys were good at their jobs. They'd tracked an international terrorist here to this out-of-the-way island. And not merely a bomb-toting suicide killer, to hear them tell it, but a mastermind assassin. While his radical counterparts were flapping their beards and wagging their fingers at the Great American Satan, our man went quietly and professionally about his job, and few were ever the wiser.

Except for the people he terminated.

His kills were strategic—not meant for public exploitation. They were designed to accomplish specific political or economic ends, rather than to generate mass hysteria. Rogue generals were decommissioned for good; opposition government leaders brought down; whole governments toppled with one well-aimed long-distance rifle.

Qamar Mohammed was known for his cunning and chameleon-like ability to fit in anywhere. And in some quarters—I thought shamefully—for being a great kisser.

I suddenly realized that Agent Bland was talking to me.

"Sorry?" I said. "What did you say?"

"I asked when you first encountered Mohammed." His cheap navy sport coat was open, the belly straining at a light blue, button-down Oxford shirt. I glimpsed a white T-shirt between the buttons.

The question brought to mind my first sight of those long, lean legs in work boots. I suppressed a sigh of longing.

"Right here," I said, pointing to the table. "As I'm sure Deputy Whitehorse has told you, she brought my sister and me here to identify that man up there." I pointed to the Wanted poster on the wall, with the hand-drawn facsimile of Beaver.

"You'd never met him before that?" Blander asked.

I shook my head.

"Never seen him?"

"Not that I'm aware of."

"Then he asked to see you again?"

"He invited me to the Casino to view the job he was working on. I didn't go, but he showed up at the Christmas party that night, taking pictures."

"Was he acting as an official photographer?"

"I don't think so. You'd have to ask the organizers."

"And afterward?" Bland asked.

Oh boy, here we go.

I'd have to tell them everything about the make-out session.

Could I be shipped off to Guantánamo and charged with tongue kissing an international baddie?

"Yes. Afterward, I went with him to see the mural he was restoring, a mermaid scene. We climbed the scaffolding to see it up close."

"Mermaid scene?" Blander threw Bland an amused look.

"That's rich." Bland chuckled. "Okay, so you were on the scaffolding looking at the pretty mermaid?"

Eat dirt, I thought.

"Yes, sir," I said.

"And what did he say to you then?" Bland inquired.

I closed my eyes as if trying to remember, but I really wanted to shut out the sight of their inquisitive eyes. I didn't have to watch their reaction to my story, adding humiliation to the pain of being duped. "He said I was beautiful, he wanted to make love to me. Stuff like that."

When I opened my eyes again, the two of them were looking down at their notebooks. At least they had a smidgen of empathy.

"And what did you say in reply?"

"I said I would."

"Would what?"

"You know," I said in a choked whisper. "Go home with him."

The next questions came quick, shotgun style. I lost track of who was asking what. Didn't care, to be honest. Now that they'd extracted the most embarrassing part of my statement, they went steamrolling straight to the heart of the matter.

"And did you go home with him?"

"No, someone shot at us. It kind of put a crimp in our plans."

"Do you know where he lives?"

"No."

"Did you think you were being fed a line?"

I flinched inwardly. "Not at the time."

"Did he ask you any personal questions?"

"We talked about my boyfriends. Well... they're not really boyfriends, currently. It's hard to explain."

They raised their eyebrows.

"I told him that I was sort of involved with a police detective and an FBI agent."

They were taken aback. "Did he react to your mention of the FBI?"

I suddenly remembered. "Actually, he did seem surprised."

"I'll just bet he was," Blander said, smirking.

I wanted to hit him. Very hard.

"And then what?"

"Then we were shot at, like I said. By that goon up there." I pointed to Beaver's picture again.

"Any idea why?"

"We had identified him. He was a suspect in the murder of Nikki Edwards."

"Did Mohammed ask you anything about Steven Petty?"

"Um, no. But he knew I was looking for Petty's runaway bride."

And just how did he know that? I found myself wondering.

Oh, yes. Terry had told David when she was out shopping for poodle beauty supplies, just before he called me to make a date for coffee. The date he didn't keep.

"And did you find the wife?"

"Twice. The first time she ran away. The second time she approached me when I was at a sidewalk café, waiting for... waiting for coffee." I didn't mention the aborted date with David. I wasn't sure why I omitted this, but sometimes you had to trust your subconscious to know more about a particular situation than you. Just as my feet had started running after Anna before I'd consciously recognized her, and just as my intuition had led me to the online photo of the diamond. Now my tongue was telling me it preferred to lie still on that particular issue, so I let it lie.

The agents frowned, sensing I was holding back. Now I wished my tongue would share its insights with me, because I wanted to know why I'd risked lying—even by omission—to federal investigators. I had a sense that some bit of information was teetering on the edge of my memory, in danger of falling into the chasm of forgetfulness to be lost forever.

But I knew this much: They were wrong about David. Or Qamar, or whoever he was. Call it a hunch. Call it wishful thinking. Just don't call it *smart women, stupid choices*.

Bland took up the questioning again.

"And what did Anna Petty say to you?"

I snapped back to attention. "She said she believed her husband had murdered Nikki Edwards, and that he wanted to kill her, too, because she had witnessed him kissing Nikki."

"And did you believe her?"

"I hadn't decided who to believe. I was still processing it all."

"And have you *processed* it now?" Bland asked sarcastically.

"Not completely."

"Please fill us in on your thought *processes*."

I took a moment to organize my thoughts before I spoke, hoping I could nudge the teetering puzzle piece into place.

Beaver had killed Nikki—I was convinced of that. But just beforehand, Max had seen her leaving the apartment with someone. A beach bum, according to him...

The stray piece of information was suddenly jolted into place. *Terry had been right.*

No one, not even cranky old Max, would describe Steven Petty as a 'beach bum.' He wore expensive clothes, sported a Rolex, exuded an air of entitlement. That meant that the person Nikki had left with that night could not have been Petty. However, it could have been someone with long dark hair, wearing baggy shorts and work boots. Someone who resembled that original wandering hippie who spouted his radical philosophy to stragglers up and down the Galilee coast.

For some reason I couldn't explain to myself yet, I knew this was the key to everything. Just then my wily old tongue did something terribly impulsive.

"You've got the wrong man," it announced.

"I beg your pardon?" Bland said.

"David Solomon is not this Qamar Mohammed person. I don't care what you say."

The two of them shook their heads. Then Blander turned mean, pointing a finger at my face.

"Listen, lady. You máy be hot for this character, but I can tell you, the Department of Homeland Security does not make that kind of mistake."

"Oh yeah? What about the Los Angeles filmmaker who sat in a Baghdad lockup for fifty days on suspicion of being an enemy combatant?"

"That was the Pentagon, not us," Bland muttered. "Mistakes happen."

"Thank you, that's exactly my point!"

"You're wasting your point on us, Ms. McAfee," Blander shouted.

"Something's not right, here," I insisted.

"Yeah, and what's wrong is some little girl trying to tell two counterterrorism experts how to do their jobs."

"I'd like to see my lawyer before I say any more." I folded my hands on the table.

"We don't have to let you see a lawyer," Bland said ominously.

"Yes, you do!"

"No," Blander said with a menacing smile. "We don't."

"This is America." I stabbed the table with my finger, as if it were a map of the U.S. and I was pointing straight at Kansas. "We still have *some* rights in this country, do we not? What's the point of fighting the War on Terror if we have to give up everything that was great about being American in the first place?"

I leaned both palms on the table, coming out of my chair. "And *as* a tax-paying, law-abiding citizen of this great and free country, I'm telling *you* Bozos that I want my constitutionally guaranteed advocate, and I want his ass now! *So, go get him!*"

My knees weakened and my hands began to shake. I had no frigging idea where that speech had come from. But if I had expected my audience to burst into thunderous applause or a spontaneous rendition of *America the Beautiful*, I was sadly mistaken. The agents glared at me in frosty silence as my words echoed off the walls.

Bland stood up and started walking around the table. Was he going to start right in on the torture? *Let's knock out a few of those pretty little teeth and just see how tough she is.* I sure hoped they had good dentists at Guantánamo.

I flinched, eyes shut tight, waiting for a fist to my jaw or a sucker punch to the gut. But he just kept on walking right past me.

"Your lawyer's busy talking to the sheriffs," Bland said. "He'll be here in a minute."

I looked up to see him poised next to the coffee station, holding up the carafe. "Want a cup of coffee while you wait? It's fresh."

"Yes." I fell back into my chair, completely spent. "Yes, I would, please."

thirty-five

They brought Terry into the interview room to wait with me. The two of us sat at the table staring at our novelty coffee mugs. The legend on mine said, *Smarter than the Average Mushroom.* Terry's said, *Kiss Me, I'm Kickapoo.*

"Thought she was Shawnee," I said.

"Probably a gift from someone who wouldn't know the difference. Deputy Young, maybe?"

"He of the mushroom IQ."

"Yeah." She chuckled. "Hey, I've been doing some thinking."

"I'll alert the Darwin Society."

Terry let that one go by. "And you know what? I've decided you were right. I shouldn't have commandeered that cart."

I regarded her with suspicion. Terry never admits a mistake without an ulterior motive. "I'm over it," I said. "Yesterday's news."

She gave me an ultra-sincere smile. "Still, it was wrong of me."

"Your apology is accepted." I prayed that would be the end of it.

234

But no…

"Okay, now you apologize," she said.

"For what?"

She put a finger to her cheek. "Let me see, what should Kerry apologize for…? Oh, I know!" She kicked a chair, causing it to squeak across the linoleum. "For porking a terrorist!"

I slumped down on the table, head on my arms. "I didn't pork him."

"Then why are we here? Let me put it this way: Why am *I* here? I never put my country in jeopardy because I had hot pants for some terrorist. It's guilt by association, that's what it is. I'm identical to a terrorist-porker, so here I am."

"Zip it, Ter."

"You have the nerve to suggest I should zip it?" She jumped up and circled the room, arms flapping. "I can't believe you would even use the word 'zip,' when it was your failure to keep your low-riders zipped that got us into this mess in the first place!"

"Terry, please. Let's not play the blame game."

"It is not a game! For once and truly, it is not a game!" She got up in my face. "Maybe you want to think a little harder before you go traipsing off with some tall, dark stranger, huh? A man you know nothing about!"

I pushed back from the table. "I'm sorry, all right? I'm very, very sorry I got us involved in this whole thing."

She fumed at me, her eyes ablaze. Then at long last, she took a breath and eased herself back into a chair. "That's all I wanted to hear."

"Fine. I said it."

"Good. Now say, 'I'm a horny little slut.' "

Her hand whipped up just in time to catch my fist before it connected with her face.

"Ow!" She rubbed her hand. "I was only kidding."

The door opened and our white knight wafted in on a cloud of cigar smoke—Eli Weintraub, defense attorney extraordinaire, friend to working girls and unrepentant criminals, and all around *mensch*. Who else would hitch a helicopter ride across the bay as soon as he was summoned by two desperate femmes?

235

"Eli!" Terry ran to him with her arms open.

I felt tears in my eyes as I watched her hug him around the neck. Once again, I was thanking my lucky stars that I had found Eli when Terry was brought up on drug charges.

He scuffed toward the table with Terry still clinging to him, dragging her across the floor like a dead weight. Then he stopped halfway to the table. "Are we done hugging?"

"Sorry." Terry released him, straightening his shirt. "Just happy to see you."

He stretched his neck and sat down, smiling at me. "I hear you gave quite a 'Come-to-Jesus' speech to the Homeland Security grunts."

"Somebody had to. Jesus wasn't here."

"Don't be too sure about that." Eli tossed his bashed-up briefcase on the table. "Somebody up there likes you. They're letting you go."

Terry pumped a fist. "Yay!" Then on second thought: "Me, too?"

"You, too."

"Yay!" She pumped her fist again.

Eli extracted a yellow pad from his briefcase and flipped to a clean page. "For the record, why don't you tell me how you got into this situation? Give me everything from the beginning."

I spent the next ten minutes recapping everything that had happened to us from the time of our arrival. He listened intently, scribbling notes, occasionally asking for clarification. I wrapped everything up with my fake arrest by Whitehorse.

"Okay." He clicked his silver Cross pen and returned it to his coat pocket. "It's pretty clear you guys were innocent bystanders. I don't think we're going to have any problems. I'll have these notes typed up, then get Homeland Security to sign off on them. That way they can't change their story or yours."

"Thanks, Eli," Terry said.

I recalled Whitehorse's threat. "Did they mention anything about me spying on David?"

Eli shook his head. "That's out. I told them they're going to have to handle the espionage themselves. That's why they get the big bucks. If the guy calls, Kerry, you tell him you're busy, you got your period, whatever. You do not make plans to see him. You'll have a contact number. If he does call, you'll notify your contact immediately, then leave the rest to them. Your phone will be bugged from now until doomsday, anyway, but it'll show them you're being cooperative."

"What? They can't bug my phone!"

"Ever heard of the Patriot Act? The NSA?"

"I protest that invasion of my privacy!"

He gave me a jaundiced look. "We're done with the righteous indignation for today, all right? You're lucky you're not facing a military tribunal for consorting with a known terrorist."

"Oh, yeah? Well, he's not a terrorist!"

Eli closed his eyes, shaking his head.

"I'm telling you, they've got the wrong guy."

"The wrong guy," Eli repeated, opening his eyes again. "How do I put this gently?" He came halfway out of his chair. "I don't give a rat's patooty! He's their problem. You're mine. You got it?"

"Eli, hear me out, please?"

He sat back down and crossed his arms over his belly, daring me to continue.

"The agents wanted to know if David had mentioned Steven Petty to me." I was putting it together in my mind even as I spoke. "Why was that?"

"They know you're working that case. You told them. So what?"

"But what relevance does it have? If the Petty thing is a murder based on a mistaken identity or an act of jealousy—choose your pet theory—why do they care? Spousal murder isn't exactly their bailiwick."

"Don't think I follow you," Eli said.

"Don't think I want to," added Terry.

"I'm saying, what if David Solomon is one of theirs and they don't know it? Homeland Security is a huge bureaucracy. He could be deep undercover with the CIA, and these guys might not be aware of it because they're in a different division."

Terry *tsk-tsked* at me. "Kerry, admit it. You fell for a terrorist. He did a great job of misrepresenting himself and the man is *mighty purty*. Hell, I almost fell for him myself, and he's not my preferred gender."

"I'm not done," I said.

Eli waited for me to continue, his patience nearly tapped out.

"Why did Beaver take a potshot at us? He had no reason to shoot me. I was only one of several witnesses. What if his intended victim was actually David? They could have been working the same case, but from two different angles. What if they're after the same thing?"

"And what would that be?" he asked.

I paused for dramatic effect. The two of them leaned forward and I left them in suspense for as long as I dared, and then made my pronouncement.

"The ring."

They slumped back in their chairs.

"The ring, the ring!" Terry laughed mockingly. "I got a news-flash, Ker. This isn't Middle Earth, it's California! Everybody in the world is not running around looking for some stupid ring!"

I pushed ahead, in spite of her reaction. "David made a date with me for coffee, then didn't show. But Anna Petty did. She said she'd spotted Steven Petty and Nikki kissing on the first night of her honeymoon."

"What?" Terry became visibly nauseous at the thought of this coupling. She stuck out her tongue and made a wiping motion over it. *"Ick, ick, ick!"*

"Anna ran away because of that, and because she had a sus-picion Petty wanted to kill her. She's freaked out and pissed off, but I think she may have been right."

"Why would he want to kill his new wife?" Eli asked.

"That was always his plan from the very beginning, the reason he married her in the first place. They're both guilty, Terry. Steven Petty only married Anna as bait for Paige. Our bet is a draw."

Terry sat there frowning, taking it all in. "Holy moly. I hate to admit it, but this is starting to make sense."

"Great," Eli said. "Make it make sense to me."

"Steven Petty swept Anna off her feet and married her immediately," I explained. "Then he brought her here with the green diamond on her finger. He knew his ex-wife Paige was a loaded weapon—unstable, violent, crazy with jealousy. If Paige murdered Anna, she'd be locked away forever and he'd be free. He probably even called her in advance to let her know where they'd be staying. He was going to spend his nights boinking his new wife, then leave her vulnerable during the day while he played golf. The golf would provide him an alibi when Paige finally did kill the girl."

I saw I was getting through to Terry, at least.

"Paige *is* dangerous," she agreed. "And if she had the added incentive of the, you know—"

"The ring, Frodo?" I folded my arms.

"She'd be ripe for going postal."

"But what has this got to do with our terrorist friend?" Eli wanted to know.

I took a breath. "I'm not sure, but there's a connection somewhere. And here's how I know."

I described once again the phone call I'd had from David. "He wanted me out of the room so he could find the ring. Only trouble was, Whitehorse showed up and caught him in the act."

"But how would he even know we had it?" Terry asked, then it hit her. "Oh no, you didn't."

"It slipped out."

"Loose lips, much?"

"So the guy's a sneak thief as well as a terrorist," Eli said. "Way to pick 'em."

"Does that sit right with you?" I asked him. "Since when do radical Islamists go in for jewelry theft? They're religious fanatics. What do they care about enriching themselves on earth when their reward is in the afterlife?"

"But what about those guys who lived high on the hog in Orange County before September eleventh?" Terry said. "They went to gentlemen's clubs, drank booze, did drugs—" she looked at me sideways, "fooled around with girls."

"Yes, but with strippers. Not with regular women."

"So what are you saying? Because you're not a stripper, he couldn't be what they say he is?"

"No, because he's all wrong for it. A Middle Eastern terrorist who knows his way around Art Deco murals? I don't think so."

"Maybe he wanted the ring so he could sell it," Eli suggested. "Needed money for his arsenal or something."

"Aha! I'm so glad you said that, and you know why? Because I believe that there *is* a connection between diamonds and weapons, and I bet you would like to know what that is."

Eli rolled a hand in the air. "Bring it, baby."

"Petty Investments was strictly domestic real estate, then all of a sudden they went out and bought a diamond mine in Namibia, supposedly to provide a tax write-off. "

"So?" Eli said.

"So, what if Petty's interests have expanded to doing business with international bad guys? He could be laundering money through the mine, or providing industrial diamonds for trade on the arms market. Banks everywhere are freezing the terrorists' assets. What if this is a new way to finance their hand-held missile launchers and M-16s?"

"Pure speculation." Eli closed his legal pad. "Anyway, what's it got to do with your dream boy?"

I ignored the dig. "If I'm right and he is CIA or something, he might have been trying to flush out the arms ring."

"There's nothing like a woman making excuses for her man," Eli said to Terry.

"I understand your skepticism. All I want is a chance to work it out, put a few more pieces of the puzzle together. And Terry and I know just how to do it."

"We *do*?" she said.

"Yes. We proceed with our plan."

"What plan?" Eli asked.

I laid the whole thing out for him, the arrangement with Steven and Paige Petty. I explained that Paige would get the ring back, and Steven would supposedly get her assurance that the stalking had ended.

"But what if you're right, and he's been trying to get the old wife to kill the new one?"

"The new wife won't be there."

"What's the point, then?"

"The point is that one of them killed Nikki, and we're gonna figure out which. And when we find out why everyone wants this diamond ring so bad, we'll know why Nikki was killed."

"I'm in," Terry said.

"You're absolutely determined to do this?" Eli looked back and forth between us, as if we were a couple of prize boneheads.

"Yes," we said together.

The dynamic duo was back!

"As long as there's no contact with the Mohammed dude, I see no reason to interfere. Still sounds risky, though."

"We've talked about that," I told him. "We figure the risk is minimal because both Steven and Paige will be satisfied in the deal."

"Would you like to share your insights with Homeland Security?" Eli nodded to the door.

"This is none of their business."

"If you're right and the guy's in the international arms trade, it *is* their business. They've probably been listening to this whole conversation on a hidden mike anyway."

Terry was appalled. "They can't do that! This is a privileged conversation. You're our lawyer!"

"Brave new world." Eli's eyes lit on the Kickapoo mug. He picked it up and spoke into the base. "Right guys?"

Seconds later, the door opened and the Homeland Security agents strode in, followed by Whitehorse.

"Right," Agent Bland said.

Blander smiled at me. "You have a very interesting mind, young lady. I like the way you think."

thirty-six

"Remind me never to go on vacation again," Terry said, as we headed back to the hotel in the dark.

"Hey, Ter?"

"Huh?"

"Never go on vacation again."

"Thanks."

The Homeland Security agents had finally convinced me that David was who they said he was. I was forced to come to terms with the fact that I'd had my head turned by a pretty face. My only consolation was that the face resembled one that was usually adorned with a halo. Anybody could have made the same mistake.

When we got to the room, we planned to see if the ring was still in place. If it was, the exchange with the Pettys would go on as planned, but with Homeland Security backing us up. We had a phone number to call as soon as the rendezvous was set.

Eli had checked into the Sunspot Motel, refusing to leave until he had signed affidavits confirming our deal. The documents needed to be sent up the food chain for approval, so he was going to wait for them. I could only hope that the meeting with Paige and Steven would finally put a cap on the whole affair, allowing Terry and me to resume our normal lives. I'd decided that international espionage was definitely not my thing.

The honeymoon suite didn't appear to have been disturbed since I'd been apprehended by Whitehorse. Terry lifted the lid on the toilet tank, smirking.

"You know, this is the dumbest, most adolescent place to hide something. And nobody thought to look there."

She was washing the ring in the sink when a knock came at the door.

"Probably Eli." I crossed into the bedroom and peered out through the peephole. But it wasn't Eli; it was Steven Petty standing in the hallway, giving me a little wave.

Damn, I thought. *Double damn. Triple damn.* This wasn't how it was supposed to go down. We were supposed to fix a meeting place, and then let our contact know where it was for certain. Now I wouldn't have the opportunity.

Neither could I take a chance on blowing the whole operation. I opened the door and pretended to be delighted to see him.

"I was in the neighborhood." He sidled into the room. "Thought I'd see how things were going."

"We got the ring," I said.

"Excellent!"

To her credit, Terry betrayed no surprise when she walked in to see Petty standing there. She showed him the ring on her finger. "Here it is, Steven. Spit-shined and ready to go."

Petty's eyes widened at the sight of the diamond, an expression of hunger crossing his face. Terry started to pull the ring off her hand.

"No, don't!" he said.

She stopped at mid-knuckle. "You don't want it?"

"You might was well wear it until we meet Paige. It's safer there than in someone's pocket."

Terry pushed the ring back into place, throwing me a surreptitious glance.

Petty clapped his hands. "This is wonderful! Anna agreed to the exchange, then?"

I nodded. "She told us she never really liked that ring."

"Really?" His mouth went tight. "I thought she loved it. Oh well, women are so fickle."

"Aren't they just?" Terry said. "Those flighty *gals*."

"Sorry," he said. "Didn't know you were so sensitive."

"I'm not sure Terry should wear the ring," I said to him. "What if Paige gets violent?"

"She may pull your finger off, but believe me—getting the ring will put an end to all her madness."

"She wouldn't kill to get it?"

"She might if she had to. But now she won't have to, will she?"

I shook my head slowly.

"All right then, I'll get her." He punched a speed-dial number on his cell phone, and it was answered immediately.

"Hello, dear. It's me."

There was some screeching on the other end. Petty held the phone out at arm's length while Paige ranted, then put it back to his ear. "Listen, Paige, I've got the ring… Yes, that's why I'm calling… I'll give it back, but you must promise to end the stalking… Where shall we meet?" He looked over in my direction, his hand over the microphone.

"Coffee shop?" I said.

He shook his head. "Too public."

"What's wrong with public?"

"She won't go for it."

"There's a copse of trees up on the bluff above town. It's very private, nothing but buffalo as far as the eye can see."

"Can you get there by golf cart?"

Terry told him you could, so he repeated her directions to Paige. "I'll be with my private investigators." He chuckled, smiling at us. "Yes, the 'little redheaded bitches'… Hold on."

He covered the phone again. "She says she'll only come if Anna's along."

"That's impossible," I said. "Anna hitched a ride out of here after she gave us the ring. She said to tell you she'd be in Newport Beach. You'd know where to find her."

Petty stared into my eyes, unsure whether to believe me.

I didn't blink.

"She's not here anymore," he said into the phone. "I don't know, maybe you scared her off... Look Paige, do you want the ring or not? All right, fine. You do understand the conditions? You are to leave us alone from now on." More screeching leaked from the phone. "We'll be there in ten minutes. Drive carefully." He closed the phone.

Terry gave him an odd look. "Drive *carefully*?"

"Reflex," he said with a shrug. "Now, I wish to be clear on one thing. Anna said she'd return to me if Paige agreed to back off?"

"Yes," I said. "But you'll have to work on the marriage. There's been a lot of damage."

"Of course. We'll go into couples counseling, if need be. I'll do whatever it takes." He leapt on the bed, shaking his fists at the ceiling, "I love that woman!"

Terry turned to me, poking a finger down her throat.

"C'mon," I said. "Let's get this over with."

Petty jumped back down off the bed and headed for the door.

I held him back. "Wait. Are we sure Paige doesn't have a gun?"

He dismissed the notion with a wave. "How would she get a gun to the island? They wand all the passengers getting onto the ferry. Anyway, she doesn't know how to shoot."

"Let's say for argument's sake she smuggled one in."

Petty thought a moment, then cracked a smile. "Bring your poodle with you. Paige is insane about animals. She won't shoot you if you have a dog."

"We only have one poodle," Terry pointed out. "And there's three of us."

"Whoever gives her the ring should hold the dog."

"Won't you be giving it to her?"

"No, I'll stay a few yards behind, just in case she's inclined to scratch my face off."

Terry kicked her foot in the air. "Well, I'll be ready with a few of my famous Karate moves if she gets funny with us."

"That's the spirit!" Petty said.

thirty-seven

Robert was more than happy to let us have Jacques when we told him we were going to the croissant shop. We didn't think it wise to confess that the poodle was being used for a furry flak jacket. Jacques was still wearing his sailor sweater as we left the hotel, with the addition of a new red collar and matching leash.

A half-moon glowed overhead, casting an enchanted light on the cobblestone street. Terry and I knocked knuckles for luck, then climbed into Petty's golf cart. I kept an eye out for the agents as we headed to the bluff, but never saw a trace of them.

Petty followed Terry's directions to the bluff. Three quarters of the way up the hill, Jacques started sniffing the air excitedly—picking up on the scent of the buffalo again, no doubt. I tightened my grip on his leash, not wanting a replay of *Dances with Poodles*.

When we reached the top, he crossed the plain to the rendezvous spot. Paige's golf cart was visible next to the stand of trees. I could just make out a pale fleshy leg with pink anklet socks inside the cart.

Petty stopped a hundred yards away.

Terry and I climbed out of his cart. Paige stepped out of hers, shining a flashlight directly into our eyes as we approached.

"Let me see the ring!" she shouted.

Terry waved the diamond in the shaft of light. Green sparks flitted across the tree trunks like the afterimages of wood sprites. Paige's lips curled up in a greedy smile as she beheld the stone. I moved over in front of Terry as we got nearer, holding Jacques tightly against my chest.

Finally we were five feet away from her.

"Give it." Paige grabbed spasmodically at the air.

Terry took her time removing the ring. "What? This?"

"Give it here!" The woman was practically hyperventilating. "Give it! Give it here!"

"All right, all right." Terry extended it to her.

Paige grabbed for the ring, but her fingers closed on nothing when Terry whipped it back at the last second.

"What's wrong with you, you skinny little twerp? We had a deal!"

Terry first made sure Steven was out of earshot, and then she looked Paige straight in the eye. "Tell us why you want it so bad, Paige. Tell me why it was worth killing Nikki Edwards."

Paige bounced on the balls of her feet. "I didn't kill the little bitch!" she shrieked.

"You hired the man who did," I said.

Paige inched closer. "Give me that ring or I'll—"

"You'll what?" Terry took a step backward. "Kill me, too?"

"All right, I'll tell you why I want it." Paige licked her lips. "It's proof!"

"What do you mean, proof?" Terry asked.

"Proof that my ex-husband is a mass murderer."

"What?" Terry and I said in unison.

"The diamond's radioactive." Paige gave a deranged giggle. "That son of a bitch owns a mine in Africa that's poisoning the workers with radiation. That's why the stone's colored. When a diamond is exposed to radiation during its development, it turns green."

Terry looked down at the stone as if it were a live grenade.

"It's not enough to hurt the person wearing it, but the workers are dying like flies. Horrible deaths." That thought caused her to giggle again. "Steven doesn't think I know about it, but I do. And I'm going to ruin that bastard. He'll never get out from under the lawsuits." She took another step closer. "Once Amnesty International and the World Health Organization and all the rest of the bleeding hearts get wind of it, he'll be tied up in the international courts forever!"

Her hand went around her waist, then whipped back in front holding a revolver.

"Dammit, Terry. I told you she'd have a gun!"

Paige was holding the gun upside down. She fumbled it to an upright position, clutching it with two hands as she'd seen on TV, poking her index finger through the trigger guard.

"Now give me the ring or I'll shoot!"

I stepped in front of Terry with Jacques covering my heart. Paige probably wasn't a good enough shot to get me in the head.

"You won't shoot," I said. "Not with the innocent doggie here."

Paige made a face. "I hate yappy little dogs. Especially yappy little dogs in sweaters. I might go ahead and shoot him on principle. It looks like he's got one paw in the grave, anyway."

Why had we believed Petty about this when he'd lied about absolutely everything else? Probably because most people, even murdering thugs, tend to love dogs.

"Leave him alone," I said to Paige. "He's done nothing to you."

Jacques sensed I was being threatened.

"Arf," he said. "Arf arf arf."

Damn it, Jacques. You're a poodle, not a Rottweiler!

Paige's left cheek twitched. She stared at Jacques with abject hatred, her hand jerking each time he barked. I feared the next yap might cause her to have a psychotic break. Slowly I lowered Jacques to the ground.

"I'm letting him go now, Paige. Forget about him. He's gone."

Part of me was hoping Jacques would run after the buffalo and cause another diversion. But he just sat there, growling up at the woman holding the gun.

"Grrrrrrrr."

"Make him stop or I'll wipe that nose off his nasty little face!"

I prodded Jacques with my foot. "Run, boy! Run!"

But instead of escaping, Jacques took off like a shot, headed straight for Paige. Maybe he'd mistaken *her* for a buffalo.

"Not another step!" she yowled.

Before I knew what was happening, she fired off a round, hitting Jacques square in the rump. He gave a heart-rending yelp as the bullet sent him sailing backward through the trees. Then he hit the ground and lay there completely still, paws up.

Terry went mad with rage.

"You monster!" she screamed, rushing at Paige.

Paige turned the gun on her, firing inches away from Terry's abdomen.

The explosion knocked Terry back. Time froze as she hung there, suspended in space with her hands on her belly, the scene becoming watery and unreal.

Then I sank to my knees and Terry collapsed in my arms.

"No!" I screamed.

Paige aimed the gun at me. "You're next!"

"And then comes you, honey." Petty sauntered up to Paige, aiming his own gun at her face.

Paige's head whipped around with so much loathing in her eyes, I was surprised his gun barrel didn't melt.

"Quick," I said. "She shot the dog and my sister. We have to get help. Call an ambulance!"

He gave me a regretful smile. "Sorry, sweetheart. Not gonna happen. What's going to happen is that Paige here is going to finish what she started—killing you two girls—after which I'm going to finish *her*. Then I'll call the cops and tell them how sorry I was I didn't get here in time to help you."

"You... you set me up!" Paige glowered at him. "You're the one who put this gun in my room."

"Yes, but I don't think the law would have bought the 'he set me up' defense, dear, since the gun has your fingerprints on it. I knew you wouldn't use it to kill *me*, because then you wouldn't have the pleasure of seeing me go to prison."

"You deliberately provoked me. Calling to let me know you'd be here with your little whore. Telling me how you'd screwed her brains out while she was wearing my ring..."

"Brilliant, wasn't it? Thanks for playing your part to perfection. The insane wife who would rather kill than allow her ex-husband a moment's happiness."

"You're not gonna have any happiness, asshole! You're going down for your radioactive mine!"

"You're the one with a gun pointed at her head, Paige. Think about it—that is, if you *are* still capable of rational thought. There's no way out. I've won at last." He pointed at me. "Now, shoot her! Shoot the little tramp, Paige!"

"You hired Beaver to kill Nikki!" Terry was limp in my arms, her breathing shallow. "It's been you all along!"

He nodded. "Nikki was double-crossing me."

"Double-crossing you how?"

"I signed over my shares in the diamond mine to her, so Paige here couldn't get her hands on them in the divorce. Then I found out Nikki was going around me. She was trying to make her own deal for the uranium deposits." He sighed. "Pity. She was a great lay."

"Her own deal? With who?" I had to get him to say it.

"An international consortium. What do you care?"

"What kind of consortium?"

"I assume it's a terrorist front."

I stared at him in amazement. "You would provide uranium to mass murderers?"

"A few dirty bombs here and there. It's not the end of the world. If not me, someone else would sell it to them."

"You are beneath contempt."

"And you are beneath a gun!" He grinned at his own cleverness. "Now Paige, be a good girl put the little redhead out of her misery. She wouldn't want to live without her twin, would you, sweetie? To say nothing of your little pooch."

"Thanks, but I won't have to live without my twin," I said, pushing Terry off my lap. "She's just fine, aren't you?"

Terry lifted her head, smiling in the direction of the trees. "Officers! So glad you could make it!"

And then like Robin Hood's Merry Men, they materialized out of the forest—six of Catalina's finest, led by Deputy Whitehorse—their Mag lights blazing, semiautomatic handguns aimed at the toxic couple from Orange County. This location was our backup option, if either Steven or Paige had refused the coffee shop for the rendezvous. We didn't have a backup to the backup, so it was a good thing they'd agreed to this one.

"Thanks for the confessions," Whitehorse said. "Now kindly drop your weapons."

Paige's whole body began to tremble. She stumbled back, reflexively pulling on the trigger. *Click click click.* But there were no rounds to fill the chamber. Sweat trickled down the side of her jaw as she realized her mistake.

Whitehorse snatched the gun from her unresisting hand. "I'll take that, now. Why don't you learn to shoot, next time? And how to tell whether the gun's loaded?" She spun Paige around and slapped the cuffs on her wrists. "Paige Petty, you're under arrest for attempted murder. You have the right to remain silent. Anything you say can be used against you in a court of law. You have the right to an attorney. If you cannot afford an attorney…"

Steven played it smarter, handing over his gun butt-first to Deputy Young. He put his arms behind his back compliantly.

"Steven Petty, you're under arrest for illegal trafficking in uranium ore," Young announced, as if it were the proudest moment of his life.

"Don't waste your breath. I know that business about being entitled to an attorney. And wait until you get a load of mine."

A black SUV with tinted windows zoomed up to the scene. The doors flew open and four SWAT officers piled out with automatic rifles, headed straight for Petty.

His face fell. "Who are these guys? Wait a second," he said to Young. "I'm going with you, right?"

Young shook his head, backing away from him.

The SWAT team swarmed Petty and hustled him, protesting fiercely, over to their vehicle.

"Just a goddamned minute! You haven't read me my rights! I want–I want a lawyer!"

There was only muffled laughter as the SWATs shoved Petty into the backseat of the armored car. Then they were gone just as quickly as they'd arrived.

Terry rubbed her belly. "You said blanks didn't hurt!" she complained to Whitehorse.

The deputies and Homeland Security had kept Paige and Steven under surveillance the whole time. When they saw Steven breaking into Paige's room to plant the gun, they went in afterward and substituted blanks for the bullets. They'd done the same to Steven's gun.

"I said they didn't hurt *much*," Whitehorse replied.

"Well, it was too much for poor little Jacques."

Terry and I walked over to where he lay on the pile of leaves.

"I don't think croissants are gonna work this time," she said sadly. "But he gave his life in a good cause."

"Wait a second!" I said. "Are we forgetting what season this is?"

I fell to the ground and lifted Jacques' little mouth to mine, covering his wet nostrils with my thumb. I took a deep breath and blew gently into his itty bitty lungs. The whole group of officers pressed in, watching his rib cage expand and deflate, expand and deflate.

"Breathe!" a deputy urged him.

"Die!" Paige shouted.

"Don't go into the light, *garçon*!" said Terry.

Suddenly, Jacques gave an *Arf*! and bit me—well, gummed me—on the nose.

"Thanks a lot, fella."

He jumped to his feet, shaking himself as if he'd just come from a swim, or from the big dog groomer in the sky. The law enforcement officers hooted and hollered, moving in for a group hug. "It's a Christmas miracle!" one of them said.

"No," I muttered, rubbing my nose. "It's Christmas in *The Twilight Zone*."

Terry leaned into me, whispering behind her hand. "I'm not even going to tell you what I saw Jacques eating earlier."

"What?"

"Buffalo patty."

I smacked her on the top of the head. "Liar!"

She grinned at me. "But I had ya going. *I had you going.*"

thirty-eight

$\mathcal{J}$erry and I lounged around the honeymoon suite, treating ourselves to mani-pedi's. We figured we were due that much for bringing two arch criminals to justice. Paige Petty had been hustled off to the station to be interrogated by the sheriffs, while Steven Petty was out there somewhere, getting acquainted with rubber hoses.

We'd ordered room service. Buffalo burgers, fries, beers, and extra pickles.

Our mood was celebratory, even though we'd receive no credit for the arrests. This one was going to be kept under wraps. There'd be no medals for valor, no banner headline: *Twins Save Civilization*! But it was good enough knowing that we'd kept uranium out of a few evil hands.

"How's your side?" I asked Terry.

She felt her ribs with her fingers. "Sore. But it was totally worth it to see their faces when I came back to life."

"What a couple of losers, huh?"

"Yeah." Terry coated her big toenail with powder blue polish. "I have to admit, though, I'm surprised about Nikki."

"I guess we both got snookered by sexy bad guys, huh?"

"Fools for love."

The phone rang and I rose to answer it. "It's probably Eli."

"Every time you say that, it turns out to be trouble."

I picked up the handset. "Hello?"

"Kerry, it's David."

No, it's not! I wanted to say, but remembered to play my role. "Hi," I said. "Where are you calling from? L.A.?"

"No, I'm still in Avalon."

"You didn't go for supplies?"

"I wanted to see you first."

"Oh."

I let him stew for a minute. "I'm not sure that's such a good idea, David."

"It's really important. I need to explain something to you."

I wondered what sort of self-justifying crap he wanted to lay on me. It might be fun to see him get arrested right in the middle of some speech about his holy mission.

"Where would you like to meet?" I said.

Terry waved her arms, mouthing *No, no, no!*

"The same café?"

I turned my back on Terry. "You mean the one where you stood me up?"

"Yes, that one."

"Sure you'll to be there this time?"

"I swear on the Bible."

"Swear on the Koran. I might believe you."

"I swear on the Koran and the *I Ching* and the World Encyclopedia. Okay?"

"Ten minutes." I laid down the receiver.

Terry jumped up from the floor. "What are you doing? You're not supposed to meet him!"

"I'm not supposed to meet him without telling them first." I reached for the cell phone. "That's what I'm about to do."

"You're going to turn him in?"

"I have to, don't I?"

I scrolled down to the contact number, which I'd filed under

X. The call was answered, but no one spoke.

"I'm meeting him at the café on Whittley." I listened, waiting for a response.

"Roger," a man said, then he disconnected.

"You shouldn't do it, Kerry. What if he pulls out a gun or a knife? What if he holds you hostage and demands a jet to take you to Riyadh?"

"We'll be surrounded by lots of people with lots of guns."

She searched my face. "Is it gonna be hard, watching him go down?"

I wanted to say no, but the truth was something else. I nodded for an answer, a lump forming in my throat.

She chucked me on the chin. "It's for your country."

"Yeah, I know."

But I didn't feel like a national heroine now. I felt more like Mata Hari.

I walked to the café, spinning out various contingencies in my mind. If David pulled a gun on me, I'd dive for cover in the alcove next door. Hopefully, the agents would bring him down before he could blast me. But if he threw his arms around me, bending me back into a movie screen kiss and telling me he how much he loved me…?

No contingency plan presented itself for that.

David waved to me from his table, where the candlelight reflected on two glasses of red wine. He was dressed beautifully in a crisp, white button-down shirt, gray slacks, and a camel-hair jacket. Quite a contrast to the scruffy Bohemian style. I had wondered whether I'd ever see my gentle artist again. Now I realized he'd never existed to begin with.

I sat down at the table. "You look handsome."

"Got myself decked out for you."

"Wine, how nice."

"My favorite shiraz."

I took a whiff. "Delightful bouquet. Full-bodied, with subtle notes of deception."

He held out the label for me to read. It was written in a script I didn't recognize. Hebrew?

"It's Israeli. From my private cellar." He clinked my glass. "Cheers."

I swirled the wine on my tongue. "Where'd you learn to drink Israeli wine?"

"On a kibbutz. I worked as a grape-picker."

"Yeah, right. Tell me another one."

He was through with the verbal sparring. "I know they've cracked my cover."

I almost spat out my wine. "How did you know?"

"Friends in high places."

"Like the Ayatollahs? The Imams?"

"I'm working for the Israeli government."

"Whoa, whoa, whoa." I put a hand to my forehead. "Is that some kind of terrorist humor? 'Cause I have to tell you, it's really unfunny."

He laughed good-naturedly. "It's the truth."

I slapped the tabletop. "I *knew* you weren't what they said you were!... Wait, things are starting to make sense. You were the 'interested party' meeting with Steven Petty about the uranium. You were pretending to represent some kind of rogue government or faction or something?"

He smiled. "Very good."

"And you were the one who met with Nikki when she tried to cut Petty out? You were the 'beach bum' Max saw her leaving with?"

He gave me another appreciative nod.

I was suddenly frantic. "Quick! You gotta get outta here! Homeland Security is coming to arrest you."

"I expected that. But I had to see you."

I started pushing him out of his chair. "No, really! They're on their way—"

He took my hand in his. "Relax. I'm not done."

"You are *so* done!" I yanked my hand back. "Who are you really? Is your name even David? Or can't you divulge that?"

"My name is Giulio di Parma."

The hits just kept on coming. "You're Italian!"

"Jewish-Italian."

"So you *are* circumcised."

He crinkled his brow. "Is that important to you?"

"Never mind. It's just that—"

I was interrupted by the arrival of Agents Bland and Blander. They strutted up to the table, badges in hand. Bland pointed a gun at David's chest.

"Nice and easy," he said, grinning. "Get up from the table. You're coming with us."

"He's not really—" was all I had time to say before David reached inside his jacket.

"Don't try it!" Bland thrust the steel barrel into David's— *Giulio's?*—cheek.

David held one hand the air, the other coming out of his jacket with a business card. On the card was a phone number with a 202 area code.

"Call this number," he said.

Bland chuckled. "We're not gonna call your lawyer, Qamar. You don't get one, bub."

Blander tapped his partner on the shoulder. "Um, this is a D.C. number. I think it may be the Pentagon."

"State Department," David said. "Go ahead. They're waiting for your call."

The agents swapped frowns, then Bland started in with the bluster again. "If I get the secretary out of bed for no reason, dog collars will be too good for you, Qamar."

"Please call the number and give us some privacy."

"Keep him covered," Bland said to his cohort. Then he stepped a few feet away to make the call. After a minute he returned, practically bowing and scraping.

"Sorry about that." He grabbed Blander by the sleeve and dragged him away. "Have a nice evening."

"What the hell's happening?" Blander said as he tottered after him, gun poised to shoot.

"I'll tell you later." Bland pushed down his partner's gun hand. "Put that away."

The two of them hurried down the street, casting nervous glances over their shoulders.

I grinned at David. "Way to show 'em. You're one of the good guys!"

He studied my face for a moment, then took a sip of wine. "There are no good guys, Kerry."

"Sure there are."

"There's your side and their side. You have different objectives, that's all. No one deserves to live anymore than anyone else."

"But you were working against the terrorists!" I said. "That makes you one of us."

He shook his head. "I'm independent. This time I'm working for your government in conjunction with the Mossad. Next time...?" He let the thought hang there.

I took a sharp breath. "You mean you'd do business with *them*?"

"Under certain conditions. But no women and children. Never women and children."

"Gosh, don't we have such high standards! What exactly do you do for a living?"

"They were correct about my profession. Just not about my identity."

"You're an assassin."

He nodded matter-of-factly.

"Killed anyone lately?" I said, then immediately regretted it.

"Ben Kirch."

My mouth fell open. I could not think of a single thing to say.

"Can you sincerely pretend the world isn't a better place without him?"

"You're contradicting yourself. You just said no one deserves to live more than anyone else."

"And I believe that, in the existential sense. But that doesn't mean I won't eliminate a dangerous killer or lend my services to people with a political agenda to implement. That's the practical sense."

So David was the one who'd done Beaver in. But there was still the question of his accomplice. "Who picked Beaver up in the boat the night he shot at us?"

"A stray Samaritan who probably hadn't heard the shots. I'm sure they'll eventually find his body in the bay. Beaver killed his own rescuer as soon as he was aboard. I found him before the sheriffs did, trying to meet up with Petty."

"And that's when you... terminated *him?*"

Another nod.

"Why?"

"You have to ask?"

It took me a second. "Because he took a shot at me?"

"Yes."

I felt sick to my stomach. I'd been responsible for a man's death. A truly odious man, but still.

"Petty was playing both ends against the middle," David explained. "When he realized you and your sister were going to start poking around in his wife's disappearance, he decided to hire you to make it look like he wanted her back."

I felt numb. "Makes sense."

"But he was afraid you'd figure out what he was up to, so he told Beaver to shoot at you, more to intimidate than to kill. It's kind of flattering, really. He thought you were too smart for your own good."

My head felt like it was going to explode. "I'm still not clear on your part in all this."

"I was here to make a deal with Petty for the uranium. When he'd taken the bait, the feds would pick him up. If for some reason they didn't, my job was to terminate him. It was their case to make, but if he got away somehow, I was here as back-up."

"One way or the other, he was going down?"

"Right."

"But then Nikki tried to make her own deal."

"Yes. I met with her to string her along. But Beaver was watching her on Petty's behalf and he must have seen her talking to me. After that, Petty gave him orders to kill."

"So Petty was trying to get rid of all his obstacles in one fell swoop? And those obstacles just happened to be the women in his life."

"Yep."

"And when Beaver broke into our hotel room? Was he trying to find the ring?"

"I assume so."

"Okay, but if all of this is about uranium, what about the workers in the mine? They're dying from radiation poisoning, according to Paige. Wouldn't somebody have picked up on that sooner or later?"

"Later," he assured me. "There's never any shortage of people desperate for work and no hesitation on the part of others to exploit them. Once the sale was made, the consortium would probably have used imported labor. True believers who were willing to make the sacrifice."

"Suicide miners?" I said in disbelief.

"Anything for the cause."

"But you... have no particular cause?"

His silence was answer enough.

"That makes you—"

"A mercenary." He watched for my reaction. "Not as romantic as an international spy, huh?"

I gave him a queasy smile.

"Kerry, if you want to believe in cowboys and Indians, black knights and white ones, be my guest. But where do you think the terrorists got their weapons in the first place?"

Of course I knew the answer to that.

"Your government. Your weapons manufacturers. Your society."

"No, don't lay that at my feet."

"They gave them to the Afghanis when they were 'freedom fighters' against the Soviets. Then they turned the weapons on you and became 'terrorists.' What did they think they were going to do with them when the conflict was over, go deer-hunting in Kabul?"

"I was just a kid then!"

"It's a dance, Kerry, everybody changing partners all the time. Friends one day, mortal enemies the next. Saddam and Muammar trading places like a do-si-do."

He could see he me resisting his argument, but he pressed on.

"You have a president whose grandfather traded arms to the Nazis. You had another one who was descended from a bootlegger, selling contraband to the mob. They serve you apple pie, they teach you patriotic songs from birth, and meanwhile they profit from war, making consulting deals for their own enrichment as soon as they're out of office, or not even waiting until then—"

"Okay!" I put my hands over my ears. "Enough!"

"It's the truth."

Maybe, but it was too much truth. "Where do you end up when it's all over? I mean, you personally? Where's your home?"

"I have houses on several continents, as well as private transportation to get to them." He took my hand in his once more.

"How nice for you."

"It could be nice for you, too." He suddenly became bashful. "I plan to retire in a year. I have a castle on a private island off the coast of Amalfi. It's so beautiful, Kerry. We could live there together."

I couldn't believe what I was hearing. Was he proposing that I traipse off to some island castle while the only world I'd ever known twisted in the wind? Did he really think I was capable of that?

When I didn't answer, he released my hand. "It was worth a try."

"Sure. You never know who might sell out her country and everyone she loves for a secluded castle getaway."

The candlelight shone in his large black irises. "Everyone she loves?"

"I didn't know you. Whatever I felt, it wasn't based on who you really were."

"Can you ever really know anyone?" he asked.

"I'll let you figure that out. You're the philosopher. I'm just a simple American girl."

"You're much more than that, Kerry."

"No, I'm really not."

It seems we had both harbored illusions about each other. He'd romanticized me as his "mermaid girl," someone who'd follow him to an island fortress for love. I'd believed him to be a gentle, artistic soul making the world a more beautiful place.

I let out a sigh. "And to think you reminded me of Jesus."

"I probably share some mitochondrial DNA with him."

"Don't flatter yourself."

I looked down at his hands. Hands that could produce accomplished works of art one minute and slit a man's throat the next. How did someone like him come into being?

"Where did you learn tile work and drawing?"

"I was an art student in Italy. That's where I was recruited by the CIA."

"So you *were* on our side!"

"I was a foreign operative. I did things they were prevented from doing by law. That's why I don't have any allegiance to anyone. It was trained out of me."

"Brilliant rationalization. But you always had a choice."

He had no comeback to that.

"Where were you from, originally?"

"Corsica. My father was Polish-Italian. He was in the diplomatic corps. My mother's a Turkish Jew."

"And where'd you learn to speak English?"

"Exeter."

"Sheesh. The 'preppie assassin.' Were you rich growing up?"

"Well off. Now I'm rich."

"What a world."

"Hey, I didn't make it what it is today."

I gazed at my own hands, which were useless except for gripping things, typing on the computer keyboard, other mundane tasks. They'd never produced anything of beauty the way David's had. But they'd never snuffed the life out of anyone, either.

"You're wrong." I looked back up at his face. "We do make the world, all of us. Every minute of every day, with each decision we make and every action we take. It all adds up to what you see."

He gave me a sly smile. "Now who's the philosopher?"

I shrugged back at him.

"So Kerry McAfee is going to save the world?"

"With a little help from Terry, maybe."

"I'm not sure the world doesn't need saving from *her*."

Under any other circumstances I would have laughed.

"Um, I gotta go." I rose unsteadily to my feet. "I can't deal with this kind of ambiguity."

"But you do deal with it. Every day."

"No, I solve crimes. Sometimes I even bring criminals to justice. I catch killers, David. I don't run away with them."

He stared at me, his eyes assessing. But not, I thought, judging me.

"Good luck to you." I started to walk away. "I mean, when you're on the right side."

"Think about it," he called after me. "I'll be in touch in a year, okay? Just think about it."

I shook my head as I made my way down the cobblestone street, the Christmas lights blurring through my tears.

I didn't look back.

thirty-nine

"Come on," Terry said. "Cheer up."

I lay on the honeymoon king, hands behind my head, watching her pack. "I'm cheerful."

"As an embalmer." She stuffed the last of our clothes in the duffel, and zipped it shut. "Okay, tell little sister all about it. You feeling guilty?"

I shook my head. "Nope."

"Sad?"

"Confused, actually. I've never met anyone who draws completely outside the lines before, know what I mean? Let alone had romantic feelings for him."

"Must have been a shock."

"Does the fact that he has no allegiance to anything make him a sociopath?"

"I'm no shrink."

"But you *are* an expert on abnormal psychology."

"Okay, I'll take a stab at it."

She sat in the Queen Anne chair, throwing her boots up on the desk. "I think you could say that anyone who puts himself above everyone else is disconnected somehow. He's the only thing that matters to him. If he does a job that makes him money, it's a good thing. If it costs someone else's life, so what? I guess you'd have to call someone like that a narcissist."

"But he didn't strike me that way. He seemed to really like me, so he has *some* human emotions."

"But he can't extend that to the rest of humanity."

"Guess not."

"So maybe he just has a more limited range. He can care about himself and one other person. Everyone else is just noise."

"Does that make him a bad person? Or is he a good person within certain limitations?"

"I want to say 'bad,' but if the government has a use for him, who am I to judge?"

I dragged my legs off the bed and stood up, catching my image in the armoire mirror. The blue ridge on my brow was going down. I walked over to the balcony for one last glimpse of the harbor.

The sky was cloudy, the water dark and choppy. Halyards clanked on masts. Seagulls cawed. People lounged on decks, dressed more warmly than the day before. The music of carols floated over the waves.

Oh yeah. It was Christmas morning.

"Got something for you."

I turned around to see Terry holding out a small gift bag tied with red and green ribbon.

"I feel terrible. I didn't get anything for you."

"You were busy saving western civilization."

I took the bag and reached in to find my present. It was a ceramic mermaid sitting on a rock with her tail tucked daintily beneath her, combing her long red hair with a starfish. A keepsake of my love affair with an international hit man.

I was touched. "How'd you know?"

"How do I know everything?"

She pulled another figurine out of her jacket pocket, this one riding on the back of a dolphin. "Got one for me, too. This one's more my speed, a bronco-busting mermaid. I bought them with the ten bucks we put on the bet."

"I like yours better."

"S'my mermaid!" She yanked it out of my reach.

"Why don't we put them in the bathroom? Then we can both see them every day. We'll set them next to the sink."

"Where else would you keep a pair of mermaids?"

She got up from the chair, slung the duffel over her shoulder, and we walked out of the honeymoon suite for the last time.

"*Time to go*, Jackie Collins!" I banged on Reba's door. "Ferry in twenty minutes!"

We heard heavy footsteps, then Eli swung the door open. His hair was mussed, his stocky legs bare, the chest fur peeking out of Reba's silk dressing gown. In his hand, he clutched one of the patent leather fruit shoes by the heel.

"Oh hi, girls." He hid the shoe behind his back. "Your aunt's gonna take a later ferry."

"Later?" Terry said.

He winked at us. "Tomorrow."

"Okay, you kids have fun." I shook a finger at him. "But we don't want any more cousins, hear?"

"Don't worry about it."

As we headed for the elevator, Eli leaned out the door. "Hey, I forgot to say Merry Christmas!"

"Same to you!" we called back.

Cousin Robert and Jacques were waiting for us in the first-class quarters of the ferry, a private wood-paneled cabin with champagne chilling on the sideboard, courtesy of the captain.

"Where's Mumsy?" Robert asked.

"She's taking time out for a romantic interlude," I told him.

He shook his head. "Some things never change."

Terry reached for the bottle. "Shall we?"

Robert demurred. "I'm back on the wagon. But Jacques might like a little."

Sure enough, Jacques started whimpering when he saw the bottle.

"You sure Jacques should imbibe?" Terry said, popping the cork. "You know what happened the last time."

"Surely he can't get into trouble here," Robert said. "It's not like he could capsize a whole ferry, could he?"

Nobody answered. We all stared down at Jacques, weighing the odds.

"Ah, to heck with it," Terry said, filling Jacques' bowl. "They have life jackets on board."

The four of us enjoyed some cheese and crackers and doggie biscuits along with our libations as the boat moved out into the harbor, away from the scene of the crimes.

Robert gazed out of the porthole wistfully. "Catalina will never be the same."

"Christmas will never be the same," said Terry.

"Who wants things to stay the same?" I said.

"Arf!" said Jacques.

The poodle had summed things up brilliantly.

epilogue

*W*e survived the treacherous ocean journey with Jacques, arriving by taxi at Reba's mansion at noon. We stood on the front porch, waiting for Grizzie to open the door.

Robert rang the bell a second time. "I wonder what's taking so long."

Finally, Grizzie answered.

"Merry Christmas, Griz—!"

The door slammed in our faces.

"What on earth is wrong with her?" Robert said.

Terry hit the intercom button. "Grizzie, we're here for the dogs!"

Her voice crackled over the speaker. "They're napping. Come back later!"

"Well, if that doesn't just tear it." Robert reached into his coat pocket to retrieve the house keys. "She's lost her mind."

Terry gave me a wise smile. "You were right, Ker."

"Right about what?" Robert turned the keys in their locks and the door opened, but got stuck on a chain lock.

"She's gotten attached to Muffy and Paquito."

"Griselda," Robert said through the partially open door. "Let us in at once."

We could see Grizzie in the foyer, arms crossed over her bosom. "They like it here. They don't want to go back to that drafty little house."

"Grizzie," Terry said, "they're *our* dogs."

"*Were* your dogs."

Robert held Jacques up for her to see. "Look, Grizzie, you're going to have a little dog, too. I've brought one home with me. His name is Jacques."

The door slammed again, almost flattening Jacques' snout.

"Ugly blighter!" we heard through the door.

"Arf!" Jacques said indignantly.

Robert stood there for a moment, bewildered. "What shall we do?"

"Is the taxi still there?" I asked.

"Yes, the driver's unloading our luggage."

"Why don't we go out for lunch at Canter's? Give Grizzie a couple of hours to get used to the idea. As a last resort, we can call in a hostage negotiator."

"What a scathingly brilliant idea," Terry said, jumping off the porch.

Robert trundled down the walk after her. "Do they allow dogs at Canter's?"

"Probably not, on most days." I gave Jacques a pat on the head. "But what kind of Scrooges would deny a poodle his Christmas day pastrami?"

~~The End~~

I so did not take the good bike that year. Kerry's a big fat liar.

The End

Read on for a sneak peek at

The Hellraiser of the Hollywood Hills,
the prequel to *The Con Artist of Catalina Island,*
by Jennifer Colt, coming Spring 2008.

Go to http://www.jennifercolt.com for more information.

"*Nuts!*" Terry banged on the wheel of the Rent-A-Wreck Chrysler Imperial and threw her right foot up on the dash.

"Are you unhappy about something?" I asked, knowing full well I shouldn't.

"I'm *bored.*"

"Boring is good, Terry."

"Since when?"

"Since we're not under threat of death and the tax assessor has his check and it's not going to bounce."

We were broke again, but at least we were honest broke. No ill-gotten gains, no blood money staining our hands. Terry had accepted a cash tip from a killer on a recent case, and I'd made her donate it to a women's shelter. She'd been in a sulk ever since.

True, our client had killed someone who really *needed* killing, but that didn't tip the scales of justice in her direction. You're not supposed to take the law into your own hands and there's a very good reason for that, as I'd tried explaining to Terry.

"What if one day someone decided *you* needed killing? What if they decided that you were such an ungrateful, selfish, obnoxious she-devil that they put their hands around your neck and squeezed and squeezed and squeezed until your big green eyes popped out of your bloated purple face...?"

She'd shrugged off my argument, and then went right ahead being an obnoxious she-devil without any regard for who might want to kill her because of it.

Terry pressed her boot against the windshield for the isometric exercise. "You know your problem?"

"Please. Tell me what my problem is."

"You demand too little from life."

I could tell we were headed for a bitch fight of seismic proportions, but I took the bait. Truth is, I was bored too.

"A roof, food, clothes...? Seems like a lot to demand with our finances."

"See? You can't think past the basic necessities. That's why I'm poor and doing shitty stakeouts, because I'm hemmed in by *your* consciousness."

The "shitty stakeout" was our current job. We'd been hired to get evidence of an extramarital affair, and that's why we were sitting down the block from the target's apartment in a trashed-out Chrysler. We hadn't even bothered trying to be inconspicuous after the first day of surveillance. No cops would hassle us if we sat here for hours, no well-meaning citizen would demand our ID—we'd be taken for harmless crackheads or hookers making an honest living. Lots of people in this neighborhood lived in the streets or in their cars, so we fit right in.

"Excuse me?" I blinked in the glare coming off the filthy windshield. "How is this about my 'consciousness'?"

"I'm a victim of your limited thinking. You reap what you sow, you know. It is done unto you as you believe. Your thought creates your experience—"

"And your point is?"

"You think small, therefore I reap small potatoes, 'cause my fate is tied up with yours."

This wasn't Terry's usual rant. Terry usually complained that I was a "bossy cow." Could a cow reasonably be accused of limited consciousness? *Daisy, you fat, lazy cud-chewer, get out of that pasture and make something of yourself!*

Secretly, I was giving her points for novelty. "Where are you getting this?"

She pulled out a dog-eared paperback from beneath the driver's seat, tossing it to me. The cover was a radioactive orange with big block letters screaming across the top:

Sky's the Limit! Think Big! Be a Millionaire!

"How many titles does this book have? And when did you buy it?"

We'd been on this stakeout for three days. Breathing each other's burger breath, squirming in the seat to get circulation back in our butt cheeks, occasionally answering the call of nature in the bushes. There'd been precious little time for personal development.

"It was under the seat. I read it when you went to get lunch."

"You read a whole book while I was at In-N-Out Burger?"

"It's written in a very readable style."

Terry is dyslexic. There was no way she read a full-length book while I was gone to fetch cheeseburgers. But she had the uncanny ability to absorb a book by reading random passages and then filling in the blanks intuitively. That's how she got through school. That, and buying the answers to exams.

I turned the book over to see the author's photograph. He had a lot of letters after his name: PhD, MFCC, DC. He also had receding red hair, a russet potato nose, and coke-bottle glasses. It was only a headshot, but I just knew the guy had food stains on his tie and walked on the balls of his feet. And he was going to tell *me* about self-improvement.

"Let me get this straight. You find a book under the seat of a thirty-year-old, bashed-up Chrysler—no doubt left by the last loser who couldn't afford to rent anything better—"

"Maybe he traded up for a Jaguar, ever think of that?"

"And you decide to make it your life philosophy?"

"Why don't you read it before you judge, huh?"

If I didn't humor her I'd never hear the end of it. And when I say never, I mean *never*. We'd go through endless cycles of death and rebirth working off Terry's karma, while she bitched at me: *We wouldn't be in this mess if you'd read that self-help book ten lifetimes ago!*

I sighed and opened the book to its introduction.

Thinking creates your experience. Everything begins with a thought; every action is preceded by thought. What you dwell on in consciousness becomes your experience. Allow your thoughts to get bigger, and your good experiences will expand in scope and frequency.

"Okay." I chucked the book in the back seat.

"You didn't read much."

"I think I got the message."

"And the message is?"

"Think big."

"Right. So what are you thinking now?"

I let my voice go dreamy. "I'm thinking of a palatial home in the Hollywood Hills..."

She nodded her approval. "Good."

"I'm thinking of *hundreds* of *millions* of dollars..."

A thumbs-up. "Excellent!"

"And I'm thinking they belong to Candy Spelling."

Terry groaned, falling back in her seat. "I hate my life. Wake me when it's over."

We were indeed in Hollywood, but not in the exclusive hills where the celebrities holed up in their mansions. This was down and dirty Hollyweird, a block up from Sunset Boulevard. Here, runaways lived in refrigerator boxes, seniors cashed their Social Security checks to buy beer and Lotto tickets, and people of every age, gender, and hue were out plying the sex trade.

Terry was right. It was not only boring sitting outside these low-rent apartments, it was depressing. But it was a paying gig and it was not life threatening—two big pluses in my book.

"Three whole days of this!" Terry moaned. "I don't even believe this guy has a young girlfriend. You saw him. He's a pig."

"Maybe he's a pig who *thinks big.*"

"And even if he is playing around, why would his wife care? It'd be good riddance as far as I'm concerned."

"The ways of the heart are mysterious."

Terry jerked up suddenly, yanking her feet down from the dash. "May Day...May Day... Babe alert, one o'clock."

A slender young woman was headed our way, walking with an athlete's bounce on blue Pumas, casting covert glances at the ground floor apartment of the piggish Paul Fellows.

"About time!" I dug the digital camera out of the In-N-Out wrappers on the floor, aiming it at the sidewalk. The girl wore a long-sleeved baggy T-shirt in toasty September, a fringed scarf around her neck and chin, and a racing cap pulled down over reflector shades.

I zoomed in on the target. "She's definitely *incognito.*"

"Chiquita incognitaaaaa." Terry rubbed her hands together. "Walkin' right into our trap."

Click. She slows near the apartments. *Click.* She checks a piece of paper to confirm the address. *Click.* She stuffs the paper into the pocket of her ripped-up jeans. *Click.* She looks around to see if anyone's watching. *Click, click, click.*

Terry grunted, annoyed at being left out of the action. "Lemme do some!" She scooted over in the seat grabbing for the camera, simultaneously jabbing her elbow into my left boob.

"Owww!"

The girl heard me cry out. She hesitated, then turned and stared at us. She was only a few yards away.

"She made us." Terry shoved the camera back at me. "Let's book."

"Why couldn't you stay on your side of the seat!"

"If you *ever* let me do any of the good stuff…!"

She slid behind the wheel, cranked the ignition, and the 8-cylinder clunker roared to life. Incognito Girl was on the car in a flash, thrusting her arms into the window.

"Friggin' paparazzi!" She clawed at the camera in my hands.

I slapped at her. "Get off me!"

She got a grip on the camera and started to pull. She was strong as hell—it was all I could do to hold on. The camera cleared the window and I found myself being yanked out of the car by the arms.

Terry jumped out of the driver's side. "Hey! Let her go!"

The window glass was cutting into my triceps. I was afraid it would shear off and amputate my arms above the elbows. Doing a quick calculation, I determined that a two hundred dollar camera was not worth going through life as a double amputee.

I let it go.

Incognito girl toppled backwards into Terry, who'd just come up behind her. The girl lurched away, then spun and around and bashed Terry on the side of the head, double-fisted. Terry went over on the grass. The camera flew into the air, plummeting to the ground a few feet away.

Then the girl pounced on Terry with a banshee yell, pinning her to the ground. The two of them fought—hands locked—grunting, snarling, practically spitting in each other's faces as they strained for advantage.

"Girl fight!" someone yelled from a passing car. "Woo-hoo!"

I leapt out of the Chrysler and raced over to the wrestlers. I threw my arms around the girl's waist and pulled with all my might, lifting her off of Terry's stomach while her legs kicked in the air. Her body was slim, but made of solid muscle. She flailed around in my arms, knocking off her own hat and sending her sunglasses sailing. Blond hair tumbled down around her shoulders.

I dug my heels into the grass for leverage and shoved her as hard as I could. She staggered away, tripped on a sprinkler head and fell to her hands and knees. Only then did I check on my sister.

Terry lay on the ground, her mouth open in shock.

"You all right?"

She pointed behind me. Her lips were moving but nothing came out of them. I spun around, prepared to fend off another attack, and that's when I saw what Terry had seen. I knew at once what had taken her breath away.

There, panting like a dog, with grass stains on her knees and murder in her round blue eyes, was the world's biggest pop star.

I gaped at her. "Bethany?"